Although Emily Johnson lives in western Nevada, she fell in love with England on her many visits to this country. Her novels, which include *The Contrary Corinthian*, *A Chance Encounter* and *Elizabeth's Rake*, are set in the English Regency period, a time she finds fascinating.

LORD DANCY'S DELIGHT

While returning to London to claim his new title, Geoffrey, Lord Dancy, saves Miss Amelia Longworth's life — not once, not twice, but three times, and he is relieved to complete the journey unscathed. But now Miss Longworth is determined to return the favour — even if it means disrupting Geoffrey's affairs . . . and capturing his heart.

Books by Emily Johnson
Published by The House of Ulverscroft:

THE CONTRARY CORINTHIAN
A CHANCE ENCOUNTER
ELIZABETH'S RAKE

EMILY JOHNSON

LORD DANCY'S DELIGHT

Complete and Unabridged

ULVERSCROFT
Leicester

First published in Great Britain in 2009 by
Robert Hale Limited
London

First Large Print Edition
published 2011
by arrangement with
Robert Hale Limited
London

The moral right of the author has been asserted

British Library CIP Data

Johnson, Emily, *1930 –*
    Lord Dancy's delight.
    1. Regency novels.
    2. Large type books.
    I. Title
    813.6–dc22

    ISBN 978–1–44480–558–1

Published by
F. A. Thorpe (Publishing)
Anstey, Leicestershire

Set by Words & Graphics Ltd.
Anstey, Leicestershire
Printed and bound in Great Britain by
T. J. International Ltd., Padstow, Cornwall

This book is printed on acid-free paper

Dedicated to my dear granddaughters,
Sharon and Karla Valleskey
and Jennifer Hendrickson

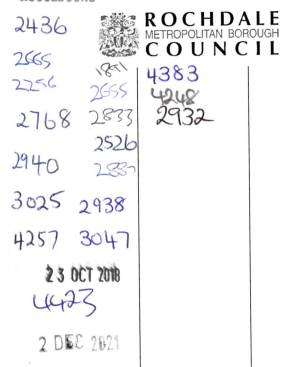

ROCHDALE
METROPOLITAN BOROUGH
COUNCIL

4383
4248
2932

Please return/renew this item
by the last date shown.
Books may also be renewed by
phone or via the web.

Tel: 0845 121 2976

www.rochdale.gov.uk/libraries

1

Amelia Longworth picked her way with great care along the filth-strewn street in Lisbon. Her pelisse was travel-strained and worn. She had no desire to bring it to further grief by a careless misstep on the wretched cobblestones. Remnants of garbage tossed by residents and discarded by dogs not only left much to be desired, but were hazardous as well.

She turned to her companion, Chen Mei, and addressed her in Cantonese. 'Mind your step. Those dogs look wild to me and certainly not to be trusted.' Amelia gestured to the dogs that swarmed toward the Praça do Commercio, noting a pack of the most vermin-ridden, ill-tempered, nasty-looking beasts she ever recalled seeing.

'The cautious seldom err,' the Chinese woman replied in agreement, looking at the dogs with disdain.

Ahead of them the square, open on one side to the Tagus River, was surrounded by government offices with an arcade beneath. The Custom Office stood on the far side of where they paused while looking about the square, supposedly one of the more splendid sights of the city.

'This is not as fine a city as I had hoped,' she commented. Not waiting to see if Chen Mei followed, Amelia strolled forward to study the scene.

She did not care for what she had found so far, but was so thankful to be on solid ground once again that she could tolerate the uncleanliness. After all, other ports they had seen on the way to England from Macao were little better.

The trip had been a tedious and extremely long six months. She understood why her father had sent her off to London, for she suspected she had a great deal to learn about the ways of society. The English in Macao tried to retain hold on the manners and the mores of society, but to make a proper come-out, a girl needed London.

Besides which, Amelia had been raised by a Cantonese woman and imbued with many of the attitudes of the Orient. Amelia suspected she might find a shade of conflict between the two cultures.

But she missed the only home she could remember. There had been strolls along the sweeping promenade of the Playa Grande, which curved along the edge of the sea. White baroque buildings had glittered in the sun while she enjoyed her amble, with the young clerks of the East India Company vying for her attention. The ground rose sharply from the sea and the water front, where Amelia had been forbidden to stray. Chen Mei had scolded her at the mere mention of that area.

When Mama died things had changed. Papa was gone more, traveling to Canton to supervise trading for the East India Company. He worried, she knew, about the whims of the Chinese. They viewed the British as foreign devils and considered the goods brought for trade with utmost contempt. Papa — Sir Oliver Longworth to others — feared Chinese reaction to the opium trading sanctioned by the British government and the East India Company as an important revenue. Papa thought the Chinese might get angry enough to wage war against the British, not that the poorly equipped and trained Chinese soldiers could succeed. But it could get nasty.

Papa would have reaped a great fortune by this time had he participated in the opium trade. Each shipload brought immense profit. Still, Amelia possessed excellent letters of credit, for he had done well enough with his investments, and she expected to have all the money she required for her come-out once she reached London.

There were a few things she would like to purchase, but the shops held little of interest for her. An apothecary shop had yielded tooth powder. A milliner to produce a truly pretty bonnet seemed beyond possibility. It would have been lovely to find a pretty straw confection so her aunt wouldn't think her too provincial. Amelia sighed.

A group of soldiers sauntered across the square, ignoring the Gallegos, or water carriers, who, Amelia had been informed by the captain of her vessel, brought water to each of the houses from one or another of the thirty-one fountains in the city. As the ship had neared the quay where they were to dock, she had glimpsed an aqueduct that came down into the city from mountain springs. In the pleasant February sun the sight of even one of those fountains would be most welcome.

Just then four of the dogs attacked one of the Gallegos, causing him to trip and drop his precious cask of water. The crash and fearful cursing in fluent Portuguese brought Amelia to a frightened halt. She froze as the cask bounded across the square and directly toward her. Behind her Chen Mei burst forth in angry Cantonese, denouncing these hapless foreigners.

Then Amelia was captured up in strong

4

arms and held tightly to a broad chest. The sensation of a man's arms cradling her legs and upper body ought to have rendered her speechless. Shocked, Amelia cried out as she was rushed to the shadows of the arcade at the side of the square.

The barrel rolled past them to smash against the wall of stone, water erupting in a fountain that cascaded everywhere. It was, Amelia considered, a peculiar way to see a fountain even if she had wished to do so. Fortunately she and her rescuer were spared a wetting. Her bonnet was quite shabby-looking as it was, and it the last of her original five.

The man who had so abruptly snatched her from the path of the barrel checked the square behind them, and Amelia wondered if he intended to cart her farther. He smelled pleasantly of eau de cologne, although Amelia could not truly appreciate it at the moment.

Behind them the square was in total chaos. The Gallegos water carrier cursed the dogs, who barked loudly in response, their numbers augmented from a side alley. Barefoot fishwives, dressed in black and carrying trays of fish on their heads, hurried to loudly offer their advice. Bakers, bowed by the enormous weight of bread slung over their shoulders, prudently avoided the mob and skirted the square. The other soldiers laughed at the mêlée, offering their own pithy observations on the accident.

Geoffrey placed the young woman on her feet in what he deemed a safe enough spot not too far from the remains of the broken barrel. Then he studied the slender damsel who had frozen from fear, and in so doing, had endangered her life.

'I suppose I ought to thank you, sir, but I fear it is quite beyond me at the moment.' She didn't appear to appreciate the rough handling, even if he did sweep her out of the barrel's path.

Her pelisse was out of date, but well-made and of a becoming color. That bonnet, now somewhat crushed, lacked style from what he had seen here in Lisbon. But when she raised her head to stare at him, he received a shock.

The girl possessed a fine pair of speaking blue eyes the color of the sky on a summer's afternoon — an English blue of a heavenly color in a face framed, by what glimpses he could detect, with hair like finest corn silk, a rich golden yellow. Her oval face was unbecomingly tanned however, and he wondered at her being allowed to wander about the city alone, with only that improper Chinese woman to chaperon her. Not gentry, he suspected, in spite of her cultured accents.

She spoke Portuguese, he recalled, and wondered at that, for she wasn't a local girl. He'd seen what Lisbon had to offer, and few English resided here what with the war and all.

He scolded, 'If you had any sense, you would have remained in your abode, out of harm's way. Young ladies do not wander unprotected about the city.' His voice carried all the anger he felt at a young chit off without adequate protection.

Then he glanced down at a sudden movement by the Chinese woman and found a curved dagger pointed at his heart, while the woman gazed up at him with a menacing smile.

'You muchee bad man. You no talkee Tian Li.' She gestured with the knife that Geoffrey ought to back away.

'Forgive me.' Belatedly he remembered his manners and swept his hat from his head. 'I am Major Dancy. I am only too happy to be of service to the young lady, who I trust is about to retreat to her inn.' He bowed to both women, then waited to see what the blonde would do next. She did not reveal her name, but the companion appeared to be satisfied at his identity.

The dagger disappeared beneath the sleeves of the full frock the Chinese woman

7

wore. The curious garment billowed about her knees above the baggy black trousers drawn together at the ankle by tasseled ribbons. Her incredibly tiny feet were compressed into black high-heeled slippers. He suspected that behind those dark eyes a suspicious mind worked at full speed, witness the swiftly produced knife. Even the long silver bodkins that were fixed into the wealth of black hair screwed up on top of her head appeared to be lethal weapons.

'Well, Major Dancy,' the young lady observed in cultured accents, 'I thank you for your kind rescue. I might have been injured,' she admitted. Her face pale, eyes downcast, she dipped the faintest of curtsies before warily backing away from him. Then head bowed, she glided along the edge of the square, her curious-looking companion tottering along close behind her.

The chit was not at all to his standards, however. She exhibited precisely the sort of behavior he'd not have in a wife: adventuresome, bold, impetuous, although she did appear to be a resolute thing. And she had lovely eyes. But she was not the girl he'd choose. Not in the least!

While Geoffrey stood staring after them, his friends came up to him, still laughing over the incident of the dogs and the water-carrier.

After months in battle it was a relief to find something to amuse.

'What ho, Dancy?' said Peter Blandford, the closest friend Geoffrey had made while in Spain and Portugal.

'Nothing much,' Geoffrey replied absently. 'A schoolgirl slipped the leash and received more than she bargained for, I'm sure. She could have been killed, silly chit.' He clapped his hat back on his head, then brushed down the plain jacket he had designed for his peculiar role while serving his government. His uniform was largely civilian in appearance, for he cared not for the fancy dress others affected, all gold tassels and braid.

'Or at the very least a nasty injury.' Peter added, looking after the disappearing figures. He motioned with a hand, and the group set off in the opposite direction, bent upon finding a decent meal.

Once around the corner Amelia rested against the cool stone of the building to catch her breath. She had not wanted to admit how the feel of those strong arms about her had affected her emotions. She'd not been close to any man before. Clerks dare not touch the daughter of the supervisor, and there were few unwed officers around that Amelia had been permitted to meet.

At the speculative glimmer in Chen Mei's eyes, Amelia hastily moved to set off down the street once again.

'Soldier save your life,' Chen Mei observed while shuttling along at Amelia's side.

'That does not make him a good man, however,' Amelia replied a bit more sharply than customary. 'Come, we had best seek out the inn where the captain said we are to await the sailing to England. I shall be grateful for a night in a real bed. We can only pray it does not have bugs.'

Her companion agreed, having a more philosophical opinion about those creatures but not wishing to disagree with her precious charge. When the dainty blonde had first appeared, casting her smiling blue eyes on all around her, Chen Mei had fallen victim to her charm. Dubbing the infant Tian Li, or Celestial Delight, because of her remarkable blue eyes and good nature, Chen Mei had attached herself to the Longworth household and remained. Nor would she permit her girl to sail away to heathen parts without Chen Mei to guard her. From what had been observed, her Celestial Delight would need every trick in Chen Mei's bag. No dragon would defend its treasure better.

At the inn designated by the captain as being suitable for a daughter of an East India

Company official, Amelia used her accomplished Portuguese to smilingly command a lovely bath and an excellent meal. Such ability with the language was rare in a foreigner, and it brought forth amazed compliance along with a desire to provide the best for the English lady who actually knew the language.

If the serving girl cast dismayed glances at the peculiar 'Chinee' who stood glaring fiercely at her each time she entered the room, it mattered not. For the first time in ages Amelia was able to luxuriate in a decent slipper bath and partake of a truly good meal.

She chattered to Chen Mei all the while she bathed, then ate in subdued thoughtfulness. She had grown accustomed to Portuguese dishes while in Macao, and the flavor of her dinner made her rather ache for her father and the home she had left. Best not to dwell on the matter, hence the murmur of conversation.

'Eat something, Chen Mei,' Amelia scolded gently. 'It is not like what you prefer, but until we reach my aunt's home you will have to make do with what we have at hand.'

Gesturing to the dish of prawns and rice with vegetables mixed in, Amelia nodded again. 'It is quite good.'

Obviously horrified at the thought of eating

while her mistress consumed her own dinner, Chen Mei reluctantly heaped food on a plate and awkwardly fed herself with a fork while kneeling on the rug. As lovely as the day had been, the evening grew cool and the small fire was most welcome. It cheered the room while Chen Mei scowled at her plate.

'You do not like to use a fork yet,' Amelia observed. 'I know you carry your sticks. Why not use them?'

Her companion hastily rooted about in a capacious bag, and with a pleased smile pulled out a pair of ivory sticks. The remainder of her meal was enjoyed with relish.

Once Amelia was ensconced in her bed for the night, with Chen Mei unhappily settled in the adjacent room instead of at the foot on Amelia's bed so as to guard her charge, she was free to consider the day's activities. Chen Mei considered these parts of the world quite heathen and was determined to guard her charge from foreign devils.

The shops in Lisbon had little to offer. It was a pity, for it would be quite dreadful to appear before her aunt in her sadly crushed remaining bonnet.

Which thought brought her to the event that lingered in the back of her mind. The memory of being carried in those strong capable arms, cradled so close to that broad chest haunted her. Could she even sleep this night? She doubted it. Having pushed the subject away the remainder of the day, she could not prevent it from filling her mind now she had nothing else to occupy her.

He had smelled of eau de cologne, she recalled. Odd. She couldn't recall that any of the naval men who came to meet with Papa had worn such a pleasing scent. It was light, yet sharp; pleasant, yet most masculine. Maybe it was only the army men who preferred to smell of something besides soap and boot polish.

He had been handsome, too. In spite of the tart words she had uttered to him and to Chen Mei, she had noticed everything about the man. His lean, sunburned face held unusual green eyes that had made her think of palace jade once viewed in Macao. Auburn hair had curled nicely about his well-shaped head. His uniform fit him splendidly, which told her that he could afford an excellent tailor. She couldn't place his uniform, but then, she was not well-acquainted with army uniforms.

He was undoubtedly a dangerous man. Surely any man who possessed such quick thinking, such manly attributes, along with a form that was more than breathtaking could only be such. He looked to be the sort that stole hearts as easily as smiling in that lop-sided manner he'd used when she had scolded him. Oh, he had been so amused with her! And she had been such a hen-witted creature.

On this unhappy reflection, Amelia drifted to sleep, determined to forget the handsome major and concentrate on her coming splash in London society.

Early the following morning, she and Chen Mei made their way down to the quay where they were to reboard the ship that would take them the final lap of their long journey to England and her father's sister, Aunt Ermintrude Spencer.

During the stop at Lisbon the cargo destined for Portugal had been removed, and port and other wines had been loaded, along with lemons, oil, cork, and leather among other goods the English wanted.

In the pale pink light of the early morning, Amelia glanced about her, taking in the sight of the men bustling about the quay, looking important as they ordered goods toted on board the ship.

The ship appeared to be fully loaded. Amelia's own small portmanteaus and bits and pieces of baggage were a mere nothing in view of all the rest of the cargo. A sailor came up to her, respectfully requesting that she come aboard. He swung her belongings up with ease, then marched off to the ship, leaving her to follow. She dawdled, fascinated with the scene about her.

There was an altercation somewhere behind her. Amelia paused, then turned to see what was going on. Lisbon was quite as noisy and smelly as any other port, and she held a scented handkerchief to her nose as she looked about to discover what the trouble might be.

Down the quay she espied the man from yesterday, the major. Again he wore the rather new-looking uniform, if that was indeed what it was. It had never seen battle, for certain. Unspotted, unfrayed, it bore no traces of duty unless duty involved nothing more than dancing.

His boots possessed great shine, but there was no sign of the gold tassels so beloved by most military men. The dashing red tailed-jacket seemed plain when compared to that of his friend. A discreet touch of gold braid at his collar and wrist made her suspect his tailor insisted upon the fancy addition, for it seemed unlike the major from what little she'd observed. Simple white pantaloons clung to strong legs.

Then she was struck with the notion that

he had bought the garb to replace one ruined in war. He turned, walking along with his friend, and Amelia noted that he had a slight limp. She was assailed with dismay that she had harbored such doubts about this man. Of course he was a true soldier, and she was a ninny to believe otherwise.

She wished she might apologize for her graceless thanks of the day before. What he must think of her did not bear considering. But then, when she had examined her appearance in the speckled mirror at the inn, she had admitted she did not present a fetching picture. He most likely was happy to be rid of her presence. And that thought rankled the girl who had twirled her parasol and flirted with gentlemen while strolling on the Playa Grande — in far better looks than what the major had seen.

Instead she ought to avoid the major, boarding the ship with all due haste. And this could be none too soon. The characters who strolled about the area appeared most unsavory as they twirled black mustachios and glared at her from beneath black hats. In fact it seemed to Amelia that the throng had increased quite suddenly. She was pushed and jostled about with most disrespectful lack of care.

Impulsively she turned to seek the major.

He had saved her yesterday; perhaps he might take pity on a rather unimportant girl, out of duty if nothing else.

The press of the crowd grew, and a flutter of fear rose within her. Where was he?

Then she caught sight of his trim form and blessed his distinctive, if plain, uniform. She slipped through the throng, Chen Mei not far behind. She had reached him, albeit his back, when she felt a distinct shove. Someone had pushed her.

Panic began to creep over her, building as she sought to catch the major's attention. She did not like this crowd in the least. The sooner she boarded the ship, the better off she would be. Why had she dawdled?

'Sir?' she began hesitantly, speaking up so as to be heard above the noise of the crowd.

This time the thrust was harder, and she lost her footing. Unwittingly she had come close to the outer side of the quay. Below her dirty water waited to receive her body as she teetered on the edge of the quay, desperately trying to regain her foothold. She'd never learned to swim, and with her heavy skirts and pelisse she'd not have had a chance even if she did know how. She stretched out a hand toward the major. In the distance she heard Chen Mei cry out.

'What the — ' The major had whirled

about at the sound of her faltering call to pull Amelia into the safety of his arms.

Amelia found herself caught once again against his firm body. They teetered for what seemed like endless seconds, then Major Dancy regained his balance and pulled her back with him in the direction of the ship.

'You again!' He glared at her with a most peculiar expression on his face, one she did not recognize at all.

'Please forgive me, Major Dancy,' Amelia said in a shaky voice, summoning all her reserve of dignity. 'I beg you will assist me to the ship. The press of the crowd became too much and I lost my balance. I did not intend to bowl you over like a tenpin, sir.'

She feared her feeble attempt at humor had failed. Then he half smiled at her and nodded, much to her relief.

'I fear your bonnet will never be the same again after seeing Lisbon. Where is your companion?'

Geoffrey clasped her elbow in a firm grip as he searched the area about them, taking note of the unusual throng of men crowding the quay.

What was going on here? He hadn't expected to see so much activity so close to sailing time. All the cargo ought to be stowed by now, with only the last-minute parcels and luggage of passengers coming on board. In fact, if the young miss he steered before him truly intended to sail this morning, she ought to have been on the ship some time ago.

Once on board, Amelia pulled free of that tight clasp, then sank into a proper curtsy. Chen Mei bustled up, smiling in relief at finding her charge safe.

'Please accept my deepest appreciation, Major Dancy. I cannot begin to tell you how that crowd frightened me.'

'You ought to have been on board long ago. Were you not informed of the sailing time? Or perhaps you had a last-minute delay, as I did?'

Even as they spoke, the sails began to billow out. Amelia could sense the now-familiar feel of the ship slowly moving out into the channel and underway. The wind was good, and they would have no trouble navigating along the Tagus and out to the ocean.

With the usual creaking of wood, the flapping of the sails, the shouts of the sailors, and the cries of the gulls that wheeled and dove about the stern of the ship as background, Amelia stared at the major, puzzled.

'I received no word from the captain, if I was to have been called. It has been my custom these many months to either remain on board — when the port looked unsavory — or present myself as early as possible. I trusted it would be the same here.' She gave the major a speculative look. 'Is there a problem, sir?'

'No, none,' he assured her, hoping to calm any fears she might have. After seeing her walk apart and converse with her companion, Geoffrey turned to stare back at the quay. Something didn't set right with him.

Why the devil would a Portuguese want to push a strange female over the edge of the quay, most assuredly drowning her if not rescued in time. Why she had been shoved so forcefully that she had nearly taken him with her.

Then Geoffrey stiffened as possible implications struck him. Was the real target himself, and the young woman merely a means to the end? He turned his head to study her. Tian Li, the companion called her. What was that in English, he wondered.

When the moment presented itself, he inquired of the captain as to the girl's identity. They chatted briefly, then Geoffrey properly excused himself and returned to his place at the railing.

Amelia Longworth was nowhere in sight. She must have retired to her cabin. After six months it must seem almost like home to her. Well, he had no need to worry about the chit. She was safe now. After they landed in Portsmouth, he most likely wouldn't see her again.

What a drab little thing she was, although she did have promise, he admitted. He too vividly recalled the feel of that lissome body in his arms. Pity she had such an unladylike tan, dreadful clothes, and the inclination to be where she should not.

Geoffrey utterly forgot that tan can fade, mantuamakers existed to properly dress unfashionable young ladies, and that this particular one would likely go where she pleased no matter what.

The trip to Portsmouth was uneventful. Given the indication that things tended to happen wherever Miss Longworth appeared, he was grateful for the quiet.

'You will be glad to return home, Dancy?' Peter Blandford inquired as the two stood by the railing again, wondering when they would sight their homeland.

'I should have come home long ago to take over the reins of the household. It is too much to expect that my sisters can manage the estate. Now,' Geoffrey said with a grimace and a glance at his injured leg, 'I have no choice but to obey the command to sell out

21

and tend to my family business again.'

'Your father died not too long ago. What about your sisters?'

'Julia is widowed, you see, and has returned home to keep an eye on Victoria and Elizabeth. But they all need a man in the house to take care of things. You know how women are, can't manage without us.' Geoffrey rubbed his chin, while contemplating the task before him. He knew his father had employed a good steward, but an estate needed the owner's interest to keep matters in line. He had the house in town to care for plus the estate in the country.

Peter nodded sagely, readily agreeing to the lack of capability among females in general.

'I shall have to report immediately, and hope there is nothing more they wish me to do,' Geoffrey continued. 'Then see to my sisters. Victoria is nearly on the shelf, and Elizabeth ought to be nearing the age for marriage.'

'How long has it been since you last saw them?' Peter inquired.

'A few years,' Geoffrey admitted.

'Given the mails, what makes you think they are still awaiting your guidance?' Peter grinned as his friend glanced up in frowning dismay.

'They wouldn't proceed without me.'

'Would you like to bet on that?'

Since gentlemen would bet on nearly anything and everything, Geoffrey abruptly agreed, then stared moodily at the water. Would they? He'd wagered they were still at home, dutifully awaiting their brother to come to assist them in arranging their lives.

★ ★ ★

Landing at Portsmouth was as hectic as landing at any other port, Amelia decided. However England had the advantage of being her new home, and so she eagerly leaned against the railing, searching the shore to see what her England looked like.

'I fancy you are happy to arrive at long last, Miss Longworth.'

Amelia turned to see the major moving closer along the rail. Just then the wind caught her bonnet, tearing at the worn ribands, and it went sailing over the side. Her hands flew to her head in utter dismay. How dreadful. He would think her quite the frump having one old bonnet to wear, and now that gone. For some reason she didn't care to examine she wished for the major's good opinion.

'I fear it is gone for good. It will give you an excuse to buy a new one,' he said with a teasing note in his voice.

'Oh, dear,' she wailed softly. 'It is the fifth bonnet I have lost on this journey. Between rain, wind, and other things, travel is very hard on bonnets.'

Geoffrey stared at the delicate-looking girl at his side and felt as though he were losing his grip. Beautiful thick blonde hair curled about her face, framing her now-rosy cheeks with incredible beauty — even if she dressed like a dowd and needed a proper London wardrobe.

Pity he would most likely never see her again.

'Do you intend to stay over to take the morning coach? Or do you plan to hire a post chaise to reach your destination, Miss Longworth?' Then he found himself adding, 'If I may be of any service to you, please do not hesitate to call upon me. I shall be staying at the Star and Garter.' He had named a pleasant inn not far from where the coaches departed for London.

At the sight of her frown he cursed himself for being stupid. How could a young woman arrange for a carriage, or for that matter see to her coach fare?

'If there is no one else to assist you, I shall take care of everything.'

Amelia stared in amazement, for she had

thought he would be gone the moment the ship docked. The information that the captain was to see to her arrangements somehow was forgotten as she blushed and nodded.

'I would be grateful for your help, sir.'

With that blush came common sense. Geoffrey Dancy wondered if he had taken leave of his mind.

2

The Star and Garter proved even better than Geoffrey had recalled. The host hurried forward to greet him, and when informed that the daughter of the East India Company official Sir Oliver Longworth also needed rooms, he efficiently arranged everything to their satisfaction.

'I shall write Papa to tell him of your many kindnesses,' Amelia said, holding out her hand in a desire to touch Major Dancy for a final time. Her eyes twinkled with a hint of mischief as she added, 'He promised me that English gentlemen were truly noble in character and most trustworthy. He will be so pleased to know I have found his assessment correct.'

A glimmer of worry crept into the major's eyes. 'Do not be too trusting, Miss Longworth. There are a few men who might take advantage of your innocence.'

Before Amelia might inquire precisely what that might involve, they were interrupted by the host.

'My lord, your rooms are ready if you wish. I have ordered a bath for you. Possibly the young lady wishes one as well?' It had been chilly when the ship docked, and the host knew they would want fires in their rooms and a hot bath to remove the stains of travel and warm them.

Her mind whirling, Amelia could only nod, frowning at Major Dancy while he made further arrangements with the host of the inn. Had she heard aright?

'He is, you know,' Peter Blandford said softly from behind her and to one side.

'Oh?' Amelia turned her head to listen to an explanation if one were forthcoming, while still keeping a wary eye upon the major.

'He is Lord Dancy now his father is gone aloft. I believe Geoff finds it difficult to remember his status has changed. Does it make a difference to you?'

'Why should it?' Amelia replied in an equally soft voice. 'Once we leave here, I shan't see him again most likely.' There was no clue in her voice she regretted that circumstance. Only her eyes grew wistful.

'I would make a wager on the likelihood of that, but I fancy you are not inclined in that direction.'

Amelia smiled at the amusement in his voice, banishing the frown from her face. 'No. I only bet on very sure things, sir. And I have learned that life is too unpredictable to take this sort of chance.'

'A philosopher at your tender age? Astonishing.' Mr Blandford chuckled.

'What is astonishing?' Major Lord Dancy inquired as he joined them once again.

'I suspect that being raised in the East has turned Miss Longworth into a philosopher. She views life as highly unpredictable so is unwilling to bet on her future.'

Major Lord Dancy was clearly puzzled, but merely nodded to Amelia, then gestured to the stairs located directly behind where they stood.

'Your room awaits you. I imagine your companion has already gone to inspect the place. Is she to remain with you in England?'

If Amelia thought his question intrusive, she made no indication. She imagined that quite a few people might wonder about her companion as days went by.

'I doubt Chen Mei would return to Macao if I ordered her to go. She insisted she come along to guard me from the heathen, as she views the English. You may think me unprotected, but she rarely leaves my side.'

As though to emphasize that point, the Cantonese woman emerged from the shadows of the inn entry to glide up to her charge. 'Missee go now.'

'I shall bid you gentlemen good day. And

Major' — she paused before mounting the stairs — 'I shall be extremely grateful if you can perform one last service and assist me in arranging for a post chaise for the morrow.'

Geoffrey watched her disappear to the upper regions of the large inn.

'Pity about the poor girl, all alone in a strange country. Someone ought to look after her better than that Chinese woman. Fancy her thinking us a pack of heathen.' Peter nudged him in the ribs and chuckled.

'You failed to see the dagger Chen Mei carries up that sleeve of hers. I wonder what else she has up her sleeve.' Geoffrey speculated on this for a moment. Then he clapped his good friend on the shoulder and suggested they repair to their rooms. Later they would meet in a private parlor for their dinner.

He contemplated inviting Miss Longworth to join them for dinner, then recalled he was back in England now and could not do such things. But he regretted that he must bid her good-bye. Perhaps he would call on her once in London. The poor little thing would most likely be grateful for a gentleman caller. What her aunt might be like he couldn't imagine, not having had much to do with aunts. His sisters talked about visiting their Aunt Bel, but implied she was a bit strange with peculiar superstitions.

Dismissing Miss Longworth from his mind, he relaxed in a welcome bath, then took his ease with Peter, discussing the meeting he faced with Hardinge once they reached London.

'I believe he will be pleased with what has been accomplished. Not that we shall need all those maps I drew anymore, but I think we have shown that we can gather intelligence with the best of them.'

'Meaning the Russians?'

'And the French, at least in Germany. They are meeting at Chaumont this week, and it will be interesting to see how it all ends.'

'Surely Napoleon must admit his defeat? He is being hard pressed on every side.' Peter took a sip of the excellent port provided by their host, easing back from the table following their meal.

'I believe he is not one to accept defeat willingly. If I may borrow from Miss Longworth's philosophy, never bet on any-thing unless it's a sure thing.'

'Like your sisters?' Peter teased. 'What is your Miss Longworth's destination — since you arranged for her post chaise?'

'She is not *my* Miss Longworth, and she goes to London, the same as we do. The captain informed me that she is to stay with her aunt, presumably until the aunt will arrange a suitable marriage for the girl.'

Peter fiddled with the empty glass in his hand, studying Geoff's face as he spoke. 'A poorly endowed girl, then? She'll have difficulty in firing her off?'

'You make her sound like a gun.' Geoff grinned at his friend, then sobered, reflecting. 'Actually, our good captain hinted that Miss Longworth has a generous portion, being an only child of a very prosperous East India official.'

'She might look a bit unfashionable, but she seems demure enough to pass the dragons of society.'

'It will depend upon her connections, I suppose. I thought I might drop by her aunt's place one day. Just to see how she goes on, you know.' Geoffrey waved a hand in the air in a negligent manner, then poured them each another glass of port.

Peter nodded, his eyes downcast so his expression was concealed. 'I think that would be kind and most noble of you.'

'Are you roasting me?' demanded Geoffrey, slightly insulted by his friend's tone.

'I? Roast you? Never. Now when we arrive in London, I might have a thing or two to say about your sisters.' He paused, then added, 'You could introduce Miss Longworth to them. Just a thought. She won't have any friends in the city. Apt to be lonely for a bit, you know.'

'Good thinking, Peter. By the bye, need a place to put up for a time? House has plenty of room in it for another chap.' He gave his friend a searching look, for Peter rarely spoke of his family, and then only in brief terms.

'I'll take you up on that kind invitation if necessary. My, you are turning over a leaf, becoming a regular saint.' He chuckled at Geoffrey's expression, then added, 'It's only to look over those sisters of yours. Who knows, I might take to one of them?'

'Ha!' Geoff replied, thinking he would very much like to have Peter for a relative. But even he knew he could not order one of his sisters to marry where she didn't want to.

Down the hall Amelia curled up in the good bed, tucking a wonderful down pillow behind her, then contemplated her companion who refused to be banished to the next room.

'Nothing will happen to us, Chen Mei. This is a perfectly respectable English inn, not like those others we saw. That inn in India might have been full of thieves, but once they saw your dagger, they left us alone.'

'Missee have need of mo' than dagger. I feel. I know.' Chen Mei nodded sagely, then prepared for the night ahead when she would guard her precious Celestial Delight. Remaining fully clothed, she camped close to Amelia.

Secure in the knowledge that before long she would be with her aunt in London and on the way to acquiring an English husband, Amelia settled to sleep.

She was greatly annoyed when Chen Mei shook her awake in what seemed like the middle of the night. The room was warm, the fire still burning faintly in the grate. She could see nothing out of the window, just a hint of the dawn to come.

'Chen Mei, I hope you have a good reason for this,' she scolded softly, so as not to disturb others.

'I hear noise.'

'You heard a noise and woke me to tell me that?' Amelia frowned. It wasn't like Chen Mei to do something like this. Quickly slipping from beneath her covers and wrapping the heavy satin Oriental-style robe about her, Amelia crossed the room. At the window she could see that the hour was more advanced than she had realized. Down in the inn courtyard, she spotted Major Dancy supervising the loading of his carriage. What was wrong? She sniffed the air, testing it.

'Stow that last bit of baggage in the boot and we are ready to leave,' Geoff instructed the groom. To Peter he added, 'I think a bit of breakfast will not come amiss.'

Geoffrey wanted to have another look around. When he had come down the stairs this morning, he could have sworn he saw a face he had last seen on the quay in Lisbon. He wanted to search about again.

'Do you smell smoke, old chap?' Peter inquired with the languid air of a London dandy, apparently one he intended to cultivate once he shed his uniform for good.

'Just the chimneys, I suppose. This time of year everyone wants a fire.' Geoffrey pulled his coat about him, then gestured toward the inn.

'Not the same, Geoff. I could swear I see smoke rising up from that side of the inn. Look.'

Concerned, Geoffrey allowed himself to be pulled along until they were on the far side of the building. Sure enough, the faintest trace of smoke curled up from the eaves. Wasn't that where Miss Longworth had a room? He tossed a worried look at Peter, then made a dash for the inn door.

'It may be nothing at all, but I believe I will investigate. Miss Longworth is in that section of the inn.'

Peter following closely behind, the two men ran into the inn and dashed up the stairs. The smell of smoke was stronger here. There was silence, as most of the occupants of the rooms still slept. At the far end of the hall, where Miss Longworth slept, the smell of smoke grew stronger.

All at once flames burst forth from one of the doors, revealing the room behind it on fire. Flames seemed to shoot everywhere at once. Turning to Peter, Geoffrey shouted, 'Rouse everyone you can. I'll find Miss Longworth.'

The two began pounding on doors, alerting the people before hurrying on to the next rooms. Geoffrey had begun to wonder if he had misunderstood the direction of her room, when he met success.

Amelia opened her door, staring with confusion at Major Lord Dancy even as she wrinkled her nose at the acrid scent of burning wood and fabric. With a call to Chen Mei, she held out her hand to the major.

'There is a fire. I trust you will take us out of here?' She placed her slim hand in his large capable palm, then bravely followed as he led them down the hall.

Chen Mei, her arms loaded with bags, darted past them to check the safety of the hall for her charge. At the corner where the stairs were located, she paused then said, 'Velly bad. You carry missee. She no make it otherwise.' Then she disappeared from view in the thickening smoke.

Chaos now reigned as the various occupants peeked out of the doors in horror, then pushed and shoved past Major Lord Dancy and Amelia with total disregard for their safety.

Angered as one buck nearly jostled Amelia into the path of the fire, Geoffrey swung her up into his arms and stalked past the flames, burying his face in the wealth of blonde hair to keep from inhaling the smoke overmuch.

'Hold your breath,' he ordered as they reached the staircase.

The sound of crackling flames, feeding on old and very dry timber, grew louder. Amelia closed her eyes, shrinking against her rescuer as the blaze flared up and little flames darted out as though to grab her. One hand clung tightly about his neck and her head burrowed snugly against his shoulder as they raced down the stairs.

He was all that was strong and heroic — most noble. Her *preux chevalier*, although it was as well he was not wearing shining armor at the moment, for it would have been most uncomfortable and he would have been roasted with heat. But he gallantly came to her rescue like knights of old. Even in her terror Amelia could not help but know a thrill of elation.

Then they were outside and breathing fresh, cold air. Around them people shivered and coughed, complained and worried aloud as to the fate of their belongings. The stable lads tossed buckets of water on the fire, but it looked to be a hopeless cause. They evidently decided the same, turning their attention to saving the stables. Horses were hurried away from the scene, out to a field behind the inn.

The host of the inn marched about, checking and counting to see all were present, muttering under his breath, 'Terrible, terrible, I am all undone.'

The boor who had nearly pushed Amelia and Geoffrey into the flames stomped about denouncing with equal temper the innkeeper, the other guests, and whoever had started the fire.

Chen Mei uttered something in Cantonese. At a lift of his lordship's eyebrows, Amelia hastened to translate. 'She says that human affairs are always changeable. How can you tell whether what today is a misery may not turn out to be a blessing tomorrow?'

'Dashed hard to see how this might prove to be a blessing,' Peter observed, looking back at the blazing inn.

'We had best get on our way before our coach is claimed by someone intent upon travel,' Geoff said quietly to Peter. Then with a concerned expression, he said to the girl, 'Was Chen Mei able to rescue some clothing for you, Miss Longworth?' He observed that the companion wore her customary attire, with not a hair out of place in contrast to the disheveled appearance of the others from the inn.

The blonde, her bedraggled plait of hair slipping over her shoulder as she moved, turned to consult briefly with Chen Mei, then replied, 'I have what I need to reach London. Thank you for your concern, sir.' She again curtsied to him, nodded to Mr Blandford, then turned as her companion spoke once more, this time in her faulty English.

'Tian Li safe. You save her life again. Three times you save life.' Chen Mei nodded emphatically even as she brushed down the once beautiful satin robe, restoring a semblance of order to her charge.

'Do you truly think . . . ? Oh, no! Must I?' Miss Longworth said in obvious amazement and consternation combined.

'Missee know.' Chen Mei tucked her hands up her sleeves, giving Miss Longworth a reproving look.

Dropping a lovely curtsy, the girl raised her eyes to meet his puzzled gaze. 'It is written, my lord. You have saved my life three times. I am now yours.'

Stunned, Geoffrey stared at the girl who bowed her head submissively before him. In her smudged Oriental robe of deep blue satin embroidered with flowers and dragons, she looked far out of the common way. Her blonde hair remained in a long somewhat untidy plait, draped over one shoulder in a childish way. There was nothing childish about the softly curved figure, nor the feelings she had stirred within him when he carried her in his arms, however.

'I say,' Peter muttered quietly.

'Quite so,' Geoffrey replied to his unspoken words. 'Most remarkable.'

'You aren't serious, are you?' Peter queried Miss Longworth hesitantly, keeping one eye on Chen Mei, who hovered behind her charge like the dragon he suspected she was.

'Most assuredly. I would lose face were I not to become yours, Major Lord Dancy.' She half turned to issue soft commands in Cantonese to her companion. Within moments the two women had gathered up what belongings Chen Mei had taken from the inn.

'Lose face to whom?' muttered Peter in confusion. 'I don't understand a bit of this.'

'That makes two of us, but we can't just stand here in the bloody courtyard of the inn in a freezing chill to discuss it.' Geoffrey looked about him for the groom he'd hired yesterday.

'Mind your language, Major Lord Dancy,' Amelia rebuked, looking back at him while she walked across the inn courtyard.

'Sorry, Miss Longworth.' Geoffrey rubbed his neck in a gesture of frustration, wondering what in the world he was to do now. The glance he exchanged with Peter revealed he had no ideas to offer. He looked equally bewildered.

'You had best call me Amelia, if I am yours. And could we not set out for London? I do wish to get on our way.'

'Our way?' Geoffrey echoed, a feeling that things had just taken a peculiar turn hitting him with full force.

'Naturally. If I am to be your chattel, I must be at your side.' She calmly walked to where his coach awaited him, then climbed inside.

'I do not believe any of this,' Geoffrey declared in an undertone while watching Chen Mei follow suit. 'It is a strange sort of dream, no doubt from those mushrooms in the steak and kidney pie last night. I told you they were off.'

'Not mushrooms, old chap. Just one determined young lady who has been living in the Orient for most of her life.' Peter motioned to the coach where the driver patiently awaited his command.

Geoffrey started toward the coach, after giving some instructions to one of the servants of the inn regarding the post chaise that had been ordered for Miss Longworth. He discovered that two of her trunks had been in the stables, awaiting the post chaise, so a delay occurred while they were loaded on his coach.

Amelia, she had instructed him to call her. Did she have any notion of how this all might be viewed in London? He groaned, then gave Peter a dirty look when he laughed out loud.

When he climbed into the coach after Peter, he discovered that the two women sat facing the rear, leaving the forward-facing seats for Peter and himself. He protested this arrangement.

'It is not seemly, my lord,' Miss Long-worth, that is, Amelia replied smoothly. Perhaps too smoothly? She stared at the folded hands in her lap instead of flashing those blue eyes at him, as he suspected she must yearn to do.

'What do you mean?' he said while the coach lurched forward to commence its trip to London.

'As your chattel, I must consider what is best for you and act accordingly. Also, I would have Chen Mei sit beside me. I truly believe this to be the best for all.' She glanced at him. 'Perhaps we may pause at one of the inns so I may change into a gown. There may have been no time to find another inn at Portsmouth, but I am dressed most improperly.' She touched the blue satin robe.

'Well,' he said, determined to have the last word, 'this is to be a fast trip. I wish to make London today. We shall make a stop for a meal, and I suppose you would like to change clothes before we reach the City.' This last was not said grudgingly, for Geoffrey was most impressed by her lack of fuss. Any other woman of his acquaintance would have been up in the boughs, demanding they stop over so she might regain her sensibilities. It seemed that Miss Longworth was down-to-earth. Her practical nature seemed providential to him if he was indeed to be saddled with her.

A glance at Peter revealed that his friend was equally at a loss. The coach dashed along the Portsmouth Road, with only murmured comments between the two women, and an occasional remark between the men.

The stop at Horndean went rapidly, the coachman passing along the news of the fire at the inn at Portsmouth with relish. Then he swung up, and they were off once again, barreling along the road at great speed.

Chen Mei stared out of the window at the passing scenery with curious intent.

'I say, those must be some of Featherston-haugh's race horses. Can't be far from Uppark at this point,' Peter said, leaning forward to study the animals as they raced past them. 'They look as though they might give us a good run.'

That brought up the subject of horse racing, which kept the gentlemen entertained all the way to Liphook.

As they entered the small town, Amelia took note of the attractive inn where they were to pause while the horses were changed. With its ivied walls and sparkling windows it made her long to leave the coach for a bit.

'Might I change my clothes here. Major Lord Dancy?' she hesitantly inquired. Since she and Chen Mei had thrust themselves upon this gentleman, she hated to put him out, especially when it seemed he was in a tearing rush to arrive in London.

'I can't imagine what the proprietor will make of you two in your most unusual garments, but I expect this place will be as good as any.' He ushered the two women from the coach, arranged for a room to be placed at Amelia's disposal, then joined his friend. Looking over her shoulder as she walked up the stairs, Amelia could see them plunge into conversation.

It was the first time she had found a chance for a private talk with Chen Mei since the dramatic outburst at the inn following the fire.

The blue satin robe quickly fell to the floor. Chen Mei untangled the plait of blonde hair and rapidly brushed it while Amelia bathed her face with a soft cloth, trying to refresh herself after feeling embarrassed for her disarray.

'Major Lord Dancy was most kind not to object to my appearance,' she observed while watching Chen Mei work wonders with a gown that had been carefully rolled up in one of the portmanteaus.

'He good man,' the Chinese woman observed. She held out the blue sprigged muslin for Amelia to slip over her head.

'Chen Mei, are you quite certain I must do this thing?' She didn't define the matter, for they both knew what was meant. Wiggling into the gown, then holding still while Chen Mei fastened the tapes and adjusted the dress took but moments. Once that was accomplished, Amelia folded her blue robe to place in the portmanteau so they might leave the room.

'Hold faithfulness and sincerity as first principles,' the companion stated in Cantonese with a nod of her head. 'You know what written. He save your life three times, now — you his.' A crafty look flittered across her face. 'Fire no bad thing, for it give you him. Now you have family.' It was obvious that Chen Mei considered family to be of first importance.

Amelia sighed, wondering how she was to make Chen Mei understand the more complicated ways of the West. In both cultures a young woman had a father, or older relative who arranged a good marriage for her. But other matters could be involved. Not that Amelia had one thing against the major, who was handsome, titled, wealthy — if his actions gave any clue — and kind as well.

'I shall obey, for I have no desire to have the fates punish me.' While not precisely superstitious, Amelia had seen too many instances where retribution followed failure to follow the old sayings. Unless . . . Chinese sayings lost their power once she was in England. One glance at Chen Mei decided that question. Amelia had no desire to find out. Chen Mei would heap dire predictions on her head until Amelia yielded.

'Missee be sincere, faithful to him. Good come.' Chen Mei bustled their things down the stairs and out to the coach.

Amelia sought out the men to tell them she was ready to depart. A glance at the large clock in the common room revealed she had changed in record time. At the quiet sound of their voices on the other side of a partition she halted, not wishing to intrude on a private conversation.

'I tell you Peter, it was the same face I saw in Lisbon. The more I think on it, the more certain I am. Why he would want to start a fire at the inn I can't fathom, but start it he did. I'm certain of that as well. A hunch, if you will, but *that* I'd bet on.'

'You believe he'll follow you to London? Is that why you are in such haste?' Peter replied softly.

'The sooner I report to Hardinge the better. We have received information from the royalists and others disenchanted with Napoleon that is to our advantage to use. And Hardinge is dashed clever in utilizing it. Wellington will be prepared for anything Napoleon can think up.'

'Well, we best see if your Amelia is ready to leave here. I suppose it's too much to hope for, but we can look.'

She heard the sound of chairs scraping against the stone floor, so slipped back toward the stairs. What she had heard them say needed to be considered at length, and she did not wish them to know she had overheard their conversation. It seemed that

Major Lord Dancy needed someone to look after him. Amelia had a task to perform.

Well, she thought, as the men started in surprise when they saw her waiting for them, he would have her — and Chen Mei as well, for that matter.

'Gentlemen, I await your pleasure.' She curtsied, then hurried to the coach where she resumed her place.

'She's a rare one,' Peter observed quietly.

Geoffrey contemplated those words from Amelia and what it might be like to have her pleasure him. One look at the Chinese dragon and he put it aside. No one would touch the Celestial Delight as the captain had translated for him, until the dragon gave permission.

It was late when they clattered past the Robin Hood gate hard by Richmond Park. Shortly after that came the Vauxhall and Newington gates before they raced across London Bridge into the City.

'Glad to be home?' Peter inquired as the coach drew up to the Dancy residence at No. 15 Berkeley Square.

'Yes,' came the fervent reply.

Few lights showed from the house other than the entry. The door opened in response to the groom's urgent knock. Geoffrey hurried from the coach and up the steps to the house leaving Peter to cope with the ladies.

'Evenson, my sisters around? I have guests for them.' It had been decided that the ladies from Macao would stay with his sisters until he could locate Amelia's aunt.

'Oh, my Lord, your sisters are from home.'

'From home! Where?'

The portly butler rubbed his chin, then said, 'Miss Victoria, now Lady Hawkswood, has been in Switzerland on her honeymoon after marrying Sir Edward, you see. Lady Winton has gone to visit at the home of Lord Temple, painting. And I believe Miss Elizabeth is to shortly marry Lord Leighton with your Aunt Montmorcy's blessing.'

'The devil you say,' Lord Dancy breathed, feeling Peter's not so gentle nudge in his back.

'I ought to stay here with you,' Amelia said in a small voice, 'but I daresay it would not look at all the thing. We had best find my aunt. Do you know where Mrs Ermintrude Spencer resides?' she inquired of Evenson. 'I lost her address in the fire.'

'It wants only that,' Geoff murmured. 'Come, have a cup of tea while I sort things out. We shall have you at your aunt's home before you know it.'

'Jolly right, Geoff, or else,' Peter muttered with a knowing arch of his brows.

3

'Do you recall anything about your aunt's address in London? The area, perhaps? Or the street?' Geoffrey studied Amelia Longworth with a narrowed gaze. Dash it all, he couldn't have the chit staying here now, what with his sisters gone. Why, if word seeped out about it, he was as good as wed to the girl.

He considered the crumpled appearance of her garments, her tanned skin, the unfashionable hair style, not to mention her strange ideas, and shuddered. Not that he was so top-lofty as to judge by appearances alone, but the girl stirred something within him. She bothered him. And her blasted Chinese companion with all those peculiar notions did as well, in a different way. His chattel, indeed. Nonsense.

Miss Longworth sat demurely upon the brocade sofa, apparently mulling over his questions. At last she nodded and replied, 'I believe she lives on Brook Street. Do you know where it is? Would that be terribly far from here?'

Geoffrey exchanged a relieved look with Peter, then smiled at Miss Longworth. 'It is quite close, actually. There ought to be no problem in locating your aunt, for it isn't a very long street at all.'

At that moment Evenson entered bearing a large silver tray upon which reposed not only the requisite tea, but also coffee, sandwiches, biscuits, and thick slices of poppy seed cake.

He placed the tray on a large table, then straightened, looking at Lord Dancy with a softened expression. 'May I say on behalf of the staff that we are pleased to have you home again, milord. We are certain that your sisters will be very sorry to have missed your homecoming. They eagerly awaited news from you while you were gone.'

A slight guilt at not having written more often assailed Geoffrey before he recalled that for much of his stay on the peninsula he was unable to write because of his location and fear that his identity might be revealed.

'War does not often permit us to do as we please,' he commented. 'It is very good to be home again. I fancy I shall catch up with my sisters before long.' Then he glanced at Miss Longworth, his problem for the moment, and said, 'How can we best find out the address of Miss Longworth's aunt, Mrs Spencer? She lives on Brook Street.'

'I shall consult James, the first footman. He frequents a small tavern not far away where the servants frequently gather in their time off.' Bowing correctly, Evenson quietly marched from the room and down the hall.

'We might as well enjoy the contents of this tray. Will you pour, Miss Longworth?' He offered Peter a slice of poppy seed cake.

'Coffee, I suppose?' she said, looking at him with a smile in her eyes.

'Please.' From the corner of his eyes he could see Chen Mei fussing in one of the bags she had refused to relinquish to the groom, preferring to carry it herself.

'Chen Mei, here is your tea. I believe you will like the cake,' Miss Longworth said softly to the Chinese woman at her side.

The cup of China tea was accepted and a small parcel placed on Miss Longworth's lap at the same time. She ignored it for the moment, taking care of Peter's beverage, then pouring a cup of tea for herself.

For a few moments silence reigned while the hungry travelers consumed the food so providentially brought by a conscientious Evenson.

When Amelia had consumed sufficient sandwiches and cake to appease her hunger, she studied the packet in her lap. After a searching look at Chen Mei, who nodded solemnly back at her, Amelia rose from the sofa. She walked to stand before Lord Dancy, wondering how he would accept her gift.

'Yes? What is it, Miss Longworth?' His face was inscrutable: no clue to his inner feeling showed on that handsome countenance or in his eyes. They weren't precisely cold, more like wary, perhaps.

'Since society will not permit me to share your home so that I may look after you as I ought, I wish you to have this, my lord.' She bowed most correctly as Chen Mei had taught her, then offered the slim packet wrapped in yellow silk.

Her eyes followed his hand as they picked up the little parcel, examining it with obvious curiosity before beginning to unwind the silk. There were several layers of fabric to undo before he found the item inside. A long, thin piece of silver slid into the palm of his left hand. Several pieces of yellow silk drifted unheeded to the floor while he studied the characters inscribed onto the surface of the object.

He glanced at Peter, then returned his gaze to Amelia. 'What is it?' With a finger of his right hand, he traced the characters, frowning as though he sensed something from them, but didn't know what it was. 'It's most curious, for the silver feels cold and yet warm. Very peculiar.'

'That is very good.' Amelia shared a smile

with Chen Mei before continuing. 'This is an amulet that will protect you. You must wear it always, my lord. The characters will guard you from evil influences and accidents. That you sense the power of them means that you will find it most superior.' She bowed once again, then backed to the sofa, seating herself with demure grace.

Geoffrey gave Peter a helpless look, then turned his gaze back to the amulet in his hand. Oddly enough it was true that he did feel something when that silver piece had slid into his palm. He couldn't explain it to anyone so that it would make sense. But he could not shake off the feeling that Miss Longworth had placed some sort of spell on him. *Something* must explain the way he felt, the awareness that crept through him.

'You must wear it at all times,' she reminded him. 'Even in bed.' She looked at her companion, who produced another little packet from her sleeve. 'Here, I believe you will be able to use this.'

Placing the amulet on the table, Geoffrey opened the second packet to find a silver chain. It was obvious she intended him to thread it through the loop on the amulet, and so he did. At her gesture he then placed the chain over his head, feeling dashed silly. Men didn't wear necklaces of any sort. For instance, how could he go sparring at Gentleman Jackson's with this thing dangling around his neck?

'You wear it next to your skin,' Miss Longworth further instructed. 'It is very important, my lord.' She approached him again and appeared to be about to tuck the amulet under his collar when Evenson entered the room.

Geoffrey breathed a sigh of relief at the rescue, yet a part of him wondered what it would be like to feel the touch of Miss Longworth's gentle hands on his skin.

'Success, milord. James is well acquainted with the butler from the Spencer household. Mrs Spencer resides at No. 45.' Turning to Miss Longworth, he added as though to reassure her, 'It is a fine, large house with an excellent garden in the rear. Mrs Spencer is praised by her servants as a kindly woman.'

He had apparently observed the frightened look that had flashed into Amelia Longworth's lovely blue eyes at the mention of a large house. Had she feared it would be too grand or imposing, and that her aunt would be haughty and cold?

Geoffrey frowned as he considered the worrisome thoughts that had just popped into his head. Miss Longworth was a gentle girl, demure and perhaps too trusting. Would this

Mrs Spencer take advantage of those qualities to align her with whomever happened to be available, not seeking to find someone deserving of Amelia? This would not do in the least. He would see to it that the girl was happy before turning to his own affairs.

He had wanted to find his sisters and tend matters at his estate, but he would not be so heartless as to abandon poor little Miss Longworth to an unpleasant fate. Another look into her celestial blue eyes intensified his determination. He would champion her, perhaps help find a fellow who would appreciate a tanned, unfashionable, but obedient and demure little miss. He totally forgot that stubborn streak that had emerged on more than one occasion.

'We had best take you to your aunt immediately, before the hour is too late.' A glance at the long-case clock near the door confirmed his belief that they must hurry along.

'Thank you, Evenson, for your kindness in seeing to it we were fed so nicely,' Miss Longworth said to his butler, causing the usually unflappable man to turn red in the face. 'My lord is well served by you, I believe. Keep an eye on him while I am gone.' With these peculiar words said in the most gentle and confiding manner, the young woman drifted from the room with a dignity far beyond her years.

Geoffrey watched Chen Mei scurry after her mistress, then gave Peter a puzzled look.

'I don't understand any of this, but I'll wager any amount you wish to name that you haven't seen the last of that girl,' Peter said in an undertone.

'No wager, for I fully intend to see that Miss Longworth is safe and content with her aunt. I could hardly do otherwise. She may think she is my chattel, but really, it is my place to see that she is all right, isn't it?' Geoffrey sent Peter a rather top-lofty look, one that proclaimed him superior to a mere woman, and a girl at that.

'This situation ought to be interesting.' Peter shook his head, then strolled from the room after Amelia and Chen Mei, out to where the Dancy carriage now awaited them.

In moments Geoffrey had joined the others, first giving his coachman instructions on their destination.

The carriage rumbled off, then shortly turned a corner. Within a very brief time they had presented themselves to the Spencer butler. This august gentleman escorted them all to the salon upstairs, then disappeared from sight.

'Amelia, my love?' A dainty woman paused

in the doorway, her long draperies and several scarves fluttering around her so it was impossible to tell if she was plump or merely surrounded by yards of pink fabric. Soft gray curls framed her face beneath a modest evening cap of lace and pink satin. Beringed fingers waved at them all as she crossed the room to greet her niece with an enveloping hug.

Amelia dropped a proper curtsy, then smiled shyly at her newly found relative, sister to her papa. 'I am pleased to be here.'

'How like your dear mother you are. Oh, we shall have a famous time of it. And who are all these people, my love?'

'This is Chen Mei, my companion, who raised me after Mama died. The tall gentleman is Major Lord Dancy, who saved my life three times and has taken very good care of me since. The man next to him is Mr Peter Blandford, a friend.'

Mrs Spencer scrutinized the gentleman who had saved her niece from serious harm. 'I am much in your debt, Major Lord Dancy.'

'Just Dancy, if you please. I am to sell out and will no longer use my military title.'

'I see.' She smiled, then tilted her head like a small bird. 'Your sister pulled a coup when she up and married Sir Edward Hawkswood. Every chit in Town had been chasing him.

And Lady Winton is off to visit Lord Temple. Wonder what that dragon of a mother of his will make of that. She's been trying to push him into a second marriage for ages. Miss Elizabeth has sensibly taken herself off to your Aunt Isobel's place in the country, I hear. Odd that Lord Leighton absented himself about the same time for the same part of the country. Oh, your family has provided society with such marvelous tidbits. I do hope you intend to follow suit?'

Lord Dancy looked rather stunned at the aunt's outrageous statements by his expression. 'I shall endeavor not to disappoint you, madam.'

'I should hope not,' she murmured with a flutter of eyelashes. 'I'm accounted a shade eccentric, but after all these years, I feel I'm entitled to live a stimulating life. With dear Amelia here I shan't be bored this Season.'

Amelia darted an inquiring look at Lord Dancy, wondering if he was to be a part of her Season in London. She had no intention of losing trace of him. He needed her protection, for she had not forgotten one word of the overheard conversation regarding the menace from Lisbon.

'I am certain Miss Longworth would appreciate a night's sleep. Perhaps I may call upon you later?' Lord Dancy said, as though in answer to Amelia's unspoken plea.

'We shall look forward to seeing you, although don't rush your fences. Between the mantuamakers and milliners, and what-all-not, we should be exceedingly busy for some time.' Mrs Spencer nodded regally, then accepted his parting words and bow with serene good nature.

Once they were alone, she bustled Amelia and Chen Mei up the stairs to a large room in the front of the house. Blue silk curtains hung at tall windows and draped the wall behind a pretty cherrywood sleigh bed as well. Two comfortable-looking chairs and a cherry dressing table with a bench covered in the same blue comprised most of the furnishings. Through an open door Amelia could see a small room with a neat bed and small table, most likely for a maid. Chen Mei would take that if Aunt Ermintrude had no objections. She was unable to prevent a yawn from overtaking her.

'Now I must hear all about this rescue business. I suppose you are far too tired to explain tonight, but be assured I shall want all the details in the morning.' She surveyed her niece, frowning as she walked around Amelia.

'The skin is good but the color is not. I cannot believe you should so forget yourself as to allow the sun on your face, my love.

Had you no parasols? But then, I imagine you found it difficult, all those months on board ship.'

'I have lost five bonnets and four parasols for one reason or another. I finally gave up,' Amelia said with a shrug.

'Quite so. Well, in the morning we shall begin our attempts with cucumber solution. Sleep well.'

Most bemused, Amelia watched her aunt float out of the room. Did her aunt intend her to eat the concoction or was it merely to place on the skin?

'Leave all things to take their natural course, and do not interfere,' Chen Mei intoned solemnly in Cantonese. Then in English — for she was sincerely trying to learn that language — she added, 'Aunt velly kind. Good woman.'

'I am worried about Lord Dancy, Chen Mei. He is in trouble, and I fear he will not wear the amulet.'

Amelia divested herself of her garments, then allowed Chen Mei to undo her hair to brush it in the usual evening ritual. Their eyes met in the mirror, both concerned.

'While times are quiet, it is easy to take action; ere coming troubles have cast their shadows, it is easy to lay plans,' Chen Mei said, reverting to Cantonese once again.

'Of course,' Amelia said, while trying to hide another yawn. 'Tomorrow we shall put our heads together and devise a plan. I wonder if Aunt Ermintrude will help?'

'Good lady,' Chen Mei repeated. 'You desire to help others, you will help yourself in the end.'

'You know I don't wish to help Lord Dancy just to improve my lot,' Amelia protested after donning a dainty white cambric nightgown delicately embroidered with flowers. She slipped beneath the covers, then pulled them up to her chin while giving Chen Mei a solemn look. 'You have taught me to care about others more than myself. Therefore I must see that Lord Dancy comes to no harm.'

'It is so,' Chen Mei agreed before silently tottering off to her own bed.

Amelia hoped that her unusual aunt would see it from the same point of view, then fell into a deep sleep.

*　*　*

'Wake up, wake up, there is much to be done,' Aunt Ermintrude sang out as she floated across Amelia's lovely bedroom. She jerked aside the draperies to allow the pale light of the February sun to shine in, with the hope of encouraging her new niece to arise.

Following a modest breakfast of rolls and chocolate, Amelia's face was covered with a cucumber mixture to whiten her skin. Then she sat with her aunt to plan for the forthcoming shopping trips.

'Once we wash your hair with chamomile to bring out the color, you will see that delicate hues will suit — pale blue and violet, and pretty pinks. And I think you ought to wear lily of the valley scent.'

At that point Chen Mei brought a silken bundle to place in Amelia's lap. Giving her aunt a hesitant look, Amelia unwrapped the bundle, revealing a string of perfectly matched pink pearls, along with ear bobs and a ring holding one perfect pearl.

'Exquisite!' exclaimed her aunt with a pleased smile. 'Your father did well by you. He wrote me that his solicitors will handle all your expenses. Once we succeed in whitening your skin, we shall proceed to the mantuamaker. There is a great deal to do before we reveal you to Society. How fortunate you have already made the acquaintance of two charming gentlemen.'

'You seem to know his family well,' Amelia said with a glance at Chen Mei.

'I know everyone who is anyone in London. I have already spoken to Maria

Sefton about you. I feel assured you will have the required vouchers for Almack's when needed.'

'Almack's,' Amelia murmured, somewhat bewildered. 'I shall learn what I need to know, I suppose. I would like to employ a dancing master to learn the new dances. The rest of my come-out I will leave in your capable hands, dear aunt.'

'As is fit and proper. I am so relieved to see you are such a pretty-behaved girl. You will prove to be no problem at all with such lovely manners.'

'Aunt Ermintrude, there is something you ought to know,' Amelia cautioned.

'Ah, yes, your story. How did Dancy rescue you? I wish to hear all.' Aunt Ermintrude settled on her chair to listen to the tale. Her eyes watched carefully as she listened to what Amelia had to say.

With a commendable brevity of speech Amelia related the tale of the wild dogs in the square, the pushing throng on the quay in Lisbon, the terrible fire in Portsmouth, and her conclusion — that she owed him her life.

'Of course you do, my love. Such appreciation is only proper.'

With another look at Chen Mei Amelia continued, 'It is not just that. In China when your life is saved three times by an individual, you *owe* him your life. I am his.'

There was utter silence while Ermintrude Spencer digested this remarkable statement. After a time she said, 'And what does this mean?'

'He is in great danger. I heard him tell his friend that he fears a man from Lisbon who followed him to England, and who set the inn on fire as well. Chen Mei agrees with me that it is my duty to protect him from danger. After all, he saved me from death!'

'How in the world can a slip of a girl protect Lord Dancy from harm!' Aunt Ermintrude quite obviously found this task to be beyond Amelia's capabilities.

'If one is clearheaded and intelligent, can one be without knowledge?' Amelia said, repeating one of Chen Mei's bits of wisdom.

'Knowledge is one thing, to protect him is another.'

'I shall go where he goes, follow discreetly, and so learn much about him and his enemies. You will see. With Chen Mei at my side he shall be safe. I shall keep my ears alert, my eyes open. It is surprising what one may learn when others think you do not exist.'

Somewhat aghast at this extraordinary side of her niece, Aunt Ermintrude merely stared.

★ ★ ★

It took several days of skin treatments before her aunt would dream of permitting Amelia out of the house. Dressed in the best of her outmoded gowns and wearing one of Aunt Ermintrude's more girlish bonnets, Amelia faced the first of her trips to Madame Clotilde's establishment with commendable calm.

'I trust your Madame is not one of those haughty women who look down their noses at a girl?' Amelia said while twisting the cords of her reticule.

'I doubt she will treat you with other than utmost respect,' Aunt Ermintrude replied.

While it was true that Madame could depress the pretensions of upstart mushrooms, Amelia possessed a rather special quality, one that would intrigue Madame. Also there was the matter of Amelia's generous allowance. Even though Mrs Spencer was not the least purse-pinched, the presence of ample funds filtered through Society rapidly, often from the mantuamaker.

When the Spencer carriage stopped before the discreet gray building with a bow window picked out in gold, Amelia exchanged a wary look with Chen Mei.

Once inside they found Madame occupied in fitting a young lady for her come-out ball gown. Amelia perched on a dainty gilt chair, content to page through a fashion journal. Her aunt did likewise while Chen Mei sat quietly listening to what she heard.

At last Madame Clotilde floated into the front area of her establishment with every appearance of genuine sorrow at having kept them waiting.

'I do not mind, Madame Clotilde, for I know you will give us the same undivided attention — especially when you see the young lady I have brought to you.'

Madame Clotilde studied Amelia until she felt acutely uncomfortable. Then with a whirl of skirts, the mantuamaker beckoned to Aunt Ermintrude. 'Come with me, for I wish to show you the latest fabrics and do the final fitting on your peach sarcenet. Then I will devote the rest of the day to your niece. I believe I can find just the right way to make her unique, for her hair and those lovely eyes deserve special treatment.' To Amelia she also beckoned. 'I trust you would prefer to wait in a dressing room. One of my girls will bring you a cup of tea. Your companion, as well,' she concluded, giving the elegant long silk garment Chen Mei wore a speculative look.

Amelia and Chen Mei dutifully followed the mantuamaker, settling in the little dressing room on two of the dainty gilt chairs with resignation. After the months of sailing it seemed odd to merely sit to await the ministrations of this peculiar little woman with her fake French accent and improbably colored red hair.

The tiny room had an assortment of fashion plates on a small table and the requisite looking glasses. Amelia wondered how long she would wait when she realized that she could hear the conversation coming from the next room. Ordinarily she would not have strained to listen, but she heard a familiar name.

'Chen Mei, do you hear what I hear?' she whispered.

Chen Mei nodded, her eyes narrowing with displeasure.

Amelia shifted closer to the partition, trying to hear better.

'It is carefully planned, I tell you,' said the woman. 'Nothing will go wrong, so stop worrying your silly head about it. Mama is very particular about the matter. She discovered Lord Dancy has an excellent estate with abundant funds. It will be a pleasure to become engaged to him.'

'But I still do not understand. You are in love with Thomas Sands. How can you even think of someone else?' The second voice sounded exceedingly perplexed.

'It is absurdly simple,' said the first voice. 'I

shall contrive to arrange the engagement by means of a compromise. After all, he has been off on the Continent for some time and cannot be awake on all suits when it comes to the wiles of young ladies.'

'You love Thomas but will become engaged to Lord Dancy. Outrageous,' declared the friend.

'But you still do not comprehend the beauty of it all. Once we are safely engaged, I shall endeavor to give Lord Dancy a disgust of me, by whining, or merely making myself utterly impossible. Mama has explained just how to do it. Then he will break the engagement, for what man like Lord Dancy will wish such a wife?'

'And?' queried the second voice.

'And we will sue him for breach of promise. Is that not a wonderful plan? Then I may marry my Thomas. He is going to do the same thing. That will bring us two sums, which properly invested, ought to last for a time. Only, I believe Thomas intends to attempt an elopement with the intent of her guardian buying him off. He is exceedingly handsome, you know, so he ought not have the least difficulty.'

'That seems highly improper to my way of thinking. Who is Thomas going to deceive?'

'I understand there is a new girl in town,

the daughter of an East India Company official who has pots of money. Mrs Spencer is her chaperon, and you know how silly she is. A solicitor is her father's London agent and would have less interest in the matter than a gentleman. He would likely join the aunt in depressing any account of an elopement. And you must know that Thomas, as handsome as he is, would utterly bowl over a green girl from nowhere. Why, just the thought of his blue eyes twinkling down into mine as he requests a dance is enough to make my heart flutter.'

'That does sound utterly delicious. What a naughty girl you are, Clarissa.'

The sound of an opening door brought the conversation to a halt. Before long, farewells were made and the two wicked young women had left the establishment.

Once assured they might not hear her, Amelia turned to face her companion. 'Did you understand what that girl intends to do? Poor Lord Dancy. As for the other, I will be on the lookout for a blue-eyed man named Thomas. I believe he will receive a great surprise.'

Chen Mei withdrew the curved dagger from her sleeve, and smiled while she inspected it.

'I doubt it shall come to that, Chen Mei.

But you and I will have to take care of Lord Dancy. That terrible girl must not be allowed to get her way!' Amelia declared in Cantonese.

The two plotters put their heads together, then self-consciously drew apart as Aunt Ermintrude and Madame Clotilde entered the fitting room.

In spite of the improbable hair color, Madame proved to be a kind and talented woman.

'I shan't want white gowns, although I know they are proper for young ladies making their bows to Society,' Amelia instructed. 'White is the color of mourning in China, and I'd not offend Chen Mei.'

The Chinese nodded her agreement to the matter, settling back to watch her adored girl.

After that bolts of delicate pastels in blues and violets, raspberry and pink filled the room as Madame cleverly took charge of the challenging young miss. Once her skin achieved the suitable paleness required of young Society ladies, with her magnificent blonde hair and incredible blue eyes, she would take the *ton* by storm.

If Amelia was not quite as attentive as might have been expected, it was not noticed by her aunt or the mantuamaker. Young girls were easily tired by this sort of business.

But Amelia and Chen Mei communicated with little nods and shared looks. They were considering something else altogether. First to find out who this Clarissa might be and then to convince Lord Dancy he must take great care.

★ ★ ★

The meeting with Clarissa proved a simple matter. It was a collision, actually. Amelia's skin gleamed with the results of days of skin treatments, and she wore a pale pansy blue jaconet gown. When she heard someone mention a Clarissa Filbert, Amelia contrived to bump into her, quite by accident, of course.

'Oh, I do apologize. Such a dreadful crush,' Amelia cooed, refering to the Abvile rout they attended.

Clarissa stared with narrow eyes, as though not quite accepting Amelia's wide-eyed gaze as genuine. 'I do not believe we have met.'

'How sad,' Amelia replied, fluttering her lashes in a helpless manner. 'I am Amelia Longworth, lately of Macao and come to London to enjoy my come-out, sponsored by my dear Aunt Spencer. You are Miss Filbert. I have heard such things about you.' Amelia waved a delicate lace and ivory fan about in the air, having recognized that voice at once.

Clarissa's change of expression revealed to Amelia that the girl recognized her name immediately. Good. Amelia forced herself to chat, becoming less and less pleased with what she found.

'Tell me, Miss Filbert, are you attached to a gentleman? There is such a vast number of fine young men here in London. Such a contrast to Macao, I vow.'

'No,' Clarissa admitted. Then a feral gleam lit her eyes. 'But I expect to be promised any day now.'

The expression that glittered in Clarissa's eyes utterly repelled Amelia. It was the predatory focus of a cat about to pounce. Poor Lord Dancy. Amelia's butter-soft heart went out to the man. She must prevent his becoming entangled with the cattish Miss Filbert at any cost!

4

Geoffrey gazed about the dining room of his club while making an assessment of the occupants. The meal had been good, by peninsula standards. White's had improved since he had last been in London. He wondered what sort of meals Miss Longworth had enjoyed while on her trip to England. Six months was a long time to travel. The food must have been tolerable, or else she would have weighed even less than the delicate bundle he had carried from the inn that morning of the fire.

One of these days he would have to stop by to chat with the girl, poor thing. It was to be hoped that her aunt might find some chap who would need the dowry and not mind the lamentable appearance. And then, perhaps, Geoff might be able to get her out of his mind.

'Hello, old boy. Good to find you at last. Been trying to hunt you down for days.' Peter Blandford gave Geoffrey a cheerful smile. To any who watched, the two appeared to have not a care in the world.

'Sit down, sit down,' Geoffrey said with a

mild irritation. 'Settling in well, I take it, now that you've decided to open the house for your parents?'

Peter flopped down carelessly on the opposite chair, assuming the pose of the ultimate dandy, that of sophisticated boredom. He leaned forward as though to inspect the bottle of wine that sat on the table.

'What did Hardinge say when you reported? Haven't had a moment to discuss it with you.' Peter helped himself to wine at a gesture from Geoffrey while speaking so quietly as to be barely heard.

'He was pleased, just as we expected,' Geoffrey replied with equal discretion. 'I fancy that the proper lads were informed before the cat had cleaned its whiskers and all will be in place. No surprises — at least for our boys?'

'Well, I won't go so far as to agree with you there. But I daresay the more Old Hookey knows, the better things will go. No general likes surprises.' Peter eased back in his chair again, but still tense as though he had more information to impart and merely awaited the right moment.

'Better open your budget, old chap. I can see you are about to burst.' Geoffrey gave him a wry look while twirling his wineglass between his fingers.

'Tell me, have you visited our fair Miss Longworth?' Peter's expectant expression deserved more than a terse yes or no reply to the odd question.

'I thought I'd give her another week to settle in. It's past Easter and the Season is just coming into full swing. Do you mean to say you have heard something? I thought you went out of town to see your parents.' Geoffrey took a sip of wine, frowning at his friend.

'I've been back in Town for a few days. She is the loveliest creature, Geoff. I saw her last evening at the Sefton's. Her tan is gone, as are the frumpy clothes and hair. She has, ah, filled out a bit as well,' Peter declared with unusual relish.

'Do tell,' Geoffrey murmured, for some reason furious that Peter should have seen this vision before himself.

'Well, if you had not been so busy reestablishing yourself with certain ladies of the opera, I would not need to tell you a thing. I heard her say she and her aunt intend to attend the opera this evening. If you spent more time in the audience instead of the green room, you might see for yourself.'

'Would that I had been involved in something so pleasurable. I've been busy with my man of affairs. Lawyers can be the most bloody fools at times,' Geoffrey said in disgust. 'But at least I have the matter of my sisters' inheritance and portions straightened out, and Julia is well set. Poor girl, her husband was a rascal, make no mistake. He left her with a pittance, but I corrected that.'

'Think that she'll marry that fellow she's visiting with at the moment?'

'Have you heard anything beyond what Mrs Spencer said?' Geoffrey frowned with concern, for he'd had no news from his absent sisters, although Evenson assured him they were likely quite well with nothing to worry him about.

Peter shook his head, then gave Geoffrey a grin. 'She's a charmer, that old lady. Has the fellows eating out of her hand. Why, Thomas Sands hangs over her as though she were the one making her come-out instead of Miss Longworth.'

'Sands? Don't think I know the chap. Is he someone I ought to know?' Geoffrey gave a narrow-eyed look about the room, wondering if the fellow was present.

Peter pursed his mouth, glancing up to the ceiling as though the answer might be written there.

'Well?' Geoffrey revealed a trifle of impatience, rare in him.

'If you really want to know, I suggest you

present yourself at the house on Brook Street tomorrow during calling hours. He is to be found there every day, from what I understand.'

Geoffrey digested this information with an impassive countenance, then invited his friend to enjoy a game of cards for the low stakes they played when together.

The following day found Geoffrey presenting himself at the front door of the house on Brook Street a trifle before the customary hours for visiting. The same starchy butler showed him up the stairs into the same salon as the night he had brought Miss Longworth here. Geoffrey paced about the room, wondering just how much Amelia Longworth had changed.

'Lord Dancy!' cried a soft, delicate voice from the doorway, sounding enormously pleased.

He slowly turned about, standing utterly still as he absorbed the transformation of Amelia Longworth from a dowdy frump into a shimmering butterfly, a true diamond of the first water. Peter had not done her justice. Why, the chit stunned the eye. His hand unconsciously crept up to where the amulet rested against his chest.

'Amelia? It *is* you, is it not?' He took a step toward the vision in fragile mauve muslin.

Her simply cut round dress — trimmed only with a delicate frill at the neck and a flounce at the bottom of the skirt — hung to her ankles, below which he could see black Roman sandals of the latest design. In her hair silk lilies of the valley artlessly nestled amid her tousled blonde curls. She was quite the loveliest girl he could recall seeing.

'I had hoped to see you before this, Lord Dancy,' she chided gently, as no Society miss ought to scold a gentleman she found interesting. Come to think of it, her smile was most sisterly. He discovered he didn't find that pleasing.

He smiled gravely at her, a note of reserve in his voice as he replied, 'I have had the pressure of business, else I would have been here long ago. May I say you look very well. And are you enjoying your visit to the city?'

'Are we to be as strangers, then,' she said politely, clearly disappointed. 'I have so much to tell you. Indeed, there is a good deal you ought to know about. Come, we shall discuss what is to be done.'

Amelia beckoned to Lord Dancy to join her on the satin striped sofa after summoning the footman to request tea.

'Now, I wish to know if you have had any troubles,' she inquired with that direct manner she possessed. He had forgotten how she tended to look a fellow straight in the eyes when asking questions. It was only when being paid compliments that she lowered her eyes, or when trying to conceal something that Miss Longworth had failed to meet his gaze.

'No serious troubles other than my lawyer, who is the dreariest man alive,' he said with a smile, then recalled the man from Lisbon. The fellow must be biding his time, for Geoffrey had not caught a glimpse of him so far. But he would not relax his guard. Now that he was caught up with his desk work, he'd be out and about and need exercise more caution, he supposed.

'And you wear your amulet as promised?' she asked with the same directness.

'I do.' The weight had been distracting at first. Now he found its warmth pleasant. 'Is your aunt not to join us? I would not wish to compromise you.'

He gave her an amused look, then glanced up as Chen Mei tottered into the room, her soft-soled shoes making no sound. She stared at him, nodded, but said nothing.

'Oh, you shall not compromise me, I promise. But tell me, have you met a young woman named Clarissa Filbert as yet?'

He shook his head in bemusement. 'No, I cannot say I have. Should I seek her out?'

'No. Absolutely never.' Then Amelia revealed what she had heard in the dressing room from the girl named Clarissa. When introduced to the girl at a recent rout Clarissa had not proved more agreeable face-to-face than in the overheard conversation.

'You must be jesting,' Lord Dancy stated when Amelia concluded her recital of the overheard conversation at the mantuamaker's establishment. 'I cannot believe such an outrageous scheme.'

'Well, that odious Thomas Sands has been hanging about for days and days. I am excessively tired of him, and he pays more attention to Aunt Spencer than he does to me. I believe he is trying to get into her good graces. Any moment now I expect him to suggest that to save expenses a Gretna Green marriage would be just the thing for a girl. As though I would partake in anything so havey-cavey. Why, a girl could be ruined.' Amelia gave Lord Dancy an indignant look, hoping he would understand that he ought not take this lightly.

'I suspect that wouldn't bother Mr Sands.'

'You do believe me, then? I would not jest with you about something so serious. Oh, how I would like to teach them both a lesson they'd not forget in a hurry.'

'Does your aunt know about this?' Lord

Dancy said, his charming smile once more back in place.

Amelia was most grateful to see him relax against the sofa. She did as well, feeling as though an old and valued friend had come to call instead of the dandies and bucks who frequented her aunt's salon most days. Having odes written to her eyes and poems praising her curls seemed excessively silly.

'I doubt she would accept that anything was amiss with Mr Sands, for he flatters her shamelessly, you see.' Amelia sighed as she considered the foppish Mr Sands. How he thought she might be attracted to someone so lacking in good *ton* was beyond her.

'So you and Chen Mei have contrived to obtain the background on the two of them?' Lord Dancy shot a look at Chen Mei, then returned his attention to Amelia.

She felt warmed by his regard. Even though he apparently had not thought of her often in the past weeks, he was here now, and she hoped to make the most of it.

'It is not difficult. Chen Mei learns much, for people assume she cannot understand English and are quite free with their speech even when she is around. She is most useful, for her English improves daily.' Amelia gave her dear companion a fond smile.

They went on to chat about the places

Amelia had gone, the parties attended. However the more they talked, the greater her unease grew. Something was not right. Lord Dancy did not seem to consider the Filbert girl to be a genuine threat, and it appeared to Amelia that he totally dismissed Mr Sands as a menace.

When sounds of people were heard below in the entry, Lord Dancy arose, bowing over Amelia's hand just like one of the dandies might. 'Do not be overconcerned about this business with Miss Filbert and Mr Sands. I'm certain you misunderstood the entire matter.' He smiled into her eyes, and for one precious moment Amelia felt enormously drawn to him. Then she recalled his foolish dismissal of her concerns, and she sighed inwardly.

Amelia watched him depart with a feeling of great frustration. While she thought he had understood the danger, he had merely been placating her, intending to do not one thing. Rising from the sofa to await the approaching guests, she looked at Chen Mei with her disquiet plainly revealed.

'It is up to us, then. We shall have to save him from his own folly.' Amelia gave a determined nod, for she felt her obligation deeply.

'A man without thought for the future

must soon have sorrow,' Chen Mei observed from her corner of the room.

Amelia turned a now-composed self toward the door, but said over her shoulder, 'Knowing what is right, without practicing it, denotes a want of proper conduct. Never say that I fail to do what is right and proper.'

The remainder of the afternoon was tedious for Amelia. She was impatient to closet herself with Chen Mei and plan the downfall of Miss Filbert and Mr Sands. Instead she had to listen to the tiresome Mr Sands simper over Aunt Ermintrude's new lace cornette with its satin trim. Amelia thought the moss roses that wreathed the edge a trifle much for an older woman, but Mr Sands praised it to the skies.

What a pity that Lord Dancy considered the threat to his marital status mere moonshine. Amelia had *heard* Clarissa, *observed* the unctuous ways of Mr Sands as he poured the butter boat over her aunt's head. There was little doubt in Amelia's mind that those two were malicious troublemakers. Perhaps were Lord Dancy to see them as she did, he might change his mind.

Once the callers had left, including the dubious Mr Sands, Amelia urged her aunt to have a nice quiet rest on her bed.

'You do not wish to be too tired to enjoy

the opera this evening, dear Aunt,' Amelia gently scolded.

'Dear love, how considerate you are. I will take myself off to bed at once. You intend to rest as well?' Her aunt paused by the salon door, giving Amelia a speculative look.

'Chen Mei and I plan to retire to my room. We shall be fine.'

With that her aunt disappeared to enjoy a pleasant respite in her bed.

'Come, we must plan.' Chen Mei joined Amelia in a hurried flight up the stairs to her room.

Amelia closed the door behind them, then motioned Chen Mei to be seated. The Chinese woman preferred a low velvet hassock, finding it most comfortable.

'I have considered it from many angles,' Amelia began. 'I believe we ought to find some way to allow Miss Filbert to think she has engaged Lord Dancy's interest. Next, perhaps we could lure her to a house, or a room at one of the parties she attends? And then,' Amelia continued, 'see that she is definitely positioned in what might be a compromising situation — were a gentleman to join her. Only . . . instead of Lord Dancy, why not have Mr Sands be the man to appear? That will effectively put paid to his intentions to elope with me as well.'

Chen Mei applauded, then cautiously said, 'A plan is fine, but how you get them to do as you wish?'

'Since Lord Dancy did not believe he is in danger of being forced to marry that odious Clarissa, we must enlist the help of someone else, I suppose.'

'His fiend?' Chen Mei suggested, still unable to cope with the sound of *r*.

'Of course, his friend Mr Blandford. I shall send off a note to him at once. Perhaps he will join us at the opera this evening?' Amelia was not entirely delighted with the opera. The only circumstance that made it palatable was that the noise was so great one scarcely heard the music anyway. It seemed to her that everyone was either dying or in some tragic situation, not precisely her notion of entertainment. But everyone who was anyone attended, and the social consequence of merely being there in an excellent box was enormous.

Her aunt liked to glean the latest gossip, and the opera was a place where a great deal went on, and not necessarily on the stage.

Peter Blandford presented himself with delightful promptness when he received the note from Amelia. Once he heard she wished for his company and wanted to involve him in a plan to rescue the foolish Lord Dancy from a scheming hussy, he immediately agreed.

'I must confess that I consent to help you so that I shall know the pleasure of your company, Miss Longworth.'

'Why, Mr Blandford!' she exclaimed with genuine delight. His shy smile was most endearing to Amelia, particularly since the man who intrigued her had failed to appreciate her in the least.

That evening Amelia dressed with more than usual care. Her peach lace dress over a peach satin slip had a pretty drapery of peach lace entwined with pearls around the bottom of the skirt. Once dressed, she picked at the tight — and minuscule — bodice of the dress where it dipped very low so as to reveal perhaps a trifle too much.

'A silk rose here do you think, Chen Mei?' she asked. 'I vow I feel as though there is nothing to this gown but a skirt. Even the sleeves are tiny.'

Chen Mei shook her head, for she had been going over the fashion plates and knew precisely what was to be worn. Rather, she clasped the pearls around Amelia's neck, then placed a pretty evening hat of peach satin and lace just so on Amelia's head.

'Now go, and do not forget what you are to do,' Chen Mei reminded. She would not go along for she thought the English music very bad on the ears and declared the singing to be more like the screeching and yowling of a cat.

'If all goes according to plan, we shall set things in motion tonight.' Amelia gave herself one last inspection in the mirror before joining her aunt and Mr Blandford in the entry.

Had she not been so preoccupied with the plan to save Lord Dancy, she would have more fully enjoyed the appreciative expression on Peter's face when he first saw her. As it was, the three set off for the opera with Aunt Spencer chattering away about the latest scandal and Peter replying with great courtesy. Amelia smiled and nodded, clearly distracted.

Once settled in the box that Ermintrude Spencer considered an absolute necessity during the Season, Amelia searched the interior of the theater.

Mrs Spencer welcomed a crony of hers to the box, and they commenced to share all the latest news.

'Do you see either one of them?' Amelia whispered, leaning close to Peter. She waved her fan languidly before her while her eyes methodically took note of the occupants in each box.

'Amelia, I trust we are doing the right

thing. I'd hate to set this up only to have it rebound on Dancy or you.' Peter ignored the patrons to fix a troubled gaze on Amelia. The neckline of her gown distracted him greatly, had Amelia paid the least attention. The vast expanse of creamy skin above the delicate swell of her rather nice bosom had quite an effect on a susceptible male.

'Do think of a way that you can cross over to the far side of the theater so you may discover if they are to either side of us. And do not worry about me . . . or Lord Dancy, for that matter. These scoundrels must be taught a lesson, and how better than to use their own plan?'

'What a clever girl you are. I wonder if Dancy fully appreciates your consideration for his future.'

'I doubt it. But then, one must do one's duty.'

'You believe he is your duty?' Peter said in amazement, tossing a glance at his good friend who had just entered a box directly across from where Peter sat with Amelia. Surely no woman had ever placed Dancy in such a light.

'For the present,' Amelia replied somewhat obscurely.

Just then Mr Sands presented himself to Mrs Spencer and her crony, flattering the older lady outrageously. Peter surveyed the fellow with obvious distaste, then set about cultivating his acquaintance to learn what he could.

According to instructions, Peter managed to find out what the man's plans for the week were before he left the box. Amelia drew a sigh of relief when the door safely closed behind Thomas Sands.

Then Peter went on his errand of inquiry. Amelia had espied Miss Filbert in a box close to where Lord Dancy sat.

Within minutes she had the satisfaction of seeing Peter converse with a smirking Clarissa. Without seeming to, Amelia watched as the chat appeared to go as Peter desired.

She had not paid any attention to Lord Dancy during all this and was quite startled when he entered the box, seeking her side after bowing correctly to Mrs Spencer.

Amelia's heart fluttered in that alarming manner again, just as it always did whenever he hovered close to her.

'I am surprised to see Peter Blandford with you this evening.'

'Did you expect me to have Mr Sands as escort? I vow, sir, that is a rather harsh judgment upon your part.'

'Peter is a fine man, but you must know he has a very small estate.'

'I do not choose my friends because of their money. He is a very kind man, and he does not treat me as a silly girl.'

'You still believe that nonsense about Sands and Miss Filbert? By the bye, I met her as I came into the opera this evening. She seems a nice enough girl.'

'I understand some poison mushrooms are utterly beautiful,' Amelia responded obliquely.

'She can scarcely be labeled poison.'

'Truly, I did not say that she is such. Perhaps I cannot forget the words I heard her speak. But you are free to do as you please.'

'You have abandoned your determination to see their plan foiled? You agree with me that it's all a hum?'

Amelia turned her head to discover that Lord Dancy was alarmingly close to her, bending to speak softly in her ear so their speech might not be overheard. Her eyes sought his, and for several moments she absorbed his look. Concerned? Alarmed? Irritated? Whatever his emotions might be, they were hardly ardent.

Somehow Amelia survived the remainder of the opera. Lord Dancy returned to his box when Peter came back from his errand of inquiry.

'I say,' Peter whispered while the soprano warbled on about her tragic love, 'I hope

Dancy isn't angry with me. Near froze me with that glance of his.'

'No, I doubt it, more's the pity,' Amelia replied. 'I cannot see him being jealous of anyone, especially not one as nice as you.'

Peter seemed highly gratified at her kind regard of him and sat with a smug expression for the rest of the opera.

When she retired that evening, she related the furtherance of the plan to Chen Mei with less than might be expected relish.

'You upset. If you think things should go easy, they sure to be difficult. Best to anticipate trouble, then things not so bad,' she counseled in Cantonese.

'Well, Peter said that Miss Filbert and Mr Sands are both to be at the Twysden soirée Thursday, Lord Dancy as well. I convinced Aunt Ermintrude that we simply must attend. So, we go to Almack's tomorrow night, then the Twysden affair the next. By that time I ought to have everything well in hand.'

Chen Mei looked rather dubious, but was far too fond of her charge to point out the large holes in her plan.

The following morning found Amelia at the little desk in the morning room, nibbling on a pen while she contemplated what to put in the note to Mr Sands so it would be convincing. After all, she had avoided the man whenever possible. It would be difficult to suddenly declare she was most intrigued by him. But then, perhaps the man's conceit would ignore that fact.

At last with a bit of prompting from Chen Mei the note was written. Amelia signed and folded it with hope that her plan to save Lord Dancy from Clarissa Filbert could succeed.

'Missee write to Filbert next,' Chen Mei reminded.

Once that onerous task was completed, Amelia faced the day with a lighter heart. That evening at Almack's she found Lord Dancy in attendance and her pleasure increased tenfold. When he made his way through the crush of people to her side she found it difficult to speak, so flustered was she with his nearness. He bowed over her hand, with that charming smile Amelia found so delightful.

'I sought to request permission to dance the waltz with you only to discover you have already been approved for the dance. It seems Lady Jersey thought you a very pretty-behaved girl.'

'Well,' Amelia said judiciously, 'I did say that she was much younger and prettier than I had expected. And that I was not surprised to see most of the men sighing in her direction.'

'Minx. Sally adores flattery from all I have heard. However, it enables me to beg the next waltz.' His lazy grin sent Amelia's susceptible heart into a near frenzy of pitter-pattering.

'Of course. I am yours to command, my lord,' Amelia said with a sincerity that shook Geoffrey to his toes. He had grown accustomed to the coquetry of the young women who frequented London during the Season. Forthright behavior as Amelia displayed when with him was most unusual. He intended to watch carefully to see if she behaved like this toward other gentlemen.

He guided her onto the dance floor, slipping his arm about her with a sense of the familiar. After all, it had been mere weeks since he rescued her from the fire, carrying her to safety in his arms. He had not forgotten the sensation she created within him when she snuggled so trustingly against his chest, her arm so ingenuously curved about his neck.

Now he gathered her as close to him as proper manners permitted, enjoying her lightness in his arms, the delicate scent of lilies of the valley that wafted to his nose when he twirled her about the room.

He saw Clarissa Filbert staring at them from one of the chairs along the end of the room. Even in the light shed from the crystal chandeliers her antagonism was clear. The narrow-eyed gaze chilled Geoffrey to his bones. Could the chit actually harbor such silly notions in her head as Amelia had suggested? It seemed so absurd he would have dismissed it out of hand had he not caught sight of her countenance.

Mr Sands was not in evidence this evening, and suddenly Geoffrey wondered if the man was out arranging for the traveling coach to use while absconding with Amelia. Then sanity returned and Geoffrey dismissed the whole as too utterly fantastic.

Once returned to her aunt, Amelia watched with regret as Lord Dancy fell into the trap of inviting Miss Filbert to dance. Or . . . did he merely seek to allay her jealousy, or possibly encourage her plans?

Amelia had not failed to see the anger in Clarissa's eyes when Geoffrey had squired Amelia for the waltz. She told herself he asked Clarissa to perform the country dance with him only because it did not require intimate contact.

The remainder of the evening was less than delightful. Lord Dancy left early, as Mrs Spencer made a point of noting.

'Lord Dancy has gone. What a pity. A man who has such exceptional legs and dances as well as he ought to remain to show the others how to get on.'

'Perhaps he has an early appointment?' Amelia replied, glad to see her aunt had gathered her belongings in preparation to departure, even though the hour was not terribly advanced.

'We shall see him tomorrow at the Twysden affair. I asked him if he intends to go and he said yes. That lovely Mr Sands will be there as well. You will have a wonderful time, my girl.'

Amelia considered the odious Thomas Sands and barely repressed a shudder. She and Chen Mei would have to ensure their plot would prevail. They must. The alternative was unthinkable.

5

Aunt Ermintrude did not receive guests on the day of the Twysden's soirée. Instead she took Amelia shopping along Bond Street early in the morning before the Bond Street loungers took over, planning to rest that afternoon.

It was unthinkable that a lady should present herself on Bond Street at an hour when the fashionable gentlemen left their lodgings and hotels to saunter along to the circulating libraries and bookshops in the area or perhaps to enter Mr Truefitt's establishment for a session of barbering. An hour or two in the morning was all a lady might hope for in shopping time, and Aunt Ermintrude intended to make the best of her morning.

'I do so hope to find a lovely new evening hat or some appealing trifle,' she said with a wistful sigh. They strolled along, peering into shop windows, discussing all they found on display with keen interest.

'Come along,' Mrs Spencer said at last when convinced there was nothing tantalizing to be seen. 'I wish to go to Savory and Moore for I require some Daffy's Elixir and perhaps some distillation of willow bark. Oh, and I need more lavender water. When one has the headache there is nothing better than a soothing application of that after taking a bit of the willow bark liquid.'

Obediently following her aunt up the street, Amelia made discreet glances about her, taking note of who was out and about this day. When her aunt entered the apothecary shop, Amelia gladly followed, for she had caught a glimpse of Mr Sands exiting Long's Hotel and had no desire to have him latch on to her aunt's company. She lingered in the rear of the shop while her aunt made her purchase, hoping that Mr Sands would continue on his way without glancing in the shop window. Perhaps, considering his garb, he was on his way to play a game of tennis at the Royal Tennis Court, which was not far away in James Street. She hoped so.

'We shall stop at a perfumer's shop. There is one on Oxford Street I favor,' Aunt Ermintrude declared, her wrapped purchase tucked into the depths of her large reticule.

Relieved at escaping from Bond Street without having seen more of Mr Sands, Amelia immediately agreed.

Additional stops on Oxford Street produced a pretty fan with ivory sticks, and pink roses painted on the silk gauze.

'I wish you to have a new trifle for the Twysden soirée this evening. I believe Mr Sands will be attending,' Aunt Ermintrude said with a flutter of her lashes, for all the world like a young girl. 'You must contrive to make a better impression on him, my love. He is a most elegant and well-mannered young man.'

'Is he?' Amelia murmured. 'I thought he hinted that a Gretna Green elopement was not a thing to deplore when he visited the house the other day. Surely you cannot consider that well-mannered.'

'I do not recall such a remark,' Aunt replied, visibly confused. 'He seems such a nice person I can scarce think he actually believes *that*. Perhaps you misunderstood him? Your dear Papa desires you to make a suitable marriage, and I confess that Mr Sands is quite appealing. You should do more to attract his attention, my love.'

Amelia felt a shade guilty, for she well knew that Mr Sands had not made such a remark to her aunt. However Amelia knew he felt that way, yet she could hardly reveal her source of information, nor how she intended to deal with it that very evening.

While her aunt took her afternoon rest, Amelia sent off a note to Peter to remind him that she depended upon him to be present at the Twysden affair.

Some streets away Lord Dancy eyed the note delivered by Mrs Spencer's footman with barely concealed curiosity. He watched Peter unfold it, scan the contents, then toss the note aside on a table.

'A love letter, Blandford?' Geoffrey said idly.

'Actually, it is nothing of the sort. Miss Longworth reminds me that I am to attend the Twysden soirée this evening.' Peter added, 'You plan to go?'

'Now that you mention it, I believe I did send an acceptance to the lady.' Geoffrey fidgeted with the signet ring he wore, shifting on the chair, his manner edgy.

'Are you having difficulty with a woman, Dancy?' Peter inquired lightly. 'You know that girls, and servants as well come to think on it, are the most difficult people to handle. If you treat them familiarly, they become disrespectful; if you keep them at a distance, they resent it. Dashed hard for a fellow to know what to do at times.'

'No, no. Merely at loose ends for the moment.' Restless and annoyed at the amused glance Peter sent him at his interest, Geoffrey rose from the chair where he had lounged and chatted with his friend, making a barely coherent excuse to depart.

Out on the street Geoffrey debated on what to do. He had not planned to attend the Twysden soirée this evening at all in spite of his assurances to Mrs Spencer. They usually had the most boring of parties. But he knew he had received an invitation; it languished somewhere at the bottom of the pile of social correspondence that had accumulated of late.

Somehow Geoffrey found his feet directed to his residence, walking faster and faster the closer he came. Once there he plowed through his stack of gilt-edged and nicely lettered invitations until he found the one for the Twysden thing. Even the invitation looked boring. However he felt compelled to attend. He must know what was going on between Peter and Amelia Longworth.

He had seen their heads together too often to suit his taste. Amelia had seemed to turn to Peter ever since they had arrived in London. Yet she had declared that she belonged to Geoffrey Dancy, no one else. Never mind that he had refused her bizarre claim, he felt strong reluctance to permit anyone else to have her, either.

In short order he sent off a missive by his man to the effect that he begged Lady Twysden's pardon most humbly for being so late and prayed that he be allowed to attend her party that evening. He rather doubted that she would be annoyed, for single men were always in demand, especially for Lady Twysden.

Later that day at the house on Brook Street Amelia dressed for the evening with the greatest of care. She wanted to look seductive, yet demure; alluring, yet reserved. That was not an easy matter, she discovered quickly enough.

'It is your heart that is disturbed,' Chen Mei advised. 'Nothing seems fitting when you upset. Let the root be good and the fruit shall not be evil,' she quoted in Cantonese from her endless store of wisdom. She often managed to avoid her r problem by resorting to her native language when faced with the use of the troublesome letter.

'You know well and good that my motive is the purest. I can only pray that the fruit of my efforts will be as good as you seem to believe.' She flashed a minatory glance at her companion, then turned to the looking glass again, hoping to improve her appearance a trifle more.

At long last Amelia left her room, assured by Chen Mei that she was as well turned out as might be, considering she dressed in the English style rather than an elegant silk gown such as worn by the ladies of the Chinese court.

A quick check in the looking glass on the landing revealed to Amelia that her delicate turquoise gown of sheer sarcenet over a white satin slip and trimmed in pale peach silk roses and rouleaus of turquoise satin was all the crack. The neckline seemed shockingly low, but she knew it fashionable. Her gloved fingers touched the dainty sleeves puffed out and slashed with turquoise sarcenet over white satin. A pale peach rose nestled at the front of her bodice. Although Amelia thought it drew attention to her bosom far too much, Chen Mei muttered something about setting bait to catch a rat. After that Amelia kept silent.

'Amelia, my love, are you coming? I wish to leave early, else it will be impossible to draw near the house. The street is narrow, and I detest sitting in the carriage for an hour while my gown becomes horridly rumpled.'

'Coming,' Amelia replied and skimmed down the stairs with as much haste as seemly, followed by Chen Mei arrayed for once in a simple black gown. It was Chinese in style and made of elegant lustrous silk.

It was fortuitous that they arrived early for it presented Amelia with an opportunity to set the stage as it were. She was able to station herself so she knew precisely when Clarissa Filbert arrived and observed the hurried consultation she held with Thomas Sands. When Peter Blandford came, Amelia had little trouble catching his eye.

Aunt Ermintrude had settled herself at a card table early on, leaving Chen Mei to keep an eye on Amelia, which suited the two of them to a tee.

Since there often was no dancing at a soirée, Amelia contented herself with joining in a game of charades. She was curious to know what the surprise might be that the hostess promised her later in the evening, but having been warned by Aunt, had no high expectations. Lady Twysden apparently had no great reputation as a hostess.

Amelia and Peter Blandford had just stumped the entire group with a charade depicting the abdication of Napoleon, which Peter felt due any moment, when she sensed that someone watched her. Looking about, Amelia discovered that Lord Dancy had come. Peter had assured her that he knew how to lure Dancy into coming. He'd succeeded. She edged her way until she stood next to an elegant Lord Dancy.

'Good evening, sir.' His eyes widened slightly as he studied her, and Amelia wondered if he also found the neckline of her gown to be just a trifle shocking.

'You and Peter make an excellent combination when it comes to charades. I have the feeling that you have had more than a bit of practice.'

Amelia attended to his words with one ear while she watched Clarissa Filbert signal to Thomas Sands.

'Ah, I wonder what Lady Twysden has planned for her surprise.' Amelia knew what she intended to do. If she could just get Lord Dancy to cooperate, all would go well and she could teach Clarissa a lesson that she would not forget in a hurry.

'Having just arrived, I could not imagine what her ladyship intends to dazzle us with as entertainment.'

Amelia noted the biting tone of his voice and glanced back at him. 'I gather you do not care for Lady Twysden's games, sir. Perhaps you ought to stick to cards?'

'Oh, there are games I enjoy,' he said with a highly provocative tilt to his brows. Those eyes, the color of precious jade, danced with an intimacy that Amelia found bone-melting in intensity.

'I do believe you tease me, sirrah,' Amelia said, batting her lashes as she had observed Aunt Ermintrude do, while hoping that she might survive his bedevilment.

'There are a number of things I should enjoy doing with you, my dear. Did you have a particular game in mind?'

'As a matter of fact, I did.' She gave him what she hoped was a flirtatious look. 'Would you meet me in the first room down the hall — on the right side?'

She didn't blame him for his hastily concealed look of astonishment. It was most unlike her usual circumspect behavior to beg his company.

'Now?'

'Most definitely now.'

He studied her with that inscrutable assessment as he had once before. Chen Mei had commented that he would have made an excellent Chinese, as he could so well conceal his thoughts if he chose. Then he bowed most correctly, sauntering off down the hall just as she had hoped.

Across the room Clarissa watched his departure with an avid gaze before signaling Mr Sands once again.

Amelia caught Peter's attention by wiggling her fingers at him to bring him to her side.

'Yes, my goddess,' he teased. 'You summoned me? I noticed you in conversation with Dancy a bit ago. Things coming to a head?'

'It is so simple I fear something may go

astray. Quick, follow him to the first room on the right, get him to hide behind that screen by any means you can. I checked there earlier, and that is an excellent place to eavesdrop on all that happens. If you must, tell him that you have a surprise for him.'

'Will do,' Peter replied with commendable brevity. He circled the drawing room, then paused in the adjacent card room before slipping along the hall to where Lord Dancy waited.

Fortunately Clarissa had not noticed Peter Blandford's departure. She was undoubtedly so intent upon timing her arrival at the room where she suspected Lord Dancy was that she missed all else. She conferred a few minutes with Thomas Sands before nonchalantly walking toward the hallway.

Amelia watched, drawing Chen Mei to her side so to be poised to pounce at the proper moment. For one frustrating moment Amelia thought she would be drawn into the game of charades again, only to be reprieved by Lady Twysden.

'I want you all to meet the famous Dr. Spurzheim,' she gushed with enthusiasm. 'He lectures on the new science of phrenology and is going to demonstrate how one can determine much of the character of a person, his disposition, even his chance of success in life by the shape of his head.'

The good doctor bowed most correctly, then drew one of the young men forward to begin his demonstration.

Amelia gave thanks for the diversion offered. Although it might be interesting to hear the opinions of this man, she was wary of such fatalistic views. Why, it would seem that no one had any control over his destiny if what the man said was true. And what if a gentleman was hit on the head? A new bump might change his entire future!

She stationed herself in an alcove just outside the drawing room, ostensibly admiring a small sculpture of a horse with Chen Mei properly at her side and making snide observations on the poor quality of the supposed Ming piece.

Clarissa walked to the first room on the right after peering into those on the left side. Amelia slipped around the corner, leaving Chen Mei positioned to watch the door. Giving a message to a footman, she then watched as Thomas Sands marched around the corner and along the hall, pausing cautiously at the first door on the right before entering.

Behind the screen Geoffrey had given his friend an exasperated look. 'I daresay you have a reason for your hare-brained behavior, but I'll be dashed if I can see what it is.'

'Patience, my good fellow. Only a few moments more.'

At that the door to the room opened and Peter made a cautioning gesture.

'Lord Dancy? I must speak with you, sir. Lord Dancy?' Clarissa called again, this time more loudly.

When Geoffrey gave Peter a questioning look, his friend merely shook his head, raising a finger to his lips. So Geoffrey kept silent, wondering what this was all about and why Miss Filbert thought she must speak with him.

'Oh, bother,' Clarissa muttered. 'I made certain he was in here. Where else could he be? The other rooms are all empty.' She turned as though to depart when the door opened.

'Clarissa! What are you doing in here alone? I thought you had Dancy with you. That was the idea, if you recall,' he said in a voice that dripped with sarcasm. 'In case you have forgotten, you are to lure him in here first, *then* summon me.'

'Well, doubting Thomas, I did not summon you here, nor did I find Lord Dancy here as I'd expected. He cannot disappear, after all. He must be nearby. Quickly, you must go before someone finds us here alone. If you recall,' she hissed with matching sarcasm, 'I am to be compromised with him, not you. You have no money, my darling. He has pots of it. Speaking of which, why are you so slow with that twit Amelia Longworth. I thought you would have that matter taken care of by now. Or had you forgotten that we need a goodly sum of money upon which to live? Neither of us has common tastes.'

'True, my love. I shall flee here immediately. But before I go, allow me one small boon?' With that he stole a lingering kiss.

Precisely at that moment the door flew open and Mrs Spencer stood, utterly aghast at the sight before her. She cried out in horror, and in moments a cluster of people gathered about to stare at the well-compromised couple, Clarissa Filbert and Thomas Sands.

'Well, I never,' Mrs Spencer declared to the sorely afflicted Mr Sands. 'And to think I believed you such a gentleman. Such behavior is not at all seemly!' She turned her gaze from him to Clarissa and back again. 'I wish you well, sir. And you, Miss Filbert. I trust the wedding will occur ere long?'

There were titters of unkind laughter among the *tonnish*, gossipy gathering that flanked Mrs Spencer. That good lady was not amused, however. She glared at the culprits through narrowed eyes.

No doubt knowing that his goose was well and truly cooked, Mr Sands bowed, then bestowed a somewhat sickly smile on the lady who accused him with her gaze, not to mention a regrettable tongue. 'May you be the first to know that Miss Filbert had done me the honor of accepting my suit.'

Clarissa was speechless. In fact it seemed to Geoffrey from where he stood behind the safety of the providential screen that Clarissa looked as though she had been hit over the head with a blunt instrument and merely waited to collapse.

Things were soon sorted out, with Mr Sands escorting Clarissa to her fond mama's side. The three left shortly after that, Mrs Filbert looking as though she was about to rupture her stays.

Geoffrey eased from behind the screen, followed by Peter. 'I gather this affecting scene is what you intended me to hear, if not see?'

'Yes, well, we thought it best to handle it this way. Sands was becoming a shade too particular in his attentions to Amelia, and Miss Filbert had determined to entrap you this very evening. Amelia thought this would wrap things up quite neatly.'

'Amelia *planned* all this?'

'I suspect that Chen Mei had a devious hand in it as well. She is devilishly good when it comes to plotting.'

'Really?' Geoffrey controlled his temper with difficulty until he began to see the funny side of it all. 'Do you realize that she has paid me back one? For that Filbert girl would have been the figurative death of me, had I been forced to wed her.'

'Oh, she didn't wish to marry you. Have you forgotten? All she wanted was your money. She planned to give you such a disgust of her that you would cry off, whereupon she would take you to court with a breach of promise suit so fast it would make your head swim.'

'I'd heard of men doing something like this, but never truly expected it of a woman. And' — he gave Peter a rueful look — 'I cannot say it does much for one's dignity to be considered merely as a potential source of income.'

'Oh,' Peter said after chuckling at this sally, 'I fancy there is some woman about who will have you. The trick is to know where to look.'

'And I suppose you know just where that is?'

'No need to come over the lord with me, Dancy. We have been through far too much together.'

111

The two men strolled from the now-deserted room with rapport reestablished, intent upon finding a drink with which to seal their strengthened bond.

'Just a moment, Blandford. Find me a glass of wine. I see Miss Longworth over there and wish to speak with her.'

Peter nodded, a knowing grin crossing his face before heading in the direction of a servant from whom wine might be obtained.

As he approached Amelia, Geoffrey stared at her. That gown just bordered on the proper. Never mind that many other women wore similar gowns this evening or other evenings, for that matter. All he could think of was that Amelia ought not be revealing quite so much skin.

She seemed part angel, part devil, no doubt because of that Chinese woman's influence upon her. Certainly her aunt would never think of such connivance. What was Amelia's aim? Did she seek to ensnare him?

'I see you are quite safe from harm, my lord,' Amelia said demurely.

'If you mean Clarissa Filbert, I daresay you are correct. Blandford tells me I owe my deliverance to you?'

'No, it is I who owe you a debt, or had you forgotten?'

Geoffrey stared at her. Forgotten that he

had carried her in his arms from the blazing inn, cradled her close to him, learning the delicate shape of her with amazing intensity?

'No,' was his totally inadequate reply.

'I think you ought to consult Dr. Spurzheim.' She gestured to the man who continued to fascinate his audience. 'Perhaps he may be able to tell you about your character. I believe you are noble and kind. I hear things, of course. But . . . ' Her voice trailed off in a suggestive manner that irritated Geoffrey.

'Amelia, my love, let us depart. My nerves are utterly shattered that Mr Sands would prove to be such a naughty man. I declare, he quite deserves that frightful Clarissa Filbert and her mama.'

After bestowing a twinkling smile on Geoffrey, Miss Longworth gracefully drifted after her aunt. He watched as they made a properly reluctant farewell to their hostess. Then they disappeared from view.

Within moments Geoffrey followed suit, quite forgetting about Peter and the wine, declining Lady Twysden's offer to introduce him to Dr. Spurzheim. The notion that another female thought he needed help of any sort was entirely too much and he went home to bed, thus shocking his valet.

Geoffrey had paused outside of the

Twysden house, taking note of the number of men clustered about in the shadows. Unusually prudent, rather than walk as he had intended to do, Geoffrey took a chair home. There was something about the men that bothered him. Bah! He was turning into an old woman, thanks to that Longworth chit and all her fears. But she had saved him from a great deal of expense, not to mention notoriety that could have cost him a respectable marriage — when he finally chose to wed.

Just who that lady might be, he truly had no idea. But, he determined, she would not be an angelic blonde with positively wicked blue eyes.

★ ★ ★

Across London Thomas Sands paced back and forth in his lodgings with furious mutterings against the same young woman. To his friend and confidant, John Pringle, he declared, 'She was behind it all, of that I am sure. It is all her fault that I must be forced to wed Clarissa without two shillings to rub together when I'd counted on piles of nice shiny guineas.'

'Nothing you can do about it now, Sands.'

'Oh? You think not?' Mr Sands came to a

halt, rubbing his chin with a reflective gesture. 'I disagree. Wouldn't you say that aunt of hers would give a bundle to save her niece from a scandal? Just because Clarissa's part in this affair has gone amiss don't mean that my plan need fail. I shall proceed as soon as able.'

'By Jove,' breathed Mr Pringle in reply, all admiration.

★ ★ ★

Aunt Ermintrude was in such a state that she declined to leave the house for a day, claiming an indisposition.

Since no one suspected she had nurtured plans for Mr Sands, no connection was drawn. At any rate most of the *ton* knew Sands to be without a feather to fly with, so of course no provident parent or guardian would consider him as a potential *parti*.

Amelia did not find the enforced quiet unpleasant. She persuaded Chen Mei to take a stroll with her, intent upon the peace and greenery of Hyde Park.

When Mr Sands came into view, she gave Chen Mei a dismayed look before casting about to see if she might turn aside and avoid the man. They were truly hedged in. It seemed there was no help, unless she did an about-face and went the other way. No coward, she elected to see what he had to say.

'Ah, the fair Miss Longworth of the celestial blue eyes and exquisite blonde curls.'

'Miss Filbert is not with you this morning? I am sorry not to see her, for I had no opportunity to wish her happy last evening.'

'You were not present when I made the, er, announcement, then?' Mr Sands frowned as though trying to recall if he had seen her or not.

Amelia retreated slightly at his intense gaze. For just a moment it had seemed most malevolent.

'It looks to rain, sir. We had best make our way back to my aunt's house. I would not ruin my bonnet.' The clouds were of the type that could possibly bring a shower.

'Oh, my dear Miss Longworth, permit me to take you up in my carriage,' he replied with thoughtful promptness. 'I would not forgive myself if your bonnet is ruined because I detained you merely to chat with so charming a lady.'

Amelia gave Chen Mei a wry look. A rumble of thunder gave her earlier remark most unwelcome support. 'Well, I truly would feel horrid if I jeopardized my new bonnet simply because I do not trust the man,' she murmured to Chen Mei in Cantonese.

'The struggle for rare possessions drives a man to actions injurious to himself,' observed Chen Mei in the same language as she studied the impatient young man now awaiting them next to his carriage. 'I think we walk.'

A light mist of rain began to fall.

'Allow me to take you both home. It might be a shade crowded, but I believe we can manage.' Mr Sands hastily put up the top on his cabriolet. Although intended for two, he obviously sensed the Chinese woman would not permit her charge to go without her.

Annoyed at the weather, Amelia felt she had no choice but to accept his fortuitous offer. She quickly climbed into the cabriolet, then watched as Chen Mei scrambled up with near-unseemly haste to perch close to her.

'I not trust the man,' she said softly in Cantonese.

'We shall be on our guard,' Amelia murmured back, then gave Mr Sands a demure look. 'It shall not take long, sir? I would hurry.'

He set off at a commendable clip, the hinged leather apron protecting their clothing from the falling mist. At the corner where Amelia knew he ought to have turned, he went straight ahead out of the city.

'Precisely where do you think to take us, Mr Sands? We wish to go home,' she said firmly, her worry increasing with each block.

'Oh, you shall get there . . . eventually.'

Amelia did not think his laugh at all amusing, nor had she any inclination to join him.

'I had planned for us to take the air at Barnet,' he said casually, referring to the well-known stage on the road north to Gretna Green. 'This rain requires we change to a closed carriage, but I fancy that will do us even better.'

Her protests fell on deaf ears. If anything his speed increased. They drove madly though the countryside that stretched from Hyde Park to the village of Barnet at a pace Amelia found frightening. Trees were but a blur, and had it not been for the carriage hood behind her, she was certain her bonnet would be long gone.

When they arrived at Barnet, he pulled his winded team to a halt, obviously intending to switch carriages and cattle here. Amelia tensed as he turned to face them.

'I want you to take a hackney back,' he said to Chen Mei. 'Give this message to Mrs Spencer immediately.'

Amelia snatched the note from his hand

and scanned the contents. 'You intend my aunt to ransom me from you for a handsome sum? What a cad you are, sirrah!'

At Amelia's side Chen Mei smiled and pulled her little dagger from her sleeve.

6

'You out, Mista' Sands,' Chen Mei said, bringing the dagger swiftly to Thomas Sands's throat. 'We go home now. You velly bad man. Tian Li no like you. You want too muchee money.' Chen Mei had quickly moved from her side of the cabriolet to appear half-crouched before Mr Sands as though conjured out of the mist.

The astounded man gave a croak of anger and shock. His hand dropped from Amelia's arm. The reins fell uselessly against the hinged leather apron, now pushed aside by Chen Mei, when he dropped them in his surprise.

An ostler ran forward to pick up the reins just as a familiar figure came into view around the side of the carriage, a pistol held unwaveringly in his hand. The ostler held the horses, his eyes wide at the strange doings of the Quality.

'Amelia, are you all right?' Lord Dancy held out one hand toward her with a side nod to Chen Mei.

'Oh, Lord Dancy,' Amelia wailed, clambering hastily down from the carriage and

120

flinging herself against his broad and welcome chest. His free arm wrapped around her, offering splendid comfort, hugging her against him with an intensity that Amelia found most agreeable.

'Not trust Mista' Sands,' Chen Mei repeated. 'Lord Dancy know what do with him. Send message this day.' Obviously satisfied that a true gentleman was here to deal with the blackguard, Chen Mei removed her little dagger from the spot against Mr Sands's throat, then sat back, arms folded, to watch Thomas Sands reap his punishment.

'I am reckoned to be a dead shot, Sands, but if you contest that opinion, I should be happy to demonstrate my aim.' Peter Blandford stepped from the other side of the carriage, a pistol trained directly at the hapless Sands.

Mr Sands, now faced with two pistols aimed at his head and heart plus a quixotic Chinese woman at his side ready to slit his throat with a wicked-looking dagger, swallowed with difficulty and appeared near fainting.

Amelia withdrew from Lord Dancy's protection after that most comforting embrace, suddenly aware of the impropriety of her behavior. It had been an instinctive move on her part to turn to him, for he had saved her before and she trusted him implicitly. She tossed Mr Sands a dark look.

'That miserable creature did not give up his dastardly scheme to swindle money from my father by kidnapping me as I thought he must,' Amelia cried. She glared at Mr Sands. 'He intended to abduct me so he could obtain the money he needs to marry Miss Filbert. Surely there is a fine for kidnapping an heiress? I recall reading something to that effect not long ago.'

At this information Mr Sands turned even more pale. He clambered down from the carriage with dispatch, then stood uneasily while casting a wary eye on Peter Blandford and Lord Dancy, both of whom looked more menacing than his future mother-in-law. She was certain to give him a wigging for mismanaging this affair.

The mist eased and a pale March sun peered from behind a cloud. Amelia shivered, wishing she was anywhere but involved in such a frightful mess.

'This is too much. You gentlemen may do as you please with this creature. Chen Mei and I intend to go home.' For no reason she could think of, Amelia felt like crying and she hated to have anyone see her dissolve into a watering pot, particularly Lord Dancy. She had tried to be brave all the while the carriage had racketed from London to Barnet. She had remained calm when Chen Mei thrust her dagger at Mr Sands's throat. Now that it was all over, her knees felt thoroughly unreliable, and she longed for her bed and a cup of tea, not necessarily in that order.

There was hasty conversation between Lord Dancy and Peter Blandford, who managed to keep their guns trained on Mr Sands all the while. Chen Mei planted herself close by, her dagger again in evidence lest Mr Sands take a notion to do something unpleasant.

In short order Amelia found herself being assisted into Lord Dancy's curricle, with Chen Mei sharing the small seat behind with the affronted groom, Hemit. Since she was tiny, if intimidating, it truly did not inconvenience him. Perhaps he too vividly recalled that dagger?

'You have saved my life again, sir,' Amelia said in a wavering voice. She settled back on the seat, accepting the small rug that Lord Dancy placed over her lap and legs with a nod. She admired the manner in which he gave the horses the office to start, the carriage taking off with a smooth motion. The leather hood remained up, offering them a modicum of privacy.

'I hardly think so,' he replied blandly while

he skillfully guided the two horses along the road back to London. 'Chen Mei had things well under control. I should say that you merely completed your task of delivering me from the clutches of Clarissa Filbert. My, what a heartless little thing she is.'

'But I do not believe we could have managed without you,' she stubbornly persisted.

'No? The sight of Chen Mei with a dagger at Thomas Sands's throat would most assuredly have drawn sufficient attention for you to get all the help you need.'

Amelia gave him a thoughtful look and subsided. It seemed he did not want any part of her gratitude for rescuing her from the dastardly hands of Thomas Sands. Dancy didn't want her thanks, nor did he wish her to feel obligated to him. It seemed to her as though Geoffrey, Lord Dancy, did not appreciate her devotion. Pity, that, for Chen Mei had taught Amelia well. One fulfilled one's duty, and Amelia's duty was to look after Lord Dancy.

He competently guided the carriage through the press of city traffic until they reached Berkeley Square. Here he drew up, then handed the reins to his groom, who still looked as though he had been sucking on a lemon.

The short-lived shower had moved on to

the east, leaving the streets freshly washed; a lovely spring sun beamed down upon London. Refreshed by the rain, daffodils and primroses bloomed from pots and window boxes. Indeed, the city was beginning truly to come to life. The square bustled with others who had braved the uncertain weather to sample Mr Gunter's rightly famous fare.

'I thought you might enjoy an ice from Gunter's. Or perhaps tea, if you are chilled.' Lord Dancy signaled to the young waiter who came dashing across from the shop to take the order. 'Well? Which shall it be? Ice or tea?'

Amelia was chilled, but she had yet to enjoy an ice in the comfort of Lord Dancy's curricle. You did not have to be in London long before learning that this was one of the places to be seen. Her earlier malaise seemed to have vanished. Lord Dancy had a wondrous effect upon her.

'An ice, please. Lemon, I believe.' When the waiter sprinted back to the shop, she gave Dancy an artless smile, then added, 'I have not been here before, and I have longed to sample the ices.'

'You mean none of the sprigs who have been lingering in Mrs Spencer's salon has taken you to Gunter's?' he said in mock horror. 'What poor-spirited things they are.'

'Oh, I doubt that, merely that they are leery

of being too particular in their attentions,' she replied with surprising honesty. 'I suppose that were the amount of the dowry Papa has settled on me or the size of his fortune be revealed, I would be flooded with requests to drive out, not to mention attend plays and see Astley's Amphitheater.' Her cynicism was temporarily ignored when Dancy fastened upon one detail that worried him.

'I'd not wish to see you go to Astley's without adequate protection.' He frowned so that the young waiter looked apprehensive when he hurried up with their ices.

'If you feel I must, then of course I must,' Amelia said simply, not including the information as to where she intended to acquire that extra security.

At that moment Peter Blandford drove up in Mr Sands's carriage. He leaped out, giving instructions to the badly shaken young man who took over the reins without so much as casting a glance at Lord Dancy and Amelia.

'You are allowing him to go free?'

'What charges could we bring against him without doing you a great deal of harm in the process?' Lord Dancy argued.

'I see,' she said, thinking back to the note. Thomas Sands had calculated that her aunt would rightly desire to prevent all gossip and scandal from touching her fledgling niece.

Even though they foiled his attempt to extort money, they could not prosecute without damaging Amelia's reputation. There were so many who would titter behind their gloved hands, speculating on what had happened, had she cooperated, and to what extent.

The two men chatted while Amelia consumed her ice in silence. Peter Blandford explained what he had said to Sands, then launched into another matter dealing with a horse sale at Tattersall's.

It was most thoughtful of Lord Dancy to order an ice for Chen Mei also. But then, Amelia had observed that he was a remarkably considerate man. Fancy his charging after her when he received Chen Mei's message. It said much for that sense of duty she had observed in him before.

Amelia allowed her thoughts to wander, contemplating on what her aunt would say when informed of this escapade. Then another gentleman came up, placing his foot on one of the wheel spokes of the curricle while he spoke.

'Heard you are about to race Taunton? Think that wise? The man's a bit of a goer.'

Amelia pretended not to have paid the least attention to this remark when Lord Dancy glanced her way. She looked across the square while concentrating on what was said.

'One of those things, old fellow. You know how it is.'

'Ought to be a dashing good time of it.'

From the corner of her eye Amelia could see Lord Dancy shake his head at the two men, effectively silencing them regarding the upcoming race.

Knowing that she would not hear anything of value from now on, Amelia turned back to the men, then briefly touched Lord Dancy's arm. Placing her hands most properly into her lap, she smiled, then said, 'I expect I had best return home. Aunt Ermintrude might become worried that I am gone so long.'

'Of course, Miss Longworth,' Dancy replied correctly, for all the world as though he had not rescued her while she was wearing nothing more than a nightgown and robe, carrying her to safety while clutched tightly to his chest. That was a secret between them, and Peter Blandford, of course. Amelia tended to discount that young man, for although he was kind and pleasant, he was not Lord Dancy.

Leaving the two gentlemen gazing thoughtfully after them, Lord Dancy drove Amelia through the streets of London until he reached Mrs Spencer's home.

With a glance to the rear where she knew Chen Mei sat, Amelia faced Lord Dancy with pleading eyes. 'Could you come in for a few minutes, sir? I would have you explain all to my aunt. She is inclined to the vapors, I suspect, and I fear that Chen Mei may frighten her. If you are present, my companion will remain silent, for she holds you in great respect.'

'And your aunt would not listen to what you say?'

'Well, listen, but perhaps discount it.'

Geoffrey handed the reins to his groom, who looked somewhat relieved to see the Chinese dragon disappearing into the house. Geoffrey smiled with amusement at the reactions of the man who had been with him for years. Very few things frightened Hemit. Chen Mei not only frightened him, she rendered him speechless.

Geoffrey assisted Amelia from his curricle, considering all the while her comments on how Mrs Spencer and Chen Mei so greatly respected him. He wondered precisely how Amelia felt about him. Perhaps for the first time in his life he really wished he knew how a young woman regarded him. Respect? He was beginning to hope for something stronger than that. She had flown to him, nestling against his body in terror. He found her trust overwhelming in a way. It placed such responsibility on his shoulders. And yet . . . it also gave him the sensation of being ten feet tall, for she had gazed at him with what almost amounted to adoration in her eyes.

It was most likely the thing of a moment, the situation being highly charged with anxiety. Still, he found her dependence in his ability to right all wrongs very satisfying.

They found Aunt Ermintrude in her salon, for once alone, for it was not her afternoon to receive callers. Apparently Chen Mei elected to go up to her room, and Geoffrey felt the slim figure at his side give a sigh of what was most likely relief.

'Lord Dancy, Amelia, my little love!' Mrs Spencer exclaimed with relief.

'I feel I owe you an explanation for keeping Miss Longworth so long. You see, we went for a drive, then to Gunter's for an ice where we met friends. You know how time can fly.'

Mrs Spencer gazed at the two with a dubious look on her face. 'Ices? I was told that Amelia went haring off along Park Lane with that odious Thomas Sands in that dashing cabriolet of his. At least two people saw it.'

Geoffrey exchanged a look with Amelia, who bloomed a lovely tint of pink at the uncovering of her deception.

'It threatened to pour, as you know it eventually did, and Mr Sands insisted upon taking Chen Mei and me up in his carriage. Only he did not take us home, but rather to Barnet with the intention of holding me for ransom. He wanted a hideous sum of money to have me released.'

Here Geoffrey interposed his comments. 'Chen Mei sent me a message to the effect that she worried about Mr Sands, that he might attempt something while she and Amelia walked in Hyde Park. Fortunately it came as I was about to go out for a drive. I merely guided my horses in the direction of the park to see Sands heading up Park Lane. I followed him, thus saving Amelia the fate intended for her.'

'We are greatly indebted to you sir. I know Amelia will say that she owes you yet another obligation.'

'No, no,' Geoffrey hastily inserted into what he feared would be a long recitation of his merits. 'It was something any gentleman would have done. Blandford was there and Miss Longworth is as indebted to him as to me.'

'Aunt, Lord Dancy held a gun on Mr Sands, as did Mr Blandford. I believe they quite frightened him. I doubt if he will present himself to me again.' She turned to face Geoffrey, offering him her hand. 'Thank you, sir. You are a true hero.'

'Your servant, Miss Longworth.' He found the steady, trusting gaze from Amelia to be prodigiously unnerving. 'However, I do not think we can discount the watchful eye and faithful service of Chen Mei. She held Sands in place with a dagger, after all.'

'Amelia, I cannot like the thought of that woman carrying a dagger about with her, even if she does conceal it up one of those enormous sleeves.' Aunt Ermintrude frowned in consideration of the things she had to endure with that foreign woman beneath her roof.

'But Aunt, it undoubtedly made a great difference,' Amelia argued.

Sensing that this disagreement might continue for some time, Geoffrey begged to be excused and went on his way with the repeated thanks of both ladies ringing in his ears.

He gave his groom a nod, at which the fellow jumped up beside Geoffrey. 'Good going, Hemit. All in all it's been quite a day.'

'Think the young leddy heard that business about your race, milord?' Hemit inquired after a bit.

'Hard to tell. She appeared to be looking rather intently on the near carriage. That woman in the awful hat, you know, the one with the lime green cabbage roses and fuchsia ribbons on that enormous straw.'

'Rather,' Hemit agreed, but looked dubious.

Amelia removed her pelisse, feeling as though she had been from the house for days instead of a few hours.

'My love, you do seem to get into the most remarkable situations,' her aunt said, obviously wondering precisely where Lord Dancy stood in all this.

Amelia waved a hand as though to dismiss past events from discussion. 'I heard something ominous today.'

'Never! What?'

'While we were sitting across from Gunter's and consuming our ices — and they certainly are delicious, by the by — some man came up to Lord Dancy to inquire about his upcoming race with a man called Taunton. The way he referred to this man made me very curious. I believe I shall try to find out something about this Mr Taunton. Or Lord Taunton, as the case may be.'

'Name is familiar. I seem to recall a Lord Taunton of some years ago, which must be this man's father. Gambled away his estate, or as near as may be. Nasty creature as I recall. I wonder if his son has managed to bring his estate about?'

'All the more reason to find out what I may

about him, do you not think?'

'Oh, by all means,' Aunt Ermintrude agreed with a firm nod. The dainty roses on her daycap quivered, possibly in anticipation of another interesting series of events. Life was never dull with Amelia about the house.

Amelia left her aunt to saunter up the stairs to her room. Once there she consulted with Chen Mei.

'Mista' Blandfo'd, he know race man,' Chen Mei offered.

'Then we had best send for him, for I have very bad feelings about this, merely from their voices, you understand. That, and the interesting fact that Lord Dancy did not wish me to know about this race.'

'Maybe ladies not attend races? Not ploper?'

'Perhaps. There are a great many things considered first rate for gentlemen but not proper for ladies. It is all very confusing.'

'Send message to Blandfo'd,' Chen Mei advised.

'I believe I shall,' Amelia replied, crossing her room to sit down before the pretty little desk. She drew forth a sheet of pressed paper that was lightly scented. It took but a short time to compose the note for Peter Blandford. If she knew the young man at all, he would be here as soon as he possibly might.

It was some time after tea that Mr Blandford presented himself at Mrs Spencer's front door, requesting to see Miss Longworth, stating he was expected.

As indeed he was and the butler had been so advised.

'Mr Blandford,' Amelia caroled as she gaily floated down the stairs to where he stood in some bemusement at the sight of her.

'Miss Longworth, you continually amaze me. Where another woman would take to her bed with potions and lavender water, you appear untouched by your ordeal. In fact, you look like a veritable sprite in your green sprigged gown and the crown of flowers in your hair. Very lovely, if I may say so.' He bowed correctly over her hand, then waited for her to speak.

'What a dear you are, to come to my aid like this. As to being untouched by the day's events, well, I find it best to put the unpleasant behind me, for it does no good to dwell upon it. Come . . . we had best join my aunt in the salon where we shall confer.'

His curiosity piqued, Peter followed her up the stairs after she had requested refreshments for Mr Blandford from the stern-faced butler, a fellow aptly named Grimm.

'Now,' Amelia began once Grimm had departed after placing a tray with tea and biscuits, and an excellent canary wine for Mr Blandford on a table close by, 'I wish to know all about the gentleman who intends to race against our Lord Dancy.'

She handed Peter the wine, poured tea for her aunt and herself, then passed biscuits. Grimm would have been delighted to do all this, she knew, but since no one would speak while he was still present, she was happy to send him along.

'I gather Benedict, Lord Taunton, is the man you mean,' Peter replied, thus confirming Mrs Spencer's guess.

'Indeed, Lord Taunton,' echoed Aunt Ermintrude. 'Knew his father. What a nasty little man he was, too. Gamester, as you may know. Lost nearly everything. Would have lost the rest, but he stuck his spoon in the wall in time to prevent it.' She studied the far wall with a reflective expression on her face.

'Taunton is no great shakes, either. Oh, he does not sail quite as close to the wind as his father did, but close enough. Still has his estate, but barely, I suspect. He gambles, but with amazing success. I'd not say he cheats, for I scarcely wish to face him in a duel, but I have my doubts about his incredible luck with cards or anything else he tries.' Peter took a fortifying sip of his wine, then leaned back against his chair while waiting for the delightful ladies to astound him with whatever they intended to do.

'That puts a seal on my fears,' Amelia said, then firmed her lips with determination. 'I have this peculiar feeling, you see. I believe Lord Dancy is in danger.'

'Hardly likely in this race, Miss Longworth,' Peter said with a smile at the young lady sitting so demurely on the sofa. 'Dashed difficult to do as Hemit — he's Dancy's groom — will oversee everything, and he is as loyal as they come. I expect he will sleep with the rig just to see nothing happens to it.'

'Do things *happen* to carriages that are raced?' Amelia asked with deceptive mildness.

'Yes, I fear so,' Peter confessed. 'Why, I've seen any number of disasters, axles sawed into, wheel pins dislodged, a lot of things can go wrong with a carriage. Even the horses can be tampered with, you see. But in this case with Hemit on the job, there is no likelihood of danger. Dancy will be as right as rain.' Peter assured her with confidence.

'Forgive me for doubting you, sir. I am nothing more than a curious female, wanting to know about something I suppose most ladies do not attend?' She gave Peter a wistful smile that would have melted the heart of a marble statue, if a statue could have a heart.

Since Peter's heart was closer to butter, he

rushed to persuade her otherwise.

'Miss Longworth, let me convince you this is not so. Any number of ladies watch such a contest as this. While it would never do for a lady to take part in a race, it would be acceptable for you to sit in your carriage to watch the event. Dancy is certain to win, for his matched pair are prime goers.'

'Yes, I had noticed the horses this morning. They are beautifully matched chestnuts, Aunt Ermintrude,' she explained in the event her aunt was unaware of the excellence of Lord Dancy's horseflesh.

'You see, Miss Longworth, it is difficult to find a perfectly matched pair that also work together so well. Dancy and Hemit have turned this pair into a superb team. There is no way that Dancy can lose,' Peter added with supreme assurance in his friend.

'I expect there will be a prodigious amount of betting on the race?' Amelia said.

'I fancy so,' Peter assured her.

'Then if Lord Taunton has such an incredible ability to win when he bets, would it not seem likely that he does something to ensure that he wins this particular wager?' she demanded in her practical manner.

'I say,' Peter protested. 'That wouldn't be cricket.'

'Cricket or no, I shall not idly sit by while

Lord Dancy may be in danger,' Amelia declared.

'But, dash it all, I fail to see what you can do.'

'I have Chen Mei,' Amelia reminded her friend. 'You would be surprised at what the two of us can manage.'

A disturbed expression settled on Mr Blandford's face as he considered what this might entail. 'I say,' he began.

'Do not worry about it in the least, sir. We shall do no more than investigate, perhaps ask a few questions.' She spoke in a soothing manner, but for some reason Peter Blandford did not appear assured by her words.

He chatted about other things, confirmed that Miss Longworth was indeed not harmed by the morning's expedition, then left.

Chen Mei entered the room through the connecting door to the adjacent room, normally opened when there was a great deal of company.

'You listened?' Amelia asked.

'Man very foolish. No trust bad man in race. Dancy will lose,' Chen Mei concluded succinctly, again resorting to Cantonese.

'That is precisely what I believe,' Amelia said with a narrowed gaze. 'What utter nonsense to be sure. How in the world did Lord Dancy come to make a wager with such a man, I wonder?'

'And why would Lord Taunton desire such a race if Dancy's horses are such prime goers?' Aunt Ermintrude tossed out to the two others.

'Something mighty fishy here.'

Chen Mei nodded vigorously. 'Tian Li take care of Lord Dancy,' she said with supreme conviction.

'Oh, I must, mustn't I,' Amelia agreed with a resigned look at her aunt.

'Well . . . ' Aunt Ermintrude looked to where Chen Mei sat on the round ottoman, the picture of Oriental implacability.

'I fear he does not welcome my intervention, but dear aunt, he has saved my life so many times it is incumbent upon me to do all I can for him.'

'I suppose so,' Aunt Ermintrude said doubtfully. 'Still it seems to me that you go rather far, my love.'

'Nothing is too much for Lord Dancy,' Amelia concluded, this time with greater spirit and utter devotion.

'I fail to see how you will ascertain whether there is anything havey-cavey about this race.' Aunt Ermintrude looked first to Amelia, then to Chen Mei.

'Where there is determination, a way will be found,' Amelia declared fervently.

'We keep ears open,' Chen Mei said thoughtfully.

'True,' Amelia added. 'We can make a point of listening wherever we go. Perhaps I may be able to bring the race into conversation by some means.'

'I shall help as well by doing the very same thing,' Aunt declared with a delighted smile. 'I do so love intrigue, and this seems as interesting as my days ever get. I am very pleased your father sent you to me, my love. Think how dull this Season would have been otherwise.'

Amelia sent her dear aunt a grateful smile. She was not certain how she was to find out what she needed to know, but learn she would. Whether Lord Dancy liked it or not, she would do all she could to protect him from harm. And as far as she could see, this Lord Taunton was out to queer the race by some dastardly means. My, London was not so unlike Macao after all, where shady characters abounded.

All that remained was to discover which shady character in London intended to do Lord Taunton's dirty work and how.

7

'We shall have to find someone who is an expert at carriages to inspect Lord Dancy's for us, Chen Mei,' Amelia said thoughtfully.

'Bad man velly watchful. No want evil found light away,' Chen Mei said with shrewd insight.

'It is *right*, not light, Chen Mei,' Amelia said patiently. 'And yes, we do not need to search the carriage immediately. Lord Taunton may wait until the last moment to do the damage. We must find out precisely when the race is to be run. Mr Blandford failed to tell us that. I hope he comes to visit soon, or else I shall have to call on him for his help.'

Chen Mei murmured something in Cantonese that Amelia decided she would rather not hear. The companion was sitting on her favorite ottoman in the salon, embroidering a tiny peony on one of Amelia's plainer gowns. By the time she was finished, the gown would have an entire garden of dainty flowers embroidered here and there. Amelia felt very fortunate to have so talented an embroiderer with her as her own work, while not displeasing, couldn't compare to Chen Mei's.

An hour or so passed in peace. Amelia had just finished a letter to her dearest papa when she heard sounds from the hall.

Curious, she went to the landing to see what was going on for it was not the time for society callers to present themselves for tea and gossip.

Peter Blandford glanced up to see Amelia, then waved a hand as he murmured something to Grimm before dashing up the stairs. 'Good, you are home this morning.'

'We usually are, except for days when we get abducted to be held for ransom. Come into the salon. Shall you like anything to drink? Coffee?' She tucked her hand comfortably in the crook of his arm, tugging him along with her so they would be less apt to be eavesdropped upon. Aunt Ermintrude had loyal servants, but one never knew.

'Coffee sounds wonderful.'

Chen Mei placed her embroidery on the hassock, then slipped from the room to order the coffee for their guest. In moments she returned, picking up her embroidery and seeming to fade into the wallpaper.

Peter and Amelia chatted about the weather, which looked to be warming, and Napoleon, who looked to be fading, until one of the maids brought a tray bearing coffee and biscuits.

Once she had left, Peter took a sip from his cup then set it on the saucer with a loud clink, giving Amelia what she considered a desperate look.

'Tell me what is on your mind, Mr Blandford.'

'Please make it Peter, for you are like a sister to me. And that's the trouble.' He stared morosely at his loosely folded hands held before him.

'That you feel brotherly toward me is a problem?' Amelia replied, quite confused.

'Oh, no. 'Tis my sister who's the problem. She and m'mother came to town yesterday. She wants to attend Astley's. I am supposed to get up a party. Trouble is, I don't know any young girls suitable to present to my sister. Ain't been to Almack's; I avoid the chits who are looking for a husband. But I do know you.' Here he grinned at Amelia. 'Would you set aside your plans for the evening to join us at Astley's?'

'I should be pleased, but naturally I would have to consult with my aunt. Allow me to find her. I suspect she would enjoy a gala evening. I saw in the newspaper there is to be a special performance this evening that I believe would be quite wonderful to see,' she concluded shyly.

When Amelia left the room Chen Mei

suddenly spoke. 'You know good blacksmith? We need one to see Lo' Dancy's coach all right,' she said with care. 'Race come soon?'

'The end of this week, I believe,' Peter replied, quickly, following Chen Mei's enunciation carefully. 'I believe I know of a good fellow out near where the race is to be held. Unless Taunton wants the route changed to a different road. Since he challenged, Dancy chooses. I will look into it. You truly believe there will be something underhanded?'

'I do,' Chen Mei answered, clearly pleased that the intelligent young man would listen to her opinion.

Peter shook his head in dismay. 'I know Taunton is not the best of *ton*, but it's hard to accept he'd not act like a gentleman.'

Aunt Ermintrude was quickly found and proved most agreeable to the change in plans. She and Amelia bustled into the room, both wearing pleased smiles. Chen Mei returned to her embroidery.

'For we had planned to take in Mrs Evesham-Fowler's card party,' Aunt Ermintrude explained. 'I truly would enjoy a visit to Astley's, for I have not attended in years. And it would be a pleasure to see your mama once again. I met her a year or so ago with Lady Sefton, I believe.' If Mrs Spencer believed that the Royal Amphitheater, as Astley's was advertised, to be more for children, she gave no indication. Amelia wondered if she thought Peter might have an interest in her, hence Aunt's willingness to accompany the heir to the baronetcy of Blandford.

'Quite so, I imagine. They are good friends. I am ever so grateful to you both,' Peter beamed a smile at them. 'Mean to persuade Dancy to join us if he can tear himself away from . . . ' Peter clamped his mouth shut and turned slightly red.

Amelia wondered what it could be that caused his embarrassment, deciding it must be a woman Lord Dancy liked. Why the thought of Lord Dancy involved with some woman should cause Amelia a distinct pain in her heart, she couldn't understand. But, pain it did. To cover her peculiar reaction, she offered Peter another cup of coffee, then turned the conversation to what might be expected while at the evening performance.

'Chen Mei will most likely admire the horses, and a new song is to be introduced, 'Knowing Jerry',' he added with a mischievous glance at Amelia.

'I scarcely *know* what to make of that,' she replied primly. She joined him in a shared smile.

'There will be a lot of dashing fellows about that you must take care to avoid. A pretty girl like you is bound to attract attention,' Peter cautioned.

'It is nice to be thought pretty,' Amelia allowed, 'rather than be considered for my dowry.'

'Most of the fellows know to a penny what every young lady is worth. If they can find one who is pretty *and* well to grass, all the better,' Peter observed with brutal honesty.

'I gather Lord Dancy is not particularly interested in finding a wife,' Mrs Spencer said pensively.

'More's the pity. After what he's been through these past years, he needs the comfort of his home. His sisters are away, and the middle one married while he was gone. Wouldn't surprise me were the other two to marry within the year. Both of 'em are dashed pretty from all accounts I've heard. His parents were killed while on a trip to France to visit the *Bibliothéque Nationale* — a trip authorized by Napoleon himself. Someone accused them of treason when all they wished to do was examine a manuscript. Before anyone could rush to their aid, they were dead. Murdered, if you ask me. Why, no one knows.' Peter cleared his throat, then took a restoring sip of coffee. Since it had cooled considerably during his revelations, it lacked a certain something.

'How tragic,' Amelia murmured, her heart going out to the gentleman so alone in the world. At least she had her dear papa and Chen Mei. Aunt Ermintrude, as well.

'Well, I must be off. Want to catch Dancy before he is out and about.' Peter rose from his chair, waiting politely for his dismissal.

'Is Lord Dancy inclined to sleep late?' Amelia wondered. She rose from her place on the sofa to walk with Peter to the door.

'Actually he tends to business in the morning — correspondence, messages from his estate's steward, that sort of thing. His steward tries to persuade Dancy to come out to inspect the place he inherited. For some reason' — and here Peter looked a bit self-conscious, — 'he's reluctant to leave London.'

Although Amelia said nothing, she suspected that whatever kept Lord Dancy in London wore skirts and perfume.

They agreed upon a time to depart for the Royal Amphitheater in time to be present for the eight-thirty overture, then Peter clattered down the stairs and out to the street where his groom had patiently been walking his horse and curricle.

Amelia ran to the window, peering down to the street below. She observed that Peter drove off in the direction of Lord Dancy's home. Dropping the curtain, she stood a moment, wondering just who the lady was that had captured Dancy's interest. Most likely she would be slender, dark-haired, with shining black eyes and perfectly white skin. She would wear the most dashing gowns in seductive red satin and brazen black lace. Amelia thought she might hate the woman given the slightest provocation. And then she wondered about her intense reaction to this bit of news.

'Come, my love,' Aunt Ermintrude trilled, 'we had best decide what to wear this evening. Were it later in the year, we might have gone to Vauxhall Gardens, and that, I may tell you, is a wondrous place. When the weather turns warmer, we shall make up a party. It is something I know your dear papa would wish you to see.'

Chen Mei watched as the two women left the room, then she sank into a reflective silence. In a short while she went to the butler's pantry and, after making sure he was not around, sharpened her little dagger. One never knew. At long last she hastened to Amelia's room to see what she might do to help.

'It will not be easy, to persuade Dancy of bad man,' Chen Mei observed for no apparent reason.

At a curious look from Amelia, Chen Mei said in Cantonese, 'It is easy to convince a wise man, but to reason with a fool is a difficult undertaking.'

'You do not believe that *he* is a fool, do you? Rather believe that Taunton is the stupid one. He is the one who hopes to win by harming another,' Amelia argued.

'In your acquaintance with a man you may know his face, but not his heart. His mind is as hidden from you as by a thousand mountains. Who knows what is in Dancy's heart?'

Since Amelia would like to know that very thing, she said nothing to the topic, reverting to their foe. 'Taunton is the enemy. He cannot be considered as trivial.'

'There is no sin greater than ambition; no calamity greater than discontent; no vice more sickening than covetousness. He who is content, always has enough,' Chen Mei quoted from her store of Chinese proverbs. It never ceased to amaze Amelia how the woman could manage to think of a proverb that covered nearly every situation.

'Since Taunton gambles heavily on the race, I imagine he qualifies for nearly any one of those. He truly is an evil person, for Mr Blandford said he's not a good person. We must find a way to keep Lord Dancy from this unprincipled man,' Amelia replied.

'What did she say?' Aunt Ermintrude said with curiosity, obviously not wishing to be in the dark.

'She believes the man who opposes Lord Dancy, Lord Taunton, to be a fool,' Amelia said, arranging the facts to suit what she contended to be true. 'But even fools can win by evil measures, if only for a time.' Amelia refused to accept the notion that Lord Dancy might be thought a fool, even by Chen Mei.

'What a wise little thing you are, my love,' Aunt Ermintrude observed. Then she turned to sort through the gowns in the wardrobe in search of one that would dazzle the group this evening. She settled on a delicate blue sarcenet with silver threads woven through it. Silver ribbons enhanced the tiny puffed sleeves and the low neckline.

Amelia took one look, acquiesced, deciding she had best bring along a shawl else she might have to endure the sort of attentions Mr Blandford cautioned her against.

Later that evening they joined the Blandford trio in the commodious town chariot that the Blandfords used when in London. Evidently they were a large family, for Mary mentioned how delighted her younger sisters would be to hear her account of a visit to the famous equestrian attraction.

The crowd was far greater than Amelia had anticipated. Suddenly she was pleased that Chen Mei hovered at her side and that Lord Dancy had agreed to meet them later in the evening.

Lady Blandford audibly regretted that her husband, the baron, had not joined them this evening. 'He must go off to his club, I know, but I would feel better in this crush were he at my side.'

'The second spectacle this evening is promised to be unusually special, with a small bit of fireworks. Everyone is looking forward to it,' Mary Blandford said, giving a happy bounce as they made their way through the crowd to find their box.

'We had wonderful illuminations in Macao. The Chinese invented fireworks, you know. They do marvelous things with them; Catherine wheels, figures, cascades, even dragons,' Amelia said to Mary, rather liking Peter's enthusiastic sister.

'How wonderful to have traveled as you have. I should like to go to an exotic place someday. Have you never been in China itself?'

'English women are not permitted to enter China. I suspect the gentlemen are quite satisfied to keep it that way, for Papa has told me of the elegant dining room where they gather to eat after the day's business is over. There are servants in long robes and caps behind every chair, and the silver on the table glitters beneath the light of the chandeliers. Papa fears that nothing would get done were ladies to come. Chen Mei said English ladies are not wanted by the mandarins. They would most likely stop doing business if one of us popped up in their precious factories.' Amelia chuckled, revealing that she didn't mind the banishment in the least.

'How much you have seen,' Mary said wistfully.

'Not all is good. There is much you would rather not see, believe me,' Amelia replied, thinking of the unsavory side of Macao and the ports along their route to England.

Green curtains concealed the stage to one end of the theater, below which the orchestra sat tuning up. Around the circular performing arena people thronged in the tiers of boxes. A magnificent glass chandelier containing fifty patent lamps hung from the center, or so declared an awed Mary, who'd read up on the place. Along the second tier smaller chandeliers contributed to the excellent lighting.

With a roll of the drums and the blare of a trumpet, a silver-garbed gentleman began a rather extraordinary performance on a tightrope.

Mary clutched Amelia's arm as she stared up at the daring feats executed above them. Below in the center of the arena, two clowns in outrageous costumes presented silly skits when the tightrope performer was between his audacious tricks.

'How perfectly lovely,' Mrs Spencer exclaimed with a sigh.

'Oh, look!' Mary cried as the tightrope walker retreated to thunderous applause, and a young fellow in a sailor suit appeared on the stage at the far end of the theater. She checked her program. 'He is to sing.'

The crowd listened with more attention than Amelia thought the song called 'The Sailor's Land Voyage' deserved. It was amusing, she admitted at the conclusion. She suspected that it served to prepare for the next performance, that of the Equestrian Troop, according to the program.

That it was a trial of skill seemed to be an understatement. The men seemed to defy all reason in their fearless and bold riding exploits. She was glad when the segment came to an end and no one had been injured.

Again the young man came out to sing, this time a silly ditty called 'Timid Johnny O.' Amelia's mind wandered from the song. She looked about her, wondering where Lord

Dancy could be. Perhaps he would not appear, as he had told Peter. This fare was pretty tame for a man of his background and apparent tastes.

'Dancy ought to be along by now. I said we'd meet him here.' Peter craned his neck, looking over the audience to see if his friend had arrived and not found them. 'I think he'd find the next item on the program quite amusing.'

Amelia noted the dry note in his voice and wondered what could be amusing about 'The Heroic Battle of Salamanca' to one who had most likely been there.

She saw Lord Dancy first. She espied him in a box across the central arena deep in conversation with a strikingly beautiful woman — dark eyes, sleek dark hair, gowned in palest gray satin that, while it hung simply, revealed a superb figure.

Amelia said nothing, preferring Peter to either say something or overlook their presence. If he did that, she would know that this woman was the one who had captured Lord Dancy's interest.

Yet she could not keep her gaze from returning to him. He looked superbly handsome in his rich coat of dark blue over a pearl gray waistcoat and pantaloons. Hints of red gleamed in his auburn hair from the light overhead. The conversation must be fascinating, for he didn't even notice the man who had drawn near him. The boxes in front were quite low, and there was ample space to circulate behind them. This was where Lord Dancy elected to chat with his lady friend.

Then the man behind Lord Dancy moved so that a shaft of light struck his face. Amelia stiffened as she recognized him.

She glanced at Chen Mei, then excused herself to slip from their box, murmuring something about the necessary to her aunt. Chen Mei followed her as Amelia raced along the hall that circled the tier of boxes.

From the stage she could hear the sound of battle, the blare of trumpets, and booming of guns. No doubt flags were waving madly in the smoke-filled air with heroic soldiers dashing madly about the arena on their steeds.

That shadowy man she recognized meant danger for her lord. Chen Mei had spotted him as well, which was why the two of them scurried along, ignoring the spectacle that was supposedly the highlight of the evening.

At last they reached the area where Lord Dancy hovered close to the beautiful lady. They stood near the rear of the box behind the rest of their group. Why he had promised Peter he would join them when it was plain he intended to escort this lovely woman Amelia did not know. However she knew her duty, and that was to protect Lord Dancy no matter how painful it might be.

'He is a fool,' Chen Mei whispered, repeating her earlier opinion. 'That man — '

Amelia darted forth through the open doorway to brush against Lord Dancy, throwing him off to one side just as a loud boom came from the stage. Once he regained his footing, she apologized profusely when she saw a dark flush of anger cross his face. He stared down at her with what appeared to be utter contempt.

'Miss Longworth, may I present Lady Catherine Beaton. Lady Catherine was just telling me about my sisters.' His voice was correctly polite — polite and icy cold.

'How lovely, my lord.' Amelia blushed under his reproachful glare. 'Lady Catherine, I feel so foolish to lose my balance like that. A fold in the carpet caused me to stumble. How dangerous for a thing like that to be permitted.'

Amelia knew she was babbling like an idiot. But how could she convince Lord Dancy that a man had stood behind him with a gun, most likely with the intention of shooting him? She had glimpsed it just before throwing herself between the Portuguese man and

Lord Dancy. Chen Mei was correct. He was a fool. And Amelia thought it a pity that she was bound to serve him, for he was far too blind to recognize her devotion for what it was.

'I believe you came with Peter and his family.' His voice could have frozen cream.

'Then you observed our party,' Amelia said with equal hauteur. 'I was delegated,' she lied, 'to inform you that we shall partake of refreshments after the performance. But I see you are quite absorbed. Forgive me for disturbing you, my lord.' With that she slipped away and along the passage, following the direction she had seen Chen Mei go after the stranger when Amelia had pushed Lord Dancy out of harm's way.

Up ahead she caught sight of them in the shadows near the stairs. Chen Mei had the man back against the wall, her dagger to his throat.

'Oh, good. Perhaps we can dispatch this man once and for all. Then his lordship need not be bothered with him ever again,' Amelia whispered.

Chen Mei glanced around her as though to see if there might be a place where they could dispose of the body when they heard footsteps.

Amelia half turned to see who might be

approaching. Lord Dancy bore down on them in a furious stride.

Chen Mei let forth a spate of Cantonese that would have curled the lank hair of the Portuguese had he understood.

'My lord,' Amelia said with affected calmness, although her heart was pounding madly. 'What is it you wish?'

'Did this man accost you?' He glared at the man who cowered against the wall, his fright at the assault against him by the Chinese dragon clear.

Seizing upon the plausible explanation for Chen Mei's dagger at the man's throat, Amelia nodded. 'Yes, I was returning to our seats when he popped up demanding money. As though I would carry a handsome sum upon me.'

Lord Dancy looked suspicious. 'Another abduction attempt, Amelia?' Then he caught sight of the gun tucked in the fellow's belt. With one motion, Dancy pulled it out to inspect it. 'This has been fired recently. Who is going to tell what has been going on here?'

Chen Mei looked at Amelia, unconsciously relaxing her dagger a trifle. At this the man wrenched himself free to dash furiously down the stairs.

'You fool!' Chen Mei spat at Lord Dancy

to Amelia's embarrassment, although she quite agreed.

'What . . . ' Lord Dancy looked from one angry woman to the other. 'I think I deserve an explanation.'

'You fool, milor',' Chen Mei repeated less angrily than before. 'That man try kill you. Tian Li save your honorable life. He mean to shoot you.' She had waved her dagger around in the air, finally pointing it at Lord Dancy when she concluded her remarks.

'Good God,' Geoffrey whispered, things rapidly falling into place. He had been so absorbed in what Lady Catherine had been telling him that he had paid not the least attention to that fellow who had crowded against him.

'Now he is free again, he may try once more. Why does that Portuguese man wish you dead, sir?' Amelia asked with commendable composure, considering what she had gone through the past few minutes. 'He is the man we saw at the Lisbon docks. I believe you saw him once more in Portsmouth, am I not correct? And I doubt that is the only other time he has drawn near you. I repeat, why?'

'I cannot tell you that,' Geoffrey said in reply to a reasonable question, given the amount of information she had either seen or deduced. When she drew herself up to her full five feet and six inches, glaring at him in offence, he hastened to add, 'You see, I truly do not know why. Unless . . . ' He paused to think for a few moments.

'Unless what?' Amelia demanded.

'Unless he has been sent to assassinate me for some peculiar reason,' he said softly.

'You were a spy in Portugal. In France as well, perhaps? Also in Spain?' Amelia crossed her arms before her, tapping her foot in growing indignation, he'd wager. The silver riband on her gown glimmered in the dim light of the hall, and her eyes sparkled with outrage. Her cheeks were delightfully flushed, and that soft rose mouth was now firmed into a line.

'I believe we could have used you with us, Amelia,' Geoffrey murmured at her clever conclusion. 'Your guess is close enough to bring you problems, however.'

He felt her attraction all the while he fought it. She was not for him, no sir. He wanted a demure little thing who wouldn't dream of doing what Amelia did.

'Chen Mei was right. You are a fool. You ought to have some sort of guard. There is a distinct limit to what I can do for you, my lord.'

Affronted that a slip of a girl who looked

more like a fairy princess than an avenging angel should think to constitute herself a guard for him, Geoffrey firmly clasped her arm with his gloved hand. 'I believe you had best return to your aunt. The theatrics of this place has affected you far too much.'

He marched her along, Chen Mei trailing unhappily after them. He paused in the open doorway leading to the Blandford box.

'Perhaps it would look better were we to enter with pleasant smiles on our faces, and not as though *we* had been at daggers drawn?'

'If you wish,' Amelia said, not wanting to make him more angry with her than he already was.

Below them on the stage and in the arena the so-called Persian Festival was in progress. Not one person in the box turned to see who had entered. All the pomp and ceremony believed to exist in that part of the world together with exotic costumes and dances whirled about in a frenzy of color and pageantry.

When the players had retreated, Mary sat spellbound, unwilling to move.

'Come, Sis, we had best go,' Peter urged with success.

Mary rose, smiling broadly at Amelia.

Peter noted Lord Dancy had joined them

at long last and gave his friend a disgusted look. 'I thought you were to meet us here earlier.'

'Something came up,' Geoffrey murmured while wondering how he would see to it that Amelia and her Chinese dragon got home and stayed there. 'Why do we not adjourn to Claridge's for a light repast? From there I shall see you ladies' — nodding to Mrs Spencer and Amelia — 'safely home.'

Since Mary gasped with delight at this offering, it was quickly concluded that they would meet at Claridge's, which was just along Brook Street from where Mrs Spencer lived.

Lord Dancy elected to join them in the Blandford carriage, sitting close to Amelia. Chen Mei perched with the Blandford groom, who appeared to relish her company no more than Hemit.

Amelia was not overly pleased at this particular development. His lordship could have taken his own carriage, or he and Peter might have ridden up with the coachman.

Fortunately it was not a long trip. They assembled in the hotel, then enjoyed an elegant repast that left Mary with stars in her eyes and Amelia wishing that she did not seem to incur Lord Dancy's anger every occasion she chanced to save his life. Alas, he simply did not seem to understand that it was what she must do, like it or not.

It was becoming increasingly clear that Lord Dancy didn't like it at all. Nor her, either.

Later she climbed the stairs to her room with a lamentable droop to her pretty shoulders, dangling her blue and silver reticule from limp fingers. At her door she looked at Chen Mei.

'We shall find that blacksmith tomorrow. I wish to make certain that Lord Dancy will be all right.' She gave a tremulous sigh. 'Being a chattel isn't what I had hoped it would be.'

8

'I say, old chap, you were rather hard on Amelia last evening,' Peter said. 'She looked at you as though you were going to eat her.'

'I could,' Geoffrey muttered into his coffee cup. 'That blessed girl is behind me everywhere I turn. I was having a very nice chat with Lady Catherine Beaton last evening when Amelia and Chen Mei catapulted into the box area, nearly knocking me over in the process, then nattering on about the carpet tripping her.'

'You ought to be honored that she cares about your somewhat worthless head, my good friend,' Peter retorted, looking not at all pleased with his companion.

'I would be more pleased if she adored me from a distance.' Geoffrey took another sip of coffee, grimacing at the bitter taste. He set the cup on its saucer, then contemplated his unhappy friend.

'She does adore you, I suspect,' Peter admitted. 'More's the pity. You know, if you do not take care, she will finally have quite enough of you. I hope she does,' he declared, 'and you will find you have lost something very precious.'

With this succinct pronouncement, Peter rose from his chair and stomped from the room.

Geoffrey heard the front door slam shut and picked up his cup, taking another swallow of hot coffee in hopes the near-scalding liquid would make him feel less a cad.

That girl had rescued him again. What was he going to do about her? No other man had a delicate-looking blonde trailing after him and pulling him out of one disaster after another. It was downright humiliating. He couldn't reveal to Peter all the events of last night before he had joined the happy group at Astley's. Peter would think him daft.

Geoffrey thought *himself* daft, and he knew all the circumstances. Better that Peter merely think Geoff was a cad and let it go at that. If Peter knew that the Portuguese fellow had been so hotly on his trail and nearly succeeded in shooting him, Geoffrey would find Bow Street in his pocket before he could sneeze.

If only she wasn't so lovely. That's what made it so deucedly tough to put her where she belonged. Last night when he had been with Amelia in the hall at Astley's and she

166

had stared up at him with those celestial blue eyes so full of trust, he had almost forgotten all else that was going on — even the elegant Lady Catherine, not to mention the fellow who had intended to do him in.

What was it that the Chinese dragon lady called Amelia — Tian Li? Which he understood meant Celestial Delight — appropriate. Only she was not quite what Geoffrey would call a delight at this point.

She looked ethereal, those wide blue eyes gazing at him with such lack of guile and total faith. And he supposed her frank and open manner with him might be called delightful by some.

But . . . dash it all, a man didn't want some female — even if she was a lovely creature — to be saving his life every time he turned around.

Now Peter hinted that Amelia worried that the blasted race might be rigged in some way. Well, Geoff supposed that it might; it was not beyond possibility.

He rose from his chair and wandered along down the hall until he could stare out of his rear window at the little splash of green that constituted his garden. Meditating on his problem might bring a solution that would keep Amelia's nose far away from it all.

Taunton had the very devil's own luck. Geoffrey had yet to figure out precisely how he had been tricked into the race, for it had not been of his choice. When one is challenged, one accepts or looks a fool. Geoffrey had had quite enough of feeling like a fool without this added to his plate.

He would take care to be on his guard. Hemit had gone over his curricle inch by inch and pronounced the carriage safe. Curricle races were common enough. It seemed that every week a couple of idiots were tearing along the highway to somewhere, like a pair of demented geese.

Since Geoffrey had the pick of routes, he had selected one that seemed sound enough, given the condition of most roads at this time of year. It was a road that had traffic, yet not likely to be overwhelmed with drays and wagons from the farms as the major turnpikes might be. He had thought they could travel north out the Tottenham Court Road past Primrose Hill and Chalk Farm as far as Spaniard's Inn. Even though the road went along Hampstead Heath, the highwaymen didn't bother that area during the daylight hours. And anyway, it had been some time since one had last attacked a coach, much less curricles in a race.

It wouldn't be a long race, for Geoffrey had

no desire to injure his grays. Taunton drove a pair of roans that, while they didn't match in color — one a blue, the other a strawberry — did well enough in hand.

But the entire business bothered him. As if he didn't have sufficient to plague him — Amelia and that chap from Lisbon who seemed to think he had to put a period to Geoffrey's existence. Was ever a man so ill-fated?

* * *

Having spent a restless night, Amelia was pleased to be called to the salon to receive visitors. She was in no mood to sit contemplating her own foolishness, or what other people considered her silliness. She had kept the details of last night secret, even withholding them from her aunt. Her behavior had not been easy to explain, and so she found herself held at a distance this morning.

She floated down the stairs until she arrived at the door to the salon. Once there she was delighted to discover that Mary Blandford, accompanied by her mother and brother, had arrived for tea and a comfortable coze. At least they didn't consider her beyond the pale.

Mary rose when Amelia entered the room, a welcoming smile on her sweet face. The afternoon sun brought out pretty highlights in Mary's dark hair and revealed a happy gleam in her gray eyes.

'Mary,' Amelia said with real pleasure, for the attractive girl was the first woman her own age Amelia had been attracted to since arriving in London, 'how lovely to see you.'

'And after such a long parting, too,' Peter grumbled good-naturedly.

'Do not mind him. He has been in a grumpy mood since this morning.' Mary drew Amelia with her to a cream striped sofa at the far end of the salon.

Amelia glanced at Peter to find him studying her with disconcerting thoroughness.

'What a pity,' she said lightly. Could it be that Aunt Ermintrude was right? Could Peter Blandford entertain a tendre for her? It seemed unlikely, but then Amelia tended to concentrate on Lord Dancy, which did make her somewhat blind to others.

'Well, it is when there are so many things I long to do while in London,' Mary replied, then sighed at her brother.

'I suppose you intend to visit the mantuamaker?'

'Did that this morning.' Mary twinkled a

170

gamin smile at Amelia from beneath a stylish cottage bonnet.

'And you wish to go driving along Rotten Row in that awful crush of smart carriages and horses?'

'Peter has promised faithfully that he will take me in his curricle tomorrow.' Mary turned a hopeful look at her older brother.

Amelia smiled at Peter, amused at his resigned look. 'Silly boy, your sister will become the toast of the town. Her dark curls are quite in fashion at the moment, and her liveliness of manner is sure to inspire devotion in some gentleman's heart.'

He looked cheered at that promise, then grew wary at the speculative look Amelia sent him.

'Have you seen Lord Dancy today?' she inquired in a nonchalant manner.

'This morning.'

'I take it that you two disagreed about something?'

'You might say that.' He had a closed expression that warranted silence on the subject.

Amelia could see that she would get absolutely nowhere with Peter, so she turned her attention back to Mary. 'What else do you wish to do while in town, other than have your presentation and come-out?'

'Did your aunt mention to you that we might share a ball? Mama spoke about the terrible cost of parties in London, and when Mrs Spencer agreed, they talked about puffing us off together.' Mary bestowed a hesitant, somewhat shy look at Amelia.

Having dreaded putting her aunt to the bother of a London ball or anything resembling a come-out party, Amelia immediately saw the benefit of joining forces, as it were.

'My aunt has been involved in a domestic crisis this morning. The cook discovered that the second footman has been walking out with the upstairs maid and she is now in the family way,' Amelia said in a near whisper, for young ladies were not supposed to know about such things.

'How dreadful,' Mary replied, wide-eyed at such goings-on, although they were common enough.

'He is going to marry the girl, and they are to go to my uncle in the country. Uncle does not know it yet, but Aunt believes he will accept them. She is more tender-hearted than most of the *ton*.'

Dismissing the domestic predicament as something beyond her, Mary continued, 'So we shall plan on a modest ball? Before too long?'

'Agreed,' Amelia replied. Glancing to

where her aunt sat with Lady Blandford, heads together and smiles of satisfaction evident, she added, 'I believe they have come to the same conclusion.'

Peter rose and restlessly walked to the window to stare out.

With a look at Mary, Amelia rose to cross to his side. 'Something is bothering you today, for you are not your usual cheerful self. May I help?'

'Ain't that just like you,' he said with admiration. 'Always wishing to be of help to a fellow. Pity some don't appreciate it.'

'What brought this on?' she said, not knowing whether she ought to laugh.

'Dancy. Fellow won't listen to reason. Still going to do the race. Of course, I understand — a chap doesn't like to back off, you know. But dash it all, he will do the damndest things.'

'Mind your tongue, Peter,' Amelia scolded absently. 'One of these days it will be someone you truly wish to impress, not your sister.'

Seeing her affront, he muttered, 'Sorry. I tend to forget around you. I know you ain't my sister, but you seem like one.'

Amelia smiled, thinking that any hopes Aunt Ermintrude nurtured were far and away off the mark.

'Well, we intend to plan for a lovely ball,

and I believe we shall hire Almack's for the occasion. It's nice that such a place is usable for those of us in need. Aunt Ermintrude does not have a ballroom, and I gather you don't either?'

'True. M'father thought it a lot of nonsense. But won't Almack's be . . . ' He hesitated to finish the sentence, for it was most impertinent of him to inquire about finances.

'My dear Papa wrote me that he especially desires me to have a lovely ball, and I think that place will do quite well. I found out that when not in use for the Wednesday evening subscription balls, it is available for hire. And it will have such smashing cachet.'

'You have evidently thought it out quite well. I daresay Mary is a clever puss to have you for a friend.'

'Is that Lord Dancy approaching?' Amelia inquired softly, her eye caught by a carriage coming up the street. She looked again, more closely, and was quite certain it was his curricle.

'Dashed if it ain't. Wonder what brings him here?'

* * *

Geoffrey drove just fast enough so he did not hold up traffic, truly a snail's pace. Why he

174

found himself approaching the Spencer home, he did *not* know. The chit irritated him. She drove him utterly mad, one way or the other. And yet, here he was, meekly trotting up to her door as though he had no will in the matter. Maybe that silver amulet he wore around his neck had peculiar powers?

The trouble was that while she nearly drove him round the bend, she also beguiled him with her honest and direct manner. Loyalty such as she revealed was rare today, not to mention her devotion. He didn't know what he was going to do about Amelia, but one thing for sure, he couldn't keep away from her. However he was not going to allow her to stop his race.

When his groom rapped at the front door, Geoffrey discovered that he was welcome. After last night's business, he wasn't sure, but he marched up the stairs after Grimm. When he entered the salon, he found the Blandfords sans his lordship, Mrs Spencer, and Amelia. He held his hat and gloves in one hand, bowing to greet the ladies.

He avoided speaking to Amelia until the very last. What did he expect to see? Certainly not that expression of amusement on her face when she met his eyes.

'And how are you today, sir?' she said in

that soft, almost husky note he enjoyed hearing.

'As well as a chap can be who expects to eat crow. I trust you have one suitably boiled with a good sauce?' He spoke softly for her ears only and, without realizing it, held her hand far longer than polite.

'Oh, stuff and nonsense,' she replied irrepressibly with a charming twinkle in her fine blue eyes. 'What a lowering reflection to think that you have dreaded to come this afternoon because of a mere altercation last evening. I trust you have not seen that man since then?' she inquired in a guarded manner.

'You save my life, almost nab the fellow, then pass it off lightly? Doing it much too brown, my dear.'

'Well, and so I do, I suppose. What a piece of work about nothing. Well,' she amended at the tightening of his hand, 'almost nothing.' She glanced pointedly at her hand, then let it fall to her side when he belatedly released it.

'Well, I behaved like a veriest shatter-brain. I do apologize, my dear.' Geoffrey searched her face for some sign she accepted his tardy excuse for shabby behavior.

She laughed lightly. 'I imagine Lady Catherine considered me a very silly girl, nattering on like a magpie like that.'

'My senses were quite confused. I scarcely knew what to think when you cannoned into me like that, then Chen Mei dashed off down the hall as if chasing a dragon.'

'I only hope that wretch comes by his just desserts.'

'He will, he will. One of these days.' Geoffrey fingered his quizzing glass absently. 'By the by, I have not mentioned anything to Peter about that business with the gun and all. Dratted fellow would have Bow Street hovering over me as though I were a damned tulip.'

'Mind your tongue, Lord Dancy,' she admonished. With that, she turned aside to draw Mary into what had become a rather longer conversation than was seemly, given the circumstances.

'Hullo, Geoffrey,' Mary said with the ease of one who has known another since childhood.

'I hardly recognized you with that dash of town bronze,' he rejoined, grinning at her in a way that made Amelia swallow rather hard. Wretched man.

'Amelia and I are to have a ball together,' Mary said. 'Will you come? I shall be crushed if you do not, for you are the very kindest man I know.'

'Hush,' he reproved. 'Never let others hear

you say that. I'm supposed to have a great deal of consequence, you know.'

'How excessively droll,' Amelia murmured, but loud enough for him to overhear.

'I say,' Peter inserted, 'I think it's dashed clever that the girls will have Almack's for their ball. No fuss at all. Should be simple.'

The two girls exchanged looks, then smiled.

'I suspect it will not be quite that simple. If I know aunt, she will find a great deal to do,' Amelia said.

The gentlemen excused themselves at that point, Peter assuring his doting mama that he would see her later.

Amelia went to the top of the stairs when they ran down to the front door. She listened to their light-hearted comments while wondering where they were actually going — to discuss the route for the race? She couldn't bear to consider the dangers Lord Dancy would be exposed to on an open road. She wasn't unmindful. Anything might happen.

*　*　*

The days passed in a rush of preparation. Once Lady Blandford and Mrs Spencer ascertained that Almack's was available for their ball, they plunged into the undertaking with great relish. Gunter's was secured to cater the party, and Mrs Spencer discovered a clever little shop that did decorating for just such an affair.

Amelia and Mary allowed as how the older ladies knew precisely what they were doing and had little to say on the matter — except that Amelia insisted the punch would be a pretty pink and delicious. She agreed that she and Mary ought to have similar gowns, but in different colors.

With so little to do, Amelia found plenty of time to worry about Lord Dancy and his race. On the morning she suspected it was to take place, she persuaded Mary and Chen Mei to go with her. Peter had let slip just where the route was to be when quizzed by his sister.

They rode in the Blandford landau in tense silence, exchanging looks from time to time. Mary wore an apprehensive expression that revealed only too clearly she had more than second thoughts about the advisability of this outing.

'We must go, for I cannot like the nature of this race,' Amelia said at last. 'Whenever I have queried someone about Lord Taunton, I have heard that he is a good-for-nothing Jack Straw, a coxcomb. How can you trust a man like that to be honest in a race? I ask you!'

'Geoffrey will not thank us for interfering,' Mary cautioned. 'Gentlemen are rather fussy about things like races and wagers and the like.'

'Rubbish,' Amelia exclaimed, ignoring the frown from Chen Mei at such language from a young lady. 'Chances are there will be the devil to pay, but I must own that I don't relish a dressing-down from him. I must see that he is safe. You see, I owe him my life.' Amelia prudently did not mention the startling fact that she considered herself Geoffrey's chattel.

'Missee mind tongue,' Chen Mei scolded, sounding something like Amelia.

The carriage approached the Tottenham Court Road, and both girls fell silent again. Across from them Chen Mei appeared lost in thought as well, although Amelia noticed that Chen Mei was fingering her dagger. Most fortunately Mary did not recognize its pretty sheath and was spared the knowledge of what Chen Mei was prepared to do if necessary.

In the open landau Amelia found it a simple matter to look over the selected course for the race. The road was a busy one, and they soon found it a far different world from Mayfair. Poverty existed in abundance from the look of the buildings and people. Few private carriages traversed the street, rather drays, wagons, and hackneys. They passed by the Tottenham Street theater, giving it a curious glance for it was not one frequented by the *ton.*

The turnpike gate stood at the top of the road, and the coachman paid the fee from the money Amelia had handed to him. Then they were headed along toward Primrose Hill and the wildest part around London, Hampstead Heath.

It was a pretty prospect, and if Amelia had not been so upset about the stupid race, she would have quite enjoyed the view. She recalled a verse she had read lately. 'A steeple issuing from a leafy rise, with farmy fields in front and sloping green.' There had been more, but she was not that clever at memorizing. She had also read that a number of poets preferred to live in this area and decided that if they thought it a lovely place, it could scarcely be dreadful.

Primrose Hill — the place she'd heard was so popular with duelists — turned out to be a charming rise of some two hundred feet to the left of the road not far past the sign to Chalk Farm.

Across the field she could see laundry spread out to dry on the broom and the gorse bushes. With a gentle sun it was sure to dry quickly and have a fine fresh scent for the nobility and gentry who sent their clothes to be washed in the clean Hampstead water. Even Mrs Spencer sent her linen to a woman out here.

At the village of Hampstead she looked about with a curious gaze, then spotted Hemit on the far side of the road in front of a blacksmith shop. With a questioning glance at Mary, Amelia requested the coachman to stop. Once down from the carriage, she approached the groom without the faintest notion of what she intended to say.

'Good day, miss,' he said with a bob of his head.

'Is everything as should be?'

'Aye, nobut there might be trouble.'

'You mean you believe me?'

'Lord Taunton be known as one what allus wins. I'm thinkin' he may not be too careful as to *how* he wins.' His rather speaking look concurred with the way Amelia felt.

'The course is all right?'

'Aye. What can he do in such a public place?'

Still uneasy, Amelia left Hemit to return to the landau. Mary insisted they return home before someone they knew saw them off in such a precarious place without a gentleman to protect them.

Amelia immediately agreed with her friend,

although privately she would rather have Chen Mei than most of the dandies she had seen in London.

'What did you learn?' Mary said, most curious about her unconventional friend. The coachman set a goodly pace back into the city, evidently in agreement with his mistress as to the atmosphere.

'Nothing more than I already suspected. Since your brother will not tell us the time, we can only return to my aunt's house and wait.'

★ ★ ★

At the other end of Tottenham Court Road, unseen by Amelia and Mary, Geoffrey and Peter prepared to give the curricle its final inspection prior to the race.

'Hemit is in Hampstead, checking with a blacksmith he knows there to see if anyone has been nosing about.'

The two men exchanged looks, then motioned to the blacksmith Peter had hired to look over the carriage as well. Dancy might ignore Amelia's suspicions, but Peter felt just as strongly as she did by now.

There was silence for some time as the burly man went over the curricle, using his hands to feel and test. Finally, when Geoffrey was about to dismiss the fellow, the blacksmith straightened and gave Geoffrey a peculiar look.

'You intend to drive this today?'

'I drove it here from the mews behind my home. Why?' He drew closer to where the leather-aproned man stood.

'See that?' He pointed to the bolt that held the pole in place on the carriage. 'It's been loosened. A few more miles and you would have parted ways.'

The thought of what might have happened to his fine team, not to mention his head, brought his eyes to meet the blacksmith's in shared consternation.

'Saw that happen once,' the blacksmith said. 'Curricle tipped over, fellow had his hat smashed and his coat cut to ribbons by the horses, but he survived all right. Pretty shaken, though,' the blacksmith observed in what must have been an understatement.

Geoffrey turned to Peter and said one word. 'When?'

'Dashed if I know. With Hemit out in Hampstead, all that was needed was for us to turn our backs a trifle.'

'Aye,' the blacksmith agreed. He listened to Geoffrey's instructions, then accepted a coin from his lordship before returning to his shop.

'This gives us the excuse we want. It will be interesting to see what Taunton makes of this. Once we have it out in the open, we can get that blacksmith to do the repairs. I'll not drive it another yard until then, nor do I ever intend to race against Taunton.'

At that moment the man they sought drove up with a flourish, looking for all the world as though he fully expected to make the dash to Spaniard's Inn.

'Taunton,' Geoffrey hailed. 'Bit of a dilemma, my friend.'

At his side Peter snorted in disgust.

Taunton oozed surprise and astonishment when Geoffrey explained what had occurred to his curricle.

'Surely you don't intend to call the race off!' he exclaimed in affront.

'The blacksmith insists that the bolt could not possibly have worked its way out. Someone had to do that bit of work. Since the carriage can't be driven, I fear the race is off.'

Taunton glared at Geoffrey, but there was little he could say with so many others around listening to every word.

'Sorry, old chap. My days are rather full at the moment. Perhaps later?' Geoffrey gave Taunton a grim smile, then turned away to greet the blacksmith again. The horses slowly walked the curricle to the shop where the blacksmith unhitched it, then removed it from the street. Geoffrey found stabling for the horses not far away next to the skittle-ground.

Once in a hackney the two men breathed a sigh of relief. 'I can't understand how I got into that mess in the first place,' Geoffrey grumbled.

'Neither can I. You're usually the cool one, Dancy. Not like you to be tricked. Although from what I've heard, Taunton makes a practice of manipulating fellows into his schemes. I doubt you had a thing to say about the matter.'

'Amelia will say 'I told you so,'' Geoffrey added with a grimace.

'Aye,' Peter agreed with a laugh, 'that she will.'

9

'Well, I would never do anything so shabby,' Amelia declared in what appeared to be a miff when the two gentleman had presented themselves in the drawing room of the Spencer home.

Amelia and Mary had wisely returned to the house to await the outcome of the wager, wondering and hoping that all would be well.

What with all that was going on in London at the moment, their concerns had seemed rather trifling. The Grand Duchess of Oldenburgh was to arrive from Russia on March the thirty-first, and speculation was running wild as to her appearance and behavior. Mrs Spencer was of the opinion that the haughty duchess would snub the Prince Regent. Amelia could scarcely credit such manners, or lack of them. But Russians were deemed rather wild people, so anything was possible.

When Peter had informed Amelia that the rig had been tampered with, she had merely nodded in a knowing manner, then remained silent about her dire prediction.

'I say,' Peter said with admiration, 'I am

surprised. Thought you would come all over righteous.'

''I told you so' is not a very kind thing to say, even if it is well deserved,' Amelia replied prudently with a side glance at Lord Dancy.

'As long as you do not take to looking over my shoulder, I do not mind what you say,' Dancy observed in the most wry of tones. He had crossed to glance out of the window, presumably to see if it threatened to rain.

'Why?' Amelia said. 'Would I be likely to see something I ought not?' She looked at Peter and noted his amused expression. 'Most probably I would discover how you spend your evenings in wild dissipation. Gambling, I daresay. High stakes, I suppose? Shame on you, both of you, wasting your time and money in such foolishness. Have you never learned that in the long run the gamester loses?' Amelia offered her scold in a gentle, teasing voice, but no one doubted that she meant every word of it.

From her seat on the drawing room ottoman Chen Mei observed, 'Superior man satisfied, composed; the mean man always full of distress.'

'Then I am neither superior nor mean, for I feel no distress nor do I reek satisfaction and composure.' Lord Dancy sent the Chinese woman a narrow look. 'However, I am full of gratitude that I have so genteel a shadow to follow me about, *rescuing* me from my follies. I vow it is what every gentleman wishes he possessed, a female deliverer.' The implication of this caustic remark could scarcely be missed.

'Take note if someone praises you with no occasion, he sure to have reason fo' doing so,' Chen Mei added with a wicked gleam in her eyes. Her mastery of the 'r' sound had progressed, although at times she regressed.

'I believe Lord Dancy wishes that I would return to Macao, Chen Mei. He does not appear to appreciate his deliverance from Clarissa Filbert nor that nasty man at Astley's Amphitheater nor what could have been a disastrous curricle race.' Amelia admirably concealed the hurt she felt at what she perceived was a lack of appreciation from Lord Dancy. Or did he hold his life in so little esteem?

Mary glanced at each face in turn, then commented, 'I do wish you would all stop this quibbling. I do not like it in the least.'

'Perhaps I had best speak plainly then. Miss Longworth, while I appreciate your feeling of obligation to me, it is not necessary for you to perform repeated acts of rescue in order to redeem yourself,' Lord Dancy said abruptly. 'Besides, three good turns on your part make us even. I hereby absolve you of any indebtedness you may think you owe me.'

'In other words, you do not wish to see my face popping up at every inconvenient moment?' Amelia managed a smile, but just barely.

He had the grace to look uncomfortable, but did not refute nor deny her charge.

'What an odious man you are,' she said in a considering way. 'I shall try to respect your wishes, sir.'

He looked as though he wondered what sort of reprieve that might bring. Amelia had no intention of enlightening him.

Mrs Spencer entered the room, all aflutter and waving about one of the morning papers that contained an account of a balloon ascension to come about in two days.

'I believe you girls would enjoy seeing this. I shall take you myself as it has been an age since I last observed one of these ascensions. They are most colorful and so thrilling to see. When the balloon rises so majestically in the air, your heart nearly stops.' She sparkled with delight in offering such a treat to Amelia and Mary. 'I believe this is going to be an unusually festive spring what with the foreigners visiting and all.'

'What a famous suggestion,' Amelia said, happy to have the matter of her watch on

Lord Dancy dropped. 'Mary, you must promise to join us.' Then Amelia looked at the gentlemen and said, 'I shan't request the pleasure of your company for I suspect there are a great many places you'd rather be than at Green Park on a sunny morning to watch a balloon go up in the air.'

'You had read the article earlier?' Lord Dancy said.

'Indeed. I'd hoped to persuade my aunt to take us, and she has anticipated my desire wonderfully.' Amelia gave her aunt a fond smile, then crossed to the window where Lord Dancy had gazed out not long before. She noted what he must have seen, that the man from Astley's loitered about across the way, keeping an eye on this house. At least, it appeared to be that same man. It was hard to tell.

Dancy peered over her shoulder, seeming to follow the direction of her gaze.

'I would wager that is a familiar face to you, were you to see it closely,' Amelia murmured.

'I thought you agreed to suspend all interest in my doings, Miss Longworth,' he replied in an equally soft voice.

'Quite so,' she replied, but prudently did not tell him whether she intended to keep to her agreement.

Mary and Peter were quietly arguing about whether he ought to go along or not. Mrs Spencer persuaded them both that it might be rather nice to have an escort, particularly if Peter could find a suitable escort for Mary, thus escorting Amelia himself. She also reminded Peter that the day of the ball drew closer, and a young lady could not have too many promising gentlemen about her.

Amelia turned from the sight of the three settling just who was to be invited on the outing.

'She ought to broadcast the amount of my dowry. So far she has refused to do so, saying it is better for me to be accepted on my own merits,' Amelia said in a mocking voice.

'Cynicism doesn't become one so young. And you must admit she has a point. Most women in the *ton* would be in alt if their *protégées* had such a prodigious dowry.'

'What you do not want done to yourself, do not do to others,' Amelia quietly observed. 'I would be foolish beyond permission to argue with my aunt's plans. She has my best interest at heart, I feel sure. It is that I feel like a commodity to be auctioned off to the highest bidder, and once my value becomes widely known, I fear I may not be best pleased with the offer.'

'Yet you will obey your aunt, even though

you might have different feelings within.'

'You are perceptive about me, sir. Would that you developed the same ability regarding your enemies.' Amelia's gaze returned to the man who lingered in the street.

'You think I have so many? What a lowering reflection.' Now it was his voice that held deep amusement.

'I only hope you will not regret . . . ' Amelia did not complete her thought, for she hated to give voice to the words that lurked on her tongue.

Shortly after that conversation the gentlemen left the house, both in a peculiar mood. Peter wondered aloud where he was to find someone to escort his young sister and whether his old friend Denzil Warwick was around and available. Although he himself was clearly delighted to accompany Miss Longworth. He said this with a sidelong glance at Dancy.

Geoffrey felt mixed emotions. While he might be freed of Miss Longworth's attentions, he confessed he had rather enjoyed her concern in a way. He suspected that any number of good ladies looked after their particular gentlemen with secret anxiety, yet took care not to be discovered doing so. Amelia didn't merely worry, she became entangled in his life. He admitted, although only to himself, that he would miss the intriguing Miss Longworth from his life.

★ ★ ★

The morning of the balloon ascension dawned reasonably clear, with only a few clouds to mar the serene blue of the sky. Peter gallantly told Amelia that the sky reflected the color of her eyes.

Amelia smiled at the pretty encomium, thinking that her sky blue pelisse of kerseymere trimmed in deep blue velvet had more to do with her looks than the sky. She reached up to pat her new bonnet of the same blue velvet interlaced with levantine, with blonde lace peeping from beneath the brim. Deep blue-dyed ostrich plumes curled over the crown of the bonnet in a rather fetching manner she thought. Peter was a dear, but her interest quickly turned to the scene about them instead of her escort.

The balloonist and his assistants worked diligently to inflate the massive balloon while Mary and Amelia looked on with more than a little curiosity.

'Do you know,' Amelia confided, 'I would adore going up in a balloon.'

'I should hope not,' the more cautious Mary replied. 'But I suppose that after traveling half way around the world through storms and the like, a balloon does not appear so dangerous to you.'

'Well, any number of women have ascended,' Amelia said having read a bit on the topic. 'Elizabeth Thible, Jeanne Labrosse, and a great many others.'

'I should think they were more like circus performers, ascending for profit, not merely because they liked it. I doubt if any *lady* should attempt it,' Mary said sagely.

Denzil Warwick, the chap Peter had persuaded to escort his sister, looked at Mary with approval at her modest and retiring behavior.

'Indeed,' he agreed with a near-pompous attitude. 'Although I think it is admirable that a young lady displays an interest in the new and curious things to come our way.'

Mary beamed a pleased smile at him. They began conversing in quiet voices about the strange and wondrous things to be viewed in London. The panoramas were declared most intriguing, and they decided it would be lovely to view one or two of them. Plans were made for a few days hence.

Amelia gave them an impatient look, then turned her gaze on the balloon once again. Murmuring something particularly vague to her aunt, she slipped from the carriage where she had been sitting with Mary, her aunt, Peter, and the proper Mr Warwick to draw closer to the balloon.

By means of careful questioning and a remarkable ability to glide through the throng seemingly without any effort, Amelia gained her objective . . . the balloon.

The balloonist was a pleasant-looking man of about thirty, Amelia guessed. When she approached him about riding along as a passenger, he gave her the most horrified look she recalled receiving in her life.

'No, miss. 'Tis impossible.'

'I do not see why,' Amelia argued. 'You may leave something or someone else on the ground and simply take me instead.' It seemed quite logical to her.

The man threw up his hands, then turned to walk away from her with a haste Amelia found irritating. Why shouldn't a lady be able to go up in a balloon just as well as a performer of sorts?

'I suspected I would find you here. Contemplating stowing away in the basket? I fancy there might be a few objections to that,' came a familiar and most irritating voice from behind her — close behind her.

'Lord Dancy!' Amelia exclaimed with dismay.

'Indeed,' Dancy replied, looking down his

nose at Amelia with that infuriating smirk some no doubt called a smile. 'Caught you out, did I?'

'You have no notion as to what was in my mind,' she snapped back at the man she had been unsuccessfully trying to dismiss from her mind for two long days. How could society go into such a dither over the man. While he was handsome, wealthy, and possessed any number of other attributes, he was exasperating to the point Amelia longed to box him on the head and ship him to Macao on the slowest possible boat.

'Well, I daresay you are too much of a pudding heart to make such a passage, but I vow I would like to go,' Amelia said wistfully.

'Pudding heart!' Geoffrey said in disgust. 'Young woman, I'll have you know that I have engaged in all manner of deeds deemed dangerous by a goodly number of people. A balloon ride is a mere nothing.' With this affronted comment he stepped to the side of the basket, surveying the interior with an assessment as to the safety of the craft. That he feared heights he unwisely failed to mention.

Amelia laughed, thinking he looked rather silly in that pose of the offended expert.

'Oh, sir,' she trilled at the balloonist. 'Since you will not consider me, perhaps you will permit his lordship to ride with you?' She quite ignored the sharp inhale behind her, suspecting Dancy was more of a pudding heart than he'd let on.

Since the balloonist had been devoutly hoping for some sort of aristocratic recognition, he swooped on Lord Dancy with an enthusiasm Amelia found extraordinary.

'Of course, my lord. We know that females of the gentry are too full of sensibilities to risk taking such dangers. Gentlemen dare anything.' He beamed up at Geoffrey with a broad grin, then urged him into the basket, explaining all the while what was contained inside.

One of the assistants ran up to hurriedly consult with the balloonist who then turned to Lord Dancy.

'Well, my lord. We go aloft.'

Amelia distinctly heard Lord Dancy mutter, 'I do not like the sound of that,' as he leaned his hands on the railing, glaring at Amelia so fiercely that she was suddenly glad he was there and not beside her again.

'I shall bring you a full report, Miss Longworth. I trust that the next yearning you have in my presence will be a good deal milder.' Lord Dancy tipped his hat at her and the gentlemanly action brought a cheer from the crowd.

The last words were carried down to her from a distance, for the ropes had been released one by one and the supporting poles withdrawn. The purple and gold balloon rose majestically above the park and slowly drifted off into the distance.

'This is terrible,' Amelia murmured to Hemit, who had sidled up to her as the balloon rose into the sky. 'He ought not be up there. He hates it, I could see that. It is all my fault, for I goaded him into doing something he would never do otherwise. Oh, what a terrible girl I am. Hemit,' she declared fervently, 'we must do something.'

'Yes, miss,' He gazed at the slowly departing balloon. 'But what?'

'Follow that balloon!' she cried dramatically, pointing at the road that ran in the same direction. She dashed to the Dancy curricle — now completely restored to proper repair — and would have taken the reins had Hemit not understood she might just do such a thing and scurried after her.

'Here we go, miss. Hang on.' With a flick of the reins he directed the curricle away from the park.

Without a glance at her aunt's carriage where all occupants waved frantically at her, Amelia clung to the side of the carriage. At her side Hemit urged the horses to a full gallop along the street and out onto the road to the north.

Fortunately Amelia had her reticule and could toss the sum of money required to the keeper at the toll gate as the curricle raced through behind another that preceded them.

Craning her neck this way and that she managed to keep the balloon in sight. 'I do believe we are gaining on it,' she said to Hemit in encouragement.

The road was anything but smooth, and dust rose in the air behind them. With one hand clutching the side of the carriage and the other firmly attached to her bonnet that threatened to fly off at the least additional gust of wind, Amelia searched the sky.

'Trailing after that balloon is not the easiest of things, is it, Hemit? I believe we shall have to turn at the next road to the east. It appears that the wind is sending it that way.'

'Yes, miss,' Hemit muttered, his hands full with controlling two very prime bits of cattle.

They feathered the corner with the proper amount of dash, then charged along the country road with more fury than grace.

'Oh, he will kill me. I know he will,' Amelia murmured to herself, tugging on the ribands of her bonnet in hopes of tightening them.

Hemit threw her a wry grin, looking as

though he suspected otherwise, but he said nothing.

After what seemed like an age, although it was a more reasonable time, it appeared the balloon drifted closer to the earth.

'Oh, it is coming down. Faster, Hemit. I only hope he isn't killed.' Amelia blinked away the moisture that suddenly gathered in her eyes. 'It is all my fault if he is injured. Oh, Hemit will he ever forgive me? I doubt he will,' she replied to her question. 'How can he? What a miserable wretch I am.'

'I think you be too hard on yourself, miss,' Hemit observed mildly as he skillfully guided the horses along the lane. Their course appeared to parallel the path of the balloon which looked to be heading toward a large plowed field.

Now that they were closer, Amelia could see Lord Dancy helping the balloonist with something. It appeared they stowed away gear, and a rope dropped over the side of the basket. Hemit muttered something that sounded like, 'I believe the guv has need of a hand.'

The carriage bumped across an access to the field, then came to a halt with a jolt. Amelia tumbled off the seat to land in a heap on the floor, her bonnet all askew, pelisse a tangled mess.

'Come on, miss, if you wants to help.' The tired horses were not likely to budge an inch and were left standing where they halted.

Hemit tugged at her free hand, and without regard to her appearance Amelia struggled from the curricle, then ran along with Hemit to catch the rope.

The basket nearly touched the ground. Amelia could see Lord Dancy studying the lay of the land, yelling something to the balloonist who appeared to agree.

The basket hit the ground quite hard, bumping and dragging along while the balloonist pulled a cord to spill the air from the bag. Hemit caught the rope that had dangled over the side of the basket, Amelia joining him to pull on it in an assist to stop the forward movement.

The bag gave a sigh, collapsing on the ground as it continued to deflate, looking very much like a limp sail.

Lord Dancy leaned on the now-settled basket for a moment with both hands, then climbed from it, not appearing as shaken by the landing as Amelia suspected he ought to be.

The three men were quite occupied for a short time until the crew that had assisted with the balloon ascent rumbled up in a wagon. A group of men piled out and ran across the field to give the final assist.

Amelia retreated to the curricle, feeling definitely out of place here.

She was at the point of wondering just how she would manage to return to London when Lord Dancy approached. She wanted to shrink against the carriage, but her pride refused to encourage such craven behavior.

'Good day again, Miss Longworth.'

He tipped his hat in greeting, but she detected the grim note in his voice and trembled in her half-boots. Even his hat had stayed in place, she thought balefully.

'I am pleased to see you are in one piece, my lord. Did you enjoy your flight?' Amelia had decided that she might as well be audacious. Otherwise, he might be even worse.

He said nothing. Rather he walked to her side to stare down at her face before taking one gloved finger to trace the skin below her eyes.

'Were you worried about me, Miss Longworth? I'm touched,' he said quietly. Then he undid the mangled ribands of her bonnet, smoothed down her hair, and replaced the bonnet with judicious attention to its tilt.

Amelia gulped. This was far worse than anything she had anticipated. She suspected he longed to strangle her, a feeling reinforced when he tied the ribands rather tightly under her chin.

'I am sorry,' she said with downcast eyes. 'You must be wishing me to perdition by now.'

'Oh, I wished you even farther than that, Amelia,' he replied. 'I rather thought it would be nice to see you on a boat back to Macao.'

'I shall leave you immediately,' she said totally dispirited and wondering just a little how she would manage to walk back to London. She turned away from him to walk along the curricle toward the country lane she had jounced upon not long before.

At least there were trees along the lane, and the weather was not so hot as in summer, she consoled herself.

'Ahem,' he said, reaching out to take hold of her elbow. 'You asked if I enjoyed the ride. Well, I did. Enormously. I owe you a great debt of gratitude, Amelia. I'd always longed to try one of those things, and never quite had the courage. You cinched that for me. Allow me to express my appreciation.'

With that he tilted her face up to his, then kissed each eyelid smudged from her tears of concern with dust from the road. After that, while Amelia held her eyes tightly shut for she was certain this was a dream, he touched her lips ever so gently. Then he released her.

Amelia opened her eyes to give him a highly bemused look.

'And if you ever do anything like that again, I shall forget that I am a gentleman and beat you, my dear.'

She stood uncertainly in her tracks, debating whether or not he was serious. She decided he was. His eyes told her.

'I will try to avoid you if possible, my lord,' she croaked. Her voice broke when she tried to speak. With the most dejected heart in the world, Amelia turned away from the man she suspected she loved rather deeply and began her trudge to the road.

'Where do you think you are going now?' came a dangerously quiet voice from behind her.

Amelia stopped, but did not turn. It hurt to look at him standing there so disgustingly handsome with his hat still in place and gloves scarcely smudged. She was quite certain that she looked a veritable sight, all rumpled and dusty. One thing about air travel, it didn't leave you looking as though you'd been through a dust storm.

'You will ride back to town with me, unless of course you prefer to walk. I daresay some enterprising chap will be delighted to offer you a lift, although to where I couldn't say.

Hemit will ride behind. You will sit next to me and not do one blessed thing all the way back to town.'

She swirled around, her temper flaring. 'You enjoyed the flight in the balloon, so I fail to see why you are acting as though it was the end of the world. Men! Lords, in particular!' Her dainty fists balled up, then settled upon her hips as she glared back at him. Why had she been so broken-hearted? This man was enough to drive any sane woman to drink!

'That's more the thing,' he pronounced cheerfully. 'Now before your aunt has a permanent attack of the vapors, I suggest we depart.' He scooped her into his arms and plopped her onto the seat of the curricle. He looked over his superb team as he walked around to the other side of the curricle, then joined her.

He waited a few moments until Hemit had climbed up behind them, then guided the team carefully over the rough ground until they reached the lane. Even there the surface was rough, and the curricle jounced along until Amelia thought her teeth would come loose.

'The horses are fine, no doubt to Hemit's splendid driving.'

No thanks to you, was implied. Amelia considered ways and means of doing him serious harm. It was no use, for her brains seemed scrambled. A bit more of this road and her eyes would no doubt cross permanently. Why had it not bothered her when they came? Hemit's driving skills? Or had she concentrated so on Lord Dancy that nothing else in the world mattered? Foolish girl, she admonished herself.

At last they made the main road into London. Thanks to Mr MacAdam the road was reasonably smooth and the dust somewhat less. No water from the recent rains puddled in the road for MacAdam had decreed a crown to the road so it might drain well. Amelia decided she preferred the jouncing. At least then there was a reason not to speak.

The silence stretched on for an hour or so until they reached the toll gate where Amelia handed Lord Dancy a coin.

He glared at her, but took the coin and drove on most assuredly in a miff, she decided.

'I can pay my own tolls, thank you.'

'No trouble,' Amelia replied airily. 'I happened to have the coin in my reticule. That's the advantage of heiresses, you know. They are far more apt to have some of the ready to hand.'

She thought he was grinding his teeth, but

wasn't sure. The contact of the cobblestones with the wheels of the carriage, plus the clip-clop of the horses, plus the myriad other noises of the city quite well covered what sound he might make.

'I will say one thing, my dear,' Lord Dancy said in the mildest of tones that made her wonder if she was right about the grinding teeth business. 'Being around you is never dull.'

Slightly affronted, Amelia nevertheless took the remark philosophically. 'I have three precious things that I hold fast and prize,' she quoted from her store of Chen Mei's teachings. 'The first is gentleness; the second is frugality; the third is humility, which keeps me from putting myself before others. Be gentle and you can be bold; be frugal, and you can be liberal; avoid putting yourself before others, and you can become a leader among men. Or woman as the case may be,' she amended.

'I might have known the woman would influence you. Do you carry a dagger as well?'

'I wish I did,' Amelia retorted darkly. She smoothed the skirt of her pelisse over her knees then leaned forward in anticipation when the carriage turned onto Brook Street.

When they drew up before her aunt's home, she turned to give him a considering look. 'You are not really so bad off, you know. You had an interesting trip that you enjoyed very much, I suspect. Your carriage was not damaged in the least, thanks to Hemit's skill at driving. All in all, I believe you ought to count your blessings, the least of which is that the man who again leans against the post over there has not been able to take a shot at you yet. I trust you will be most careful, my lord.'

With that parting gibe Amelia climbed down from the curricle and marched up the steps into her aunt's home, firmly shutting the door behind her.

10

Geoffrey stared after Amelia, his mind in a whirl. A glance revealed the man, who was obviously trying to melt into the stonework across the street.

'Hemit, go around to the rear of Mrs Spencer's house. I may be some time, but I trust these nags will welcome the rest. They've had a hard day.'

With that understatement Geoffrey handed over the reins, then marched up to the front door. A firm rap brought Grimm's face to view when the door opened.

Without so much as a by your leave, Geoffrey smoothly brushed past the butler to enter the front hall. At the bottom of the stairs Amelia paused, looking quite startled. One hand clung to the oak banister. Her pretty blue bonnet, the plume on it slightly crushed, dangled from the fingers of her other hand. Her glorious blonde hair was tumbled into appealing ringlets. However her eyes blazed with a blue fire that made Geoffrey distinctly uncomfortable.

'You were right,' he said promptly. 'That fellow is lurking outside. I suspect he wants to put a period to my existence. Why, I still can't imagine.' Geoffrey glanced at her, then crossed the hall, going into the small parlor at the front of the house. From here he could see where the fellow now lounged beneath a tree as though he hadn't a care in the world. Although he hadn't told Amelia, he'd consulted with Hardinge's office. They had no lead on the man, either.

'You obviously have not put your mind to work on the matter. There must be any number of reasons someone might wish you finished.' She had followed him into the room, conspicuously leaving the door wide open. 'Think again.'

'He can bloody well find someone else to murder in any event. I'm not about to please the chap.' He studied the man, trying to figure out who it was that wished him booked. While almost everyone had someone who might dislike them, what brought about murder?

'Mind your tongue, Lord Dancy,' she reprimanded quietly.

He whirled around to stare at her, suddenly recalling the moment he had kissed those pretty tear-smudged eyelids, touched her sweet mouth with his, and wondered if he were losing his senses. With an effort he managed to control the most peculiar urge to stride across the room and clasp her in his arms. To his regret he would very much like to kiss her again, and that would never do. Not in the least. If he succumbed to necessity and married, it would be to a demure, biddable creature — certainly not the young woman who had hoodwinked him into taking that balloon ride.

Never mind that he had found it delightful once he had conquered his fear of the height. No fellow wanted a harum-scarum woman as a bride, dashing around to pull his chestnuts out of the fire. He fancied the Chinese dragon would accompany her charge when Amelia married. He wished the fellow well who acquired the pair of them. He would have his hands full.

'Oh,' Mrs Spencer trilled from the doorway, 'You are safely home. My love, I nearly had the vapors. You have been gone for hours! What a naughty girl to dash off like that.' She waggled her finger at Amelia, but her face did not appear to wear a harsh expression to match.

'I apologize, dear Aunt,' Amelia said contritely. 'There was no time to explain, you see. I had most stupidly challenged Lord Dancy to that balloon ride. Poor man, I called him a pudding heart. He took that ride as a dare. And then I feared he might be killed, so Hemit and I chased after him to see what we could do.'

'I doubt if you could have saved my hide were the balloon to have caught fire or become tangled in trees,' Geoffrey inserted, for she made him sound bird-witted.

'But you must admit it was exceedingly brave of the girl,' Mrs Spencer said with a frown at him. 'Come along, for you must tell us all about it. No doubt it will be a second hearing for Amelia, but we are all in suspense to learn the details.' She paused at the bottom of the stairs to add, 'What was it like?' She looked to Amelia as though she expected some sort of reply from her.

Amelia gave Geoffrey a rather poisonous look that he supposed he deserved. 'I have yet to be regaled with his tale, as he chose to remain silent on the matter. I would also like to hear of the horrors endured by our brave aeronaut.'

'That is what they now call them,' Mrs Spencer agreed with a nod. 'It sounds so dashing.' With a dramatic sigh she led the way up the stairs.

The others sat in the drawing room, expectantly awaiting them. Peter and Mr Warwick leaned against the fireplace surround, a glass of sherry in hand. Mary sat on the sofa, her tea cup placed on the low table close by. All eyes were fixed on those who entered the room.

'The adventurers return,' Mrs Spencer cried in her fluting voice. 'Lord Dancy is going to tell us about his experiences in the balloon.' She crossed over to join Mary, who sat perched on the edge of the sofa like a child awaiting a treat.

'Yes, Lord Dancy,' Amelia said, looking at him with a curiously unfathomable expression. 'Do tell us all about your trip.'

If the chit thought he was going to confess to those stolen kisses she was far and away out. 'Actually, it was most interesting. They fill the balloon with the hot air that's produced when they burn straw, as you may have noticed. Once aloft, I helped feed the fire until the chap spotted a likely place to land. It seems they prefer an open field away from trees and such.' Geoffrey bestowed a cautioning look on Amelia, but had no clue as to what went on in her mind.

'But,' Mary gently queried, 'what was it like? What did you see? I should have been terrified.'

'The perspective was quite fascinating,' Geoffrey said, recalling his trip. 'Everything looked very tiny, the carriages and people seemed like mere specks on the ground. I could see off to the west where the Thames winds about like a snake through the city, then the green fields and on south toward the sea. To the north I could almost think I saw Windsor. The wind felt surprisingly gentle. I saw Holland House and the Bath Road off to the west.'

Mrs Spencer gasped at this revelation, for it seemed far too fantastic. It was evident that she doubted the validity of his claim.

'How about the landing, Dancy?' Peter said, raising his glass in a toast of sorts as he spoke.

'Once the fellow decided to land, we extinguished the fire. Then he kept watch on our landing site while I made certain the rope went down on the opposite side so those who followed might grab a purchase and assist us in the landing.'

'And what did you do, Amelia?' Mrs Spencer asked her niece with a stare that seemed rather intimidating even to Geoffrey.

Amelia looked at Lord Dancy, wishing she might push him out a convenient window or something equally dire. Oh, he positively enjoyed all this fuss over him, the odious man.

'Why, Hemit and I followed the course of the balloon as best we could. And it is a good thing we did so, for the assistants were ever so slow in arriving at the field. Their wagon was no match for Lord Dancy's curricle and splendid horses.'

'Weren't you frightened?' Mary asked, her hands clenched in her lap, revealing her own apprehensions just thinking of such a mad dash.

'I fear that I was too engrossed in keeping the balloon in sight to be afraid for myself. I did feel a shade guilty for teasing Lord Dancy into taking the ride,' she confessed, again with a sidelong glance at his elegant lordship.

'What could you do when you arrived at the field where they landed?' Mr Warwick inquired with the narrowing of one eye in a highly speculative manner.

Amelia couldn't have met Lord Dancy's gaze to save her life at this point. She felt almost as though the words would be emblazoned on her forehead . . . *I allowed that fool man to kiss me, that's what I did.* Fortunately, Lord Dancy came to her rescue.

'She and Hemit ran across the field in our direction. The basket thumped along the ground, bounced a few times, then skidded toward the end of the field. At the last moment the basket toppled over on its side, and I was more than a little shaken when I crawled from it,' he revealed with a look at Amelia. 'Hemit grabbed hold of the rope, as did Miss Longworth. Once the balloon settled on the ground, Miss Longworth quite properly retired to the curricle, leaving Hemit to assist the . . . er, aeronaut, did you call him, Miss Longworth?' He met her gaze with no hint that he recalled that enticing kiss. Amelia wished she might know how he felt about it and her.

'Sounds smashing to me,' Peter said with a wistful note in his voice. The others began to voice their opinions all at once.

'I don't know,' Mr Warwick said in a momentary lull. 'I should think that if man were intended to fly, he'd be born with wings.'

'Then why do we take ships rather than swimming when we wish to cross the Channel?' Amelia wondered aloud. 'It seems to me that anything man can invent or develop to make our life easier or more interesting is certainly to the good.'

The others fell into a casual debate on the topic while Lord Dancy walked to the window to survey the scene on the street below.

Amelia followed him, keeping a proper distance, yet able to speak without the others overhearing what she said.

'He is still loitering about.' Amelia gave the fellow a disapproving look. 'Someone ought to shoo him away, for he certainly does not improve the neighborhood.'

'Does your aunt have a carriage house? Is there a way out of the back to a mews or something?'

Although Lord Dancy spoke in an undertone, Amelia could hear him surprisingly well. 'Yes,' she quickly replied.

'I shall simply avoid the fellow until a time when I am better armed to meet him.'

'Would you shoot him? A dagger is so much quieter,' Amelia offered prosaically.

'What a bloodthirsty one you are. It must come from growing up in the Orient. I feel a contest is much better when the odds are a bit more even, if you know what I mean.'

Amelia nodded, wondering a little at the feeling of camaraderie that had sprung up between them. She felt shy with him, yet oddly comfortable if such a thing were possible. She could not dismiss that gentle kiss at the curricle in the middle of a plowed field, right out in the open where anyone might have seen them. However, she'd wager that everyone present had their eyes on the balloon. She and Lord Dancy had escaped censure by means of a better attraction being around.

'Goodbye, sir,' she said at last, holding out her hand for a final contact with him. 'Perhaps I shall see you round and about.

Society being what it is, it is difficult to avoid people you know.'

'I shall take great care to refrain from any actions that might require my rescue, Miss Longworth.' He paused, then continued, 'You are a surprising creature, gentle and mild-mannered, yet fierce as a tiger. You are not a comfortable sort of woman,' he said.

Amelia noted the twinkle in his jade eyes and replied in a properly demure voice, 'Chen Mei says gentleness brings victory to him who attacks, and safety to him who defends. Those whom Heaven would save, it fences around with gentleness.'

'That obviously explains why you are still with us, Miss Longworth. You would no doubt have been strangled long ago had it not been for the wise guidance from your companion,' he said in a sardonic voice.

'Are you contemplating something hazardous in the near future, Lord Dancy? Perhaps I ought to make you a loan of Chen Mei so you might also be protected.'

'A bit of gaming will scarcely be deemed as dangerous.'

'White's this evening? Peter said something about a match with Lord Taunton. Did you not have sufficient warning of his character before, my lord? I can scarce believe my ears.'

'What I do with my time is hardly any

concern of yours, the debt you feel you owe me notwithstanding. I absolved you of that long ago, if you recall. As to Taunton, it is of no consequence if we have a congenial game of piquet. The chap insists we must have the match to compensate for the cancellation of the race.'

'Why is it that I doubt if any game of cards could be congenial with Lord Taunton? You must give me leave to doubt you there, my lord.'

Amelia withdrew from the window, returning to the others to join in the discussion of their plans for the next day. It seemed she was being caught up with the other three. And although she liked Peter Blandford very well, she knew it could never go beyond a mere liking.

'Well, I am off. I shall see you this evening, Peter?' Lord Dancy said in the most off-hand manner.

'You may depend on it, Dancy,' Peter said bracingly.

Amelia walked to the landing to see Lord Dancy lightly run down the steps, then consult with Grimm for a moment before disappearing down the hall that led to the rear of the house.

She drifted back into the drawing room, absently agreeing with the others as to the plans for the morrow. Peter decided to take Mary home, and Mr Warwick left with them.

'Well,' Aunt declared, 'all in all it has been quite a morning. I believe we ought to have our luncheon before we both collapse for one reason or another. You look rather pale, my love. Why do you not rest for a bit after we have eaten. We are to go to the Wyndham's ball this evening, and you will wish to be fresh.'

Amelia blessed her aunt's thoughtfulness and joined her in a light meal. Before she entered the breakfast room where the two of them pleased to eat when alone, Amelia slipped into the front parlor to check the street. The man was gone.

When her aunt retired to take her rest, Amelia went to her room, not to rest, but to consult with Chen Mei.

'We are to go to a ball this evening. I doubt if Lord Dancy will be there, as he contemplates a game of cards with Lord Taunton, no less. Foolish man. He thinks that he can deal with a cheat.'

'Tiger and deer do not stroll together,' Chen Mei observed from her hassock.

Amelia gave her a nod of agreement, then restlessly wandered about the room.

'What you do?'

'Oh, go to the ball, I suppose. Ladies do not frequent gambling establishments, except the ones specifically set up for them. Can you imagine what it would be like were a woman to try to gain entrance to White's? She would not only be barred from the club, but society as well, most likely.'

'Let every man sweep the snow from before his own doors and not trouble himself about the frost on his neighbor's tiles,' Chen Mei said in Cantonese with a curious glance at Amelia.

'Infamous,' Amelia snapped back. 'I owe him my very life, or do you forget? He may be the most infuriating man on earth, but I know what my duty is.'

'Mr Blandford help, maybe?'

'Of course.' Amelia sent Chen Mei a triumphant grin. 'Lord Dancy asked if he would see him there, and Mr Blandford agreed. I will write him immediately.'

'What you going to say?' Chen Mei placidly resumed her embroidery work.

'Oh . . . I shall urge him to keep watch most carefully, for I do not trust that Lord Taunton.'

'Lord Taunton most skillful cheat. No one caught him out all these many years. How Mr Blandford catch him?'

'What a pity you could not be there. You'd

see it right away. We must think on this, Chen Mei. I have heard that Lord Taunton has fleeced many a lamb of his fortune. We cannot allow that to happen to Lord Dancy.'

Chen Mei rubbed her chin in reflection. 'We see,' she concluded. 'I find way.'

With that small comfort Amelia had to be content. She carefully penned a letter to Peter Blandford, sealing it with wax while worrying all the while. Peter was not the most observant of souls. She feared that he would miss something.

The Chinese doted on gambling, and Chen Mei had quickly learned all the English games of chance from Amelia's father. Chen Mei had incredible ability to detect hand movements. She had explained about card cheats once when Amelia had wondered about such — how one might skillfully manipulate the deck so he could see the top card, or perhaps deal from the bottom, or fake a shuffle. Marking a deck of cards might be cleverly done, especially if the light was not the best. Oh, if only they could smuggle her into the club so she might watch the cheat at work. She would soon see how he managed to win so often.

Into White's? Absurd. Amelia wondered how it would be done. For she well knew that to Chen Mei precious little was impossible.

Amelia dressed for the Wyndham's ball with more than a little preoccupation. A gown of sheer peony crepe over a peony sarcenet slip with the short full sleeves trimmed in silver crepe made her feel considerably more the thing. Silver chenille was vandyked across the low front of the bodice and on the border of the skirt just below two rows of white silk roses. It was a lovely gown.

'I do believe this bodice is a trifle skimpy, Chen Mei,' Amelia complained quietly to her companion.

Chen Mei adjusted the diadem of white and silver silk roses on Amelia's hair, then stood back to inspect her charge. 'Three-tenths of good looks due to nature; seven-tenths to dress. You wish to look best this night to Mr Blandford, no?'

'No,' Amelia replied with a heart-rending sigh. 'What I wish I cannot have, it seems.'

The companion draped a delicate wisp of a scarf over Amelia's shoulders. The richly worked embroidery of silver flowers reflected Chen Mei's fondness for them, not to mention the touch of silver in the gown.

'This is the crowning touch,' Amelia said, fingering the delicate silk fabric with delight. 'Thank you so much, my dear Chen Mei. Without your help I fear I would look a sight.'

'Falling hurts least those who fly low,' Chen Mei observed with approval at Amelia's modesty.

Amelia glanced at the clock on her dressing table. 'Oh dear, the hour is late. I had best hurry downstairs.' At the door she paused. 'What about Lord Dancy?'

Chen Mei bowed, then crossed over to withdraw a very elegant but plain man's suit of clothes from the depths of the wardrobe. All was black but for a plain white waistcoat. Small black shoes and black hose were also produced along with a nutmeg wig.

Leaning against the door Amelia gasped with excitement. 'You will go! But how? One must be a member.'

In less time than Amelia had dressed, Chen Mei was transformed into a funny little man, somewhat Oriental looking in visage, with the nutmeg wig confusing it all. When the cravat was tied and affixed with a superb pin of jade, Chen Mei bowed most correctly to Amelia.

'You no go, so I go. Mr Blandford take me. He member.'

'I only hope he holds to his promise to escort me this evening,' Amelia cautioned darkly.

'I meet you at Wyndham's. No ploblem,' Chen Mei concluded. 'I fix all things.'

Leaving the transformed companion to work further magic on her face, Amelia drifted down the stairs in a highly bemused state.

'I say,' Peter Blandford said, 'you look like a peony this evening.' He chuckled at his own bon mot with Mrs Spencer adding her trill of laughter.

Lord and Lady Wyndham gave glorious parties, and this ball proved no exception. Amelia was pleased to note that peony flowers had been brought from the famed Wyndham greenhouses to decorate the ballroom. The fragrance added to the beautiful appearance of the room. Cream walls elegantly trimmed in gold with looking glasses reflected the light from the hundreds of candles in the crystal chandeliers. The flowers merely enhanced what proved to be excellent background for the colorful gowns of the ladies present. Gentlemen provided a punctuation of black and even more vivid colors.

'Miss Longworth, you must have known Lady Wyndham's intent. You carry out her theme of peony most admirably.'

'Lord Dancy! But I thought, that is, you said,' she sputtered, hope rising that Chen Mei would not have to attempt the precarious masquerade.

'I could not slight my dear friends, Miss Longworth. I see you have Blandford in tow this evening.'

'Yes, well, he and Mary and Mr Warwick make up our party along with my aunt.'

'Quite frequently, I understand.' He nodded to Peter, and the amused expression on Dancy's face was quite enough to make Amelia wish to kick him. Except she would likely hurt her toes more than his leg.

The dratted man looked superb. Black from head to toe but for a cream marcella waistcoat and a single diamond in his cravat. He put every other man in the shade. The candlelight caught fiery sparks in his hair, but his green eyes glittered at her with that look of knowing that was nearly her undoing. *What was he thinking?*

'To set your mind at ease, I intend to go on to White's sometime later. Taunton will be there, I feel sure. He has made quite a thing of it, you see I could not retreat now, Amelia.' He gazed directly into her eyes, a bit of the façade he habitually wore when in public slipping, so Amelia was able to see his uncertainty for but a moment.

She ignored his use of her given name, and merely nodded in understanding.

'Blandford? May I count on you?'

'If Amelia don't mind my leaving her.' He

looked first at Lord Dancy, then turned to Amelia.

'As if I could. Were it possible, I would go as well, just to wish you luck, my lord.'

'Then I would be certain to have a disaster!' He laughed after this remark, but Amelia felt a stab of hurt.

'One thing I ask, Blandford. A dance with your partner before her card is overflowing with names.'

'Amelia?' Peter said, refusing to be drawn into any discord that might arise. It would take a man who was deaf and blind not to see there was something between these two. Peter might be a trifle slow, but he was not stupid.

The opening notes of a familiar waltz floated across the room from where the musicians sat. Lord Dancy bowed to Amelia and held out his impeccably gloved hand.

'Shall we, my dear?'

'By all means, if you can manage to mind that odious tongue of yours,' she said in a tight little voice.

He merely laughed and swept her away from where Peter and Mrs Spencer watched.

'For a man who declares he detests the chit he shows a remarkable interest, I should say,' Mrs Spencer observed.

'Indeed,' Peter agreed.

From the dim shadows of the room a small

peculiar-looking little man watched the proceedings with a rather pained expression on his face. Whether it was the English music or a tight pair of shoes one couldn't say.

'You waltz very well for a young woman who has come all the way from Macao,' he said while spinning her about at a dizzying pace.

'You waltz very well for a gentleman who spends his time dashing about foreign countries being chased by spies, racing in curricles, ballooning, and whatever,' she replied in a remarkably calm manner.

'A direct hit, I vow,' he acknowledged with a bow of his head.

'They have balls in Macao, you know. As a matter of fact, life is not so very different there,' Amelia reflected. 'It is an attractive place, with the ground rising sharply from the Playa Grande up to where the shops and houses, convents and the Senate House are located. There are pretty trees in the bishop's garden. In the summer there are numerous parties, dances and fancy-dress balls, musical soirées, fetes, and theatrical performances. The receptions in the Portuguese governor's mansion are quite grand. I rather miss it all,' she concluded wistfully.

'I am surprised you left the place,' Dancy said with a hint of puzzlement in his voice.

'Papa wished me to have a proper English come-out.'

'And he is one person you obey?' Dancy said, amazement ringing in his voice.

'Obedience brings joy,' Amelia said with a demure flutter of her lashes.

'I wish you would desire joy when around me,' Lord Dancy muttered without considering what it might sound like to Amelia, obviously.

She debated whether she ought to comment on this statement, then decided that prudence was a better course.

'What? No clever little quote?'

'Think twice — say nothing,' Amelia snapped back.

Lord Dancy laughed in delight. Other gentlemen about the room noted his obvious enchantment with his partner and resolved to snatch a dance with the beguiling blonde who had attracted the interest of the notable Lord Dancy.

It was well that she had that first dance with him, for Amelia scarcely saw Dancy after that. She was besieged with partners.

It was well into the night when Amelia sensed that Lord Dancy had left the ballroom. Pleading fatigue, she begged her aunt to leave. Since Peter Blandford had also disappeared, Aunt Ermintrude was disposed to go before the night became too dangerous. It was well known that thieves lurked about to filch jewels from party-goers when possible.

Fortunately they reached Mrs Spencer's house without incident. Amelia ran lightly up to her room to discover a suit of men's clothing laid across her bed. Closing the door with care, then bolting it, she stared at the black garments with satisfaction.

There was a note of sorts in Chen Mei's crabbed writing. Amelia deciphered it with growing delight. It took some time to ease her way out of her gown. Even in her hurry she set the flowers on the dressing table, draped her gloves over her chair, and placed the precious peony gown carefully on her bed. Chen Mei would give her a horrendous scold if she failed to give them proper attention.

It was no easy matter to dress in the men's garb. Only years of helping her papa with his cravat enabled her to tie that creation with any credibility. Then she released the bolt of the door, opened it, and upon hearing silence tiptoed from her room.

It was remarkably simple to slip from the house, hail a passing hackney, and get to White's on St. James's Street. When she stepped from the carriage, she faced another matter entirely. How did she gain entrance?

The door opened and she glimpsed a pleasantly lit hall. No doubt the porter's stall was right at the opening, and there would be no way she might slink past him; he would be too canny to allow that.

A carriage drew up, then two gentlemen came out of the club discussing something in a heated manner.

'Fancy, Capel bet Brummel five guineas that Napoleon will not be head of the Frenchies within ten days.'

'Ponsonby has bet Raikes one hundred guineas to fifty that Boney enters Paris as a conqueror on or before May the first,' countered his friend as they entered the waiting carriage. 'Place is abuzz with the talk.'

Amelia took heart and sidled up to the front door, peering through the still-open doorway to the entrance hall beyond. It seemed to her that it was empty. Just when she was about to attempt to slip inside, a somewhat tipsy man approached and clapped his hand on her shoulder. 'Don't dawdle, my man. Move.'

Amelia found herself propelled past the porter and into the dimly lit card room. The room was hushed. At one of the tables near the center of the room Amelia could see Lords Dancy and Taunton seated at a small square table. Lamps with shades were placed in opposite corners of the table to shed light on their hands.

Chen Mei and Peter stood behind Lord Taunton. Amelia marveled that no one had challenged either her or her companion, yet. But she knew all those present concentrated on the game at hand.

All of a sudden Chen Mei nudged Peter, and he cried out, 'I say, the man is a cheat!'

Confusion broke loose.

11

A round of gasps was followed by outraged murmurs from the members clustered around the table.

'That's a dastardly thing to contend, Blandford,' Sir Humphrey Elson said. He had lost two hundred pounds to Lord Taunton not so long ago, yet he did not like to think the club housed a cheat.

'I demand you retract that charge, sir,' Lord Taunton said, not releasing his hand of cards. He slowly rose to face Blandford, staring at him with cold eyes.

The room grew silent as the members held their collective breath. All gazed at the two confronting each other by the side of the small table.

Peter bent his head to confer with Chen Mei, then straightened. His hand darted out to snatch the cards from Taunton's hand, followed by those on the table, then he took the cards in Lord Dancy's hand. He examined the cards with his quizzing glass, eventually nodding in satisfaction. The murmurs grew as members discussed the charge, most of them looking at Lord

Taunton with hostile eyes, for he was not well liked.

Geoffrey had not said a word, merely staring at his friend with a perplexed frown. He presumed his friend had reason to issue so daring a challenge. Then his gaze shifted to Chen Mei, and lastly to Amelia, who had edged close to her companion, retaining her hat and keeping to the shadows. Not by a flicker of an eyelash did he reveal he recognized them. If they were discovered in White's, they might as well board the next boat to Macao, for they would be ruined. He clenched one hand as he considered what he would like to do to that minx, Amelia Longworth. Then, at the change of expression on Peter's face, he returned his attention to his friend.

'Look! I'll show you how he does it,' Peter said with a certain triumph. 'See the pattern on the back of this deck of cards? The outer line is thickened near the top on the back of an ace. The line on a king is a bit lower, the queen lower still. By concentrating on the back of the cards, he can tell just what is to come up and what his opponent has if he can see those cards.'

'By Jove, I see just what he means. Look at this, Sefton. Scandalous!' Sir Humphrey handed two of the marked cards to Lord

Sefton, who in turn passed them along to Thomas Creevey, who shared them with Lords Alvenley and Worcester. All used their quizzing glasses to examine the cards closely.

The Duke of Beaufort declared, 'I believe we have a serious charge before us, my friends.'

Earl Gray, known and greatly respected for his honesty in all dealings, concurred. 'It will ruin the club if it is known that we tolerate a cheat in our midst, member or no. I say he must go.'

All were in agreement, to judge by the nodding of heads and indignant glances exchanged.

'I refuse to issue a challenge to a duel, Taunton,' Lord Dancy said quietly. 'Shooting you would be far too kind. I suggest that to save your face you consider traveling abroad for a long period of time, such as the remainder of your life.' The look he gave Taunton held a silent menace that would have intimidated a stronger man than Taunton.

Geoffrey reached over to scoop up all the counters that Taunton had amassed. 'And since these are mine, albeit fraudulently won by you, I shall keep them.'

There was absolutely nothing Lord Taunton could say to the charges other than to stalk silently from the room. The evidence was there, if one knew what to look for and examined the backs of the cards most carefully. There was no doubt in the mind of anyone that Taunton would be driven not only from London, but from the country, by his dishonesty.

'Blandford, we owe you a great debt,' Lord Sefton said fervently. 'To think that one of our members should be such a blackguard as to consider cheating all of us.'

'Indeed,' Sir Humphrey chimed in, 'I have lost a goodly sum to that scoundrel. Pity there isn't some way we could recover it.'

'If one had known what his ruse was, I suppose it would have been possible to switch decks on him, then fleece him in return. He'd have been ruined, of course,' Geoffrey said, rising from the table and moving slowly in the opposite direction from where Chen Mei and Amelia had half hidden behind Peter. He drew Blandford with him, his very action attracting others.

The other gentlemen followed, no one seeming to notice the two strangers, one oddly dark, the other rather young, who now edged out of the door of the room.

Mr Raggett, the proprietor of White's, then entered, passing that duo with scarcely a glance. 'What's this, gentlemen? Lord Taunton expelled in disgrace? Explain, please.'

Lord Sefton assumed the role of narrator, deferring to Peter every now and again, then suggested they all join in a toast to Mr Blandford for saving the club from disgrace.

Chen Mei and Amelia slipped along the hall amid the ensuing confusion and loud discussion. In the room behind them they could hear champagne called for; the waiters scurried about arranging trays of glasses and opening bottles of champagne.

Attempting to walk nonchalantly down the curving stairs with past members staring down from their frames, proved rather daunting, Amelia discovered. Somehow they managed.

The porter saw nothing amiss in their departure. He merely nodded at the two strangers, and before long Amelia and Chen Mei were out on St James's Street once again.

'Chen Mei, you did it,' Amelia crowed with delight, just barely refraining from giving her companion a well-deserved hug.

'Feel good,' Chen Mei admitted. 'We best hurry home. Lord Dancy no looked too pleased, missee.'

Amelia agreed and hailed a passing hackney.

She scrambled into the hackney that drew up before the club, followed quickly by Chen Mei. They drove in contemplative silence until they reached Mrs Spencer's house. Here they ran into problems.

'The door is locked,' Amelia observed in a dismayed voice.

'Grimm think we asleep,' Chen Mei explained. From the sleeve of her borrowed coat she withdrew her little dagger and within minutes the lock clicked. They slipped inside the house, then relocked the door.

'You are certainly a handy one to have around,' Amelia whispered while they hurriedly climbed the stairs.

They tiptoed along the hall, then into Amelia's room. Once there she bolted the door behind them and collapsed in a heap on her bed. This didn't last long. Her companion had other notions.

'Missee look not too bad in those pantaloons,' Chen Mei observed as she nudged her charge to her feet, then began the removal of the also-borrowed clothes.

Amelia surveyed her slim figure clad in the boyish black pantaloons in her cheval glass and grinned. 'They are shockingly comfortable. I would not mind wearing them more often, I vow.'

'Chinese women know this already,' Chen Mei said with a smile, referring to her usual daytime garb.

'Sensible custom, I believe,' Amelia mumbled

as her nightdress was tugged over her head.

At last she was settled in her pretty sleigh bed with her covers drawn to her chin.

'Do you think he will be angry with us again?' She gave an enormous yawn as she settled her head on her pillow.

'Maybe. Men funny. They like to think they know all. A man who knows that he is a fool is not a great fool,' Chen Mei concluded in Cantonese from her store of knowledge.

'What makes you think that Lord Dancy would admit he is a fool?' Amelia murmured, already half asleep.

'The day will come,' Chen Mei replied, then blew out the candle to retire to her own well-earned rest.

★ ★ ★

The following morning Amelia slept far later than usual. When she finally drifted down to the morning room, she discovered her aunt all a-twitter at the breakfast table, deeply absorbed in one of her morning newspapers.

'You will scarce credit this.'

Amelia tensed, wondering how in the world the news of the cheating scandal at White's could have reached the papers in time to be published.

'Some absurd man wagered that he could

240

walk blind-folded from the Obelisk at the end of Fleetmarket and Fleet Street to the iron gate in front of the Mansion House.'

Relieved that she was not to hear about the incident at White's, Amelia inquired with more interest than she felt, 'And did he?'

'Indeed. He won his ten guineas on Sunday morning, although it took him an hour and forty minutes to accomplish the deed. The account says there were a great number of spectators who followed him along his path. Fancy anyone doing something so silly,' Mrs Spencer concluded.

Amelia nodded her agreement while popping a bite of buttered egg into her mouth. Utterly starved, she managed to make a tidy meal of her eggs, crisp bacon, and toast with jam. Once her plate was clear Amelia sat back to reflect on the past evening.

Aunt Ermintrude broke into her thoughts. 'Your ball is nearly upon us, my love. Another two days and you shall make your bows to society with Mary. It is a pity there isn't a Drawing Room to be held at the Palace for ages. But be assured that Lady Blandford is sponsoring both of you girls so you may make your curtsy to the Queen.'

It was a jolt for Amelia to be brought back from all her mental wanderings to reality. 'I hope my dress will be nice. I think Papa would like to have a painting done for him, perhaps in that dress? I daresay it does not have to be a grand one, just so he may see how I look. He is so very far away,' Amelia concluded on this rather wistful note.

Immediately after this Grimm entered the breakfast room to announce in a most disapproving voice that Lord Dancy awaited Miss Longworth in the drawing room.

'Oh, dear,' Amelia murmured as she rose from the table.

'I cannot think what brings him here this afternoon. We saw him just last evening. Is there something I do not know, my love?' Aunt Ermintrude asked in a soft, most curious voice. 'Do you wish me to come with you?'

'I expect it is a mere nothing, dearest Aunt. Enjoy your papers while I tend to Lord Dancy. Chen Mei shall come with me.'

Chen Mei awaited Amelia in the hallway, and together they marched up the stairs to the drawing room. Amelia paused at the threshold, attempting to assay his lordship's mood.

'Come in, come in. And close the door behind you, if you please. I should not wish to have this business nosed about town.'

Amelia resolutely crossed the room while Chen Mei did as bade and shut the door as quietly as possible. She came up behind Amelia and said quietly, 'In every affair retire a step, and you have an advantage.'

Unsure what her companion meant, Amelia nodded, then took a final step to meet Lord Dancy. 'You wished to speak with me, my lord?'

'I ought to beat you, you impossible girl! Yet you and Chen Mei succeeded where others have failed, so how can I? But do you have any notion of the risk you took last night? Many of the premier lords of the land were there. If they had gone home to tell their wives of this amusing bit of tittle-tattle, you would not only have put paid to any hope of a respectable offer of marriage, you might as well leave the country. It simply is not done for a young woman — a woman of any age, for that matter — to enter one of the gentlemen's clubs in London. You ought not even drive down St James's Street after noon, for pity's sake. Amelia, what am I to do with you?'

She clasped her hands before her in an attitude of meekness, although she seethed inwardly. Small thanks they got for saving his hide.

'Amelia?' He looked just a trifle unsure of himself when she peeped up at him.

'I do not know what can be done now, sir.

Lord Taunton must by now be packing to leave the country. I have no desire to go with him.'

'Good lord, I never suggested that!'

'Well,' she said prosaically, 'my ball at Almack's is the evening after tomorrow. I look forward to it with great enthusiasm. I would not wish anything to spoil my aunt's pleasure in that event, sir. Perhaps if I promise never to do anything like this again, it would help?'

He gave a derisive sniff. 'That's easy enough. There will never *be* anything like this again. I thought you were to leave my life?'

Amelia tightened her clasp on her hands a moment, before allowing them to drop to her sides. 'It is written: A speck upon your ivory fan you soon may wipe away; but stains upon the heart or tongue remain, alas, for aye.'

'And you nearly tossed it aside. You charged across the country to fetch me from the balloon, last night you dared to enter a club where no woman has ever gone. What ever am I do?' he repeated in his evident frustration.

'Why, nothing, my lord. Chen Mei restored your fortune and your blessed club. I went only because I longed to see that all went well for you.' A tear escaped from one eye and she angrily dashed it away. 'I know it does not help to say that I truly meant for the best, but I did.'

He shook his head and began to pace back and forth. He thrust one hand through his hair, disarranging the carefully tousled effect his valet had spent considerable time over.

'Somehow, asking you to refrain from helping me is like adding fuel to put out a fire. Not only is it impossible to accomplish, it seems to have the opposite effect.'

'Shall you attend our ball, my lord?' Amelia said in the most humble manner possible.

Lord Dancy paused in his steps to consider her, then reluctantly nodded. 'The Blandfords will expect me. I shall request the honor of a waltz with you. At least you've been approved for that dance, and we shan't risk censure for that,' he concluded with another sigh.

Amelia allowed herself a tiny smile, then composed her face again. 'I shall await your pleasure, my lord.'

Her demure curtsy must have had an effect, for he relaxed and smiled at her.

'I'm being something of a gudgeon, am I not? Only when I saw you enter — and you do have the most splendid legs, my dear — my heart nearly stopped. I will see you at your ball, then. Perhaps we could have the supper dance as well? I do owe you something for lending me Chen Mei.'

To the Chinese woman he bowed and said, 'Many thanks, good lady.'

Gratified to be so noticed, Chen Mei nodded gravely, then said, 'Better do a kindness near home than go far to burn incense.'

Amelia watched his lordship depart, then turned to Chen Mei with great relief. 'I suspect he intended to give us both quite a wigging.'

'He right,' Chen Mei replied in Cantonese. 'You must take care to protect your name. As to Lord Dancy,' she added, 'if your desires and wishes be laudable, Heaven will certainly further them.'

'And what do you know of my wishes and desires in regards to Lord Dancy, may I ask?' Amelia queried pertly as she returned to the lower floor in search of her aunt.

'Think twice, say nothing.' If Chen Mei was puzzled when Amelia burst out in laughter at this comment, she said nothing.

The following hours saw the delivery of Amelia's ball gown, a confection of silver tissue over the most delicate of pink silk. Later Mrs Spencer bundled Amelia into her carriage and went to consult with Lady Blandford about the final arrangements. Everything proceeded smoothly.

Too smoothly? Amelia wondered a day

later on her way to Almack's. Since it was Friday rather than Wednesday, the usual flock of the *ton* had altered slightly. The acceptances had poured in until nearly all invited had indicated they would be there. Amelia suspected that a few desired to attend merely to see what the inside of Almack's looked like, since they had not managed to obtain one of the precious tickets for the exclusive Wednesday Assemblies.

The canopy at the entrance would protect all in the event of bad weather, but that was the least of Amelia's worries. She had developed a sort of trembling that was most felt in her knees. When she entered the lofty-ceilinged ballroom and gazed up at the huge chandeliers, she wondered if all who had accepted would actually present themselves. It was most frightening.

The musicians tuned up at the far end of the room, with their leader Colnet supervising them all.

Mr Willis, the guardian of the establishment and nephew of the founder, William Macall, hastened to greet them when Lady Blandford and Mary, followed by Lord Blandford and Peter entered the room to join Mrs Spencer and Amelia.

'Nervous?' Mary whispered so her mother wouldn't hear.

'Petrified,' Amelia murmured back. 'I doubt if I shall be able to dance one sensible step let alone make intelligent conversation.'

However neither proved true, fortunately. The people thronged into the rooms in a steady flow of gratifying numbers. Before long Amelia was so busy trying to keep all the names straight and noting their faces that she had no time to think of wobbly knees.

And then Lord Dancy was there. Correctly attired in black coat and knee breeches, a white waistcoat embroidered with a delicate silver thread, and his famous diamond in his cravat, he presented a handsome picture. He bowed with commendable poise while holding her gloved hand.

'Miss Longworth, I trust you have saved me a dance,' he said with a quirk of his eyebrow when he glanced up into her eyes. A glimmer of mischief lurked within the green depths of those eyes, Amelia noted with apprehension.

Glancing about her to see if anyone was close enough to overhear, Amelia replied, 'It is my pleasure and my duty as your chattel to await your every wish.'

'Doing it a bit too brown, my girl,' he retorted, although softly, still not releasing her hand.

'Well, and you know how I feel about it all,'

she replied, not quite happy with the role thrust upon her by circumstances.

'I believe I have mentioned more than once that I released you from that silly whatever it was. If it wasn't a vow, it was some sort of Chinese custom? Whatever, we need not heed it.'

'But I must, you see. It would be so terribly wrong if I failed to do all I could for you.'

'Amelia,' Lord Dancy said with a heartfelt throb in his voice, 'you totally unman me.'

'Oh, I doubt I could ever do that, sir,' she replied with such sincerity that he was sent into a fit of coughing.

He drifted away from the receiving line after earning searching looks from Mrs Spencer and Lady Blandford.

Lord Blandford, a gentleman with surprising grace, escorted Mary, while Peter stood in for Amelia's family in the first dance, a graceful cotillion. This was followed in succession by one minuet, two country dances, a Scotch reel, and a contradance. After which Amelia began to think it would be extremely nice to catch a breath of fresh air.

'Overwhelmed, my dear?' Lord Dancy said when Amelia paused to study her card to see with whom she was obliged to dance next.

'Lord Dancy, it is you,' she replied with

relief. At his puzzled expression, she explained, 'You are my next partner, sir.'

'Of course. That is why I forced my way to your side. Such a crush, my dear.'

Amelia thought it a great pity that she was not his dear, but merely extended her hand and mechanically smiled at him.

'This dance will be something to enjoy, then we shall disappear to partake of that lovely supper. Lady Blandford was so kind as to tell me in advance what treats await us. I believe we shall both do it justice.'

With those words he drew her into his arms and gracefully swung her into the waltz that had just begun.

'I do not recall we requested a waltz be played,' she mused aloud.

'I consulted with Colnet, and he confirmed my suspicion. So I requested one. You could not be so shabby as to deny me this? Now could you? After all you have said about pleasing me?' He grinned down at her, and Amelia laughed back at him, her blue eyes twinkling up into his handsome face with a happy glow.

'I believe you have made your point, my lord,' she replied with a charming little giggle.

Geoffrey whirled her about through the respectable throng, wondering what they would think if they knew that the beauty in his arms had dressed in gentlemen's clothing two evenings ago and entered the premises of White's. Oh, there would be a prime scandal, the likes of which would take years to live down. It would rival the doing of Caroline Lamb, no doubt, and she had done all manner of outrageous things.

The music was seductive, he decided. That had to be the reason he felt like drawing her closer to him in a true embrace. Her eyelids fluttered down against those ivory-tinted cheeks that had a touch of peach in them in obvious enjoyment of the dance. He wished he might dare to kiss her again. But scandal lurked too close for comfort. If one of the men present that fateful evening at White's should chance to study Amelia and detect her identity, he shuddered to think what would befall her. Especially when he saw her with Chen Mei and put two and two together.

Amelia bowed her head for a moment at the conclusion of the dance, then tucked her hand into the crook of his arm, prepared to trot along to the blue damask room where refreshments were laid on by Gunter's.

'You know,' he said in a mood matching hers, 'I believe it was once the custom for a gentleman to claim a kiss from his partner in a dance. Time of Elizabeth, as I recall.'

'You were there, of course,' she said, followed by a chuckle.

'I am not that old, my dear Amelia. Shakespeare refers to it in *Henry VIII*. Come, wait here while I fetch us plates of the delectables.' He stationed her by one of the tables, then crossed over to where a sumptuous buffet quite unlike the Wednesday evening fare of lemonade and stale cakes was offered.

Had he dared to kiss her, Amelia decided she would have made a joke of it. She lived too close to censure to contemplate otherwise. Fortunately he seemed to understand the situation, for he neither behaved with impropriety nor acted as though she had committed a crime.

Others crowded into the refreshment room, and Amelia lost sight of his lordship. People she did not recognize stood close to her, and she guessed they must be friends of the Blandfords. Indeed, most of the people who had come this evening owed more to friendship with them than her aunt.

'Look at him over there, just as though he were not responsible for the death of so many of my countrymen,' came a voice not far behind her.

What shocked Amelia was that the man spoke in Portuguese. He must calculate that no one would be likely to understand him, given how few of the English bothered to learn that language. She strained to hear more above the growing din.

'We shall strike soon now. He has been careful so far, but he grows careless. Had that stupid woman not intervened, we could have shot him that day when he took the balloon. Fool. He went sailing off, and we hadn't a hope with her chasing after him.'

Amelia's heart grew cold as she realized that she was the woman the man referred to and that Lord Dancy was the man he intended to shoot! She shifted about in order to see if she could take careful note of this person who spoke so boldly of killing an English peer. Dressed in acceptable ballroom attire, the Portuguese did not appear out of place. But his dark complexion was suited to the shadows where he lurked. Amelia wondered just when he intended to strike.

Then the crowd shifted, and she could hear no more, much to her frustration.

'Ah, there you are, waiting for me just as I requested. I must say, if you would behave like that all the time, I would be most grateful,' Lord Dancy said, that jade twinkle in his eyes most pronounced.

'My lord,' Amelia said as she joined him at the table she had stayed near while he had gathered their feast, 'I just overheard a most disturbing conversation.'

Before he could reply to this puzzling remark, Peter with Chloe Moore, Mary Blandford, and Denzil Warwick joined them, each carrying full plates and gaily chattering.

'Later on we shall discuss this conversation you overheard, my dear,' Lord Dancy murmured to Amelia in an aside.

With that Amelia had to be content, for it would not do to bruit it about that Lord Dancy was the target of an assassin. It was difficult for her to concentrate on the prattle about her. Mary and Chloe giggled merrily about the events of the evening . . . who was seen dancing with whom, the pretty gowns, and who was not paying court to you know who.

It was silly gossip, and normally Amelia would have joined in with the others, but she had too much on her mind — something Peter noticed in a trice.

He edged over close to where she sat with Dancy at one end of the table. 'I strongly suspect something is the matter. May I be of help?'

'No,' replied Dancy while at the same moment Amelia said, 'Oh, yes, please.'

'What is it?' Peter's kind gaze darted between his two good friends.

With a cautioning look at his lordship, Amelia said in an undertone, 'I overheard a rather dark-complected man say he plans to shoot Lord Dancy. He spoke in Portuguese you understand, and I greatly fear that he meant what he said. We must not leave his lordship alone for a moment. Otherwise his death would be upon our consciences for ever.'

'Rubbish,' Dancy declared, but not very fervently.

'He said he had intended to shoot you that day in the park, but you foiled his plans by going up in the balloon and blew away from him. Had I not torn after you, he would have, I believe. Shot you, that is, for he cursed me for interfering with his plans.'

'I say,' breathed Peter before turning his attention to his partner as might be expected of him at a ball.

Amelia stared at Lord Dancy for a moment, then dropped her gaze to her plate, where her lovely treats were sitting as they had been for some minutes. 'You see why I thought that conversation disturbing?'

'I forbid you to do a thing about it, my dear.'

'Of course, my lord,' she dutifully replied. And pigs will fly, she added to herself. She knew where her duty lay, and it wasn't in obeying a stupid command like that. But whom could she get to help her this time?

12

'By Jove,' Peter said thoughtfully when he could return his attention to his friend once again, 'Do you think it could be . . . '

'Most likely,' Lord Dancy replied quietly.

'Now that I think on it, I do believe his mastery of Portuguese was flawed,' Amelia mused. 'He sounded more like a foreigner who speaks the language well. I would not be surprised were he to prove a Frenchman.'

At that statement Lord Dancy and Peter Blandford exchanged concerned looks, but made no comment.

Amelia knew they felt she must be excluded and that a ball — where anyone could overhear a conversation when you least expected it — was not the place to discuss the matter. But she would very much have liked to know precisely what they were thinking.

'I wonder how he managed to gain entrance?' she continued. 'Surely he would not be on my list, and I very much doubt if Mary or your mother would have invited a person of questionable background, a man unknown to you.' She threw Peter a quizzical look before glancing at Mary who was immersed in conversation with Chloe Moore.

'That's true. Perhaps he came with someone known to us?' Peter said speculatively before he had to return his attention once again to Miss Moore.

People were filtering back into the ballroom, leaving the small group at the Blandford table somewhat alone.

'This will never do,' Lord Dancy declared. 'Miss Moore, I believe I may claim this dance. Peter, did you not say you are to partner Amelia?' Lord Dancy whisked Chloe Moore out of the room, taking Mary and the others with him. Peter remained behind with Amelia.

'I say, Amelia, you did promise not to interfere in this business. Could find yourself in a bit of a pickle, you know.' Peter eyed Amelia as though he fully expected her to go about inspecting each and every guest to see if they spoke Portuguese with a French accent.

'I shan't involve you whatever I might do, Peter,' Amelia said with a fond look. 'Indeed, his lofty lordship has made it quite plain that he does not wish my help. But they had intended to shoot him that morning of the unexpected balloon ride,' she stated firmly, defending what she had done. 'You must admit that his life has been in danger.'

'And once again you saved his life. Dash it all, Amelia, that sort of thing could truly irritate a fellow after a while. A man likes to think he can take care of himself, you know. Don't want to be having a female look after him. Downright disheartening.' Peter gave her a rather comical look of dismay.

'Well,' Amelia said, trying not to sound vastly annoyed, 'why do we not join the dancers before the ball is over. I suspect that my aunt will be concerned if she does not see me.' She rose from the table and watched while Peter jumped to his feet as though scorched.

Apparently realizing that his presence alone with Amelia might be greatly misconstrued, even if they were in an open room with servants milling about, Peter escorted her to the main room where they joined the others in a rousing country dance.

Amelia had found Peter to be an excellent dancer. Not once did he tread on her toes. She laughed up at him, with the hope that Lord Dancy might notice her attentions. Then she caught a glimpse of him going down the line with Chloe and realized he did not pay Amelia the least attention. Indeed, the redheaded Miss Moore seemed to have quite captivated Lord Dancy this evening.

Amelia firmly quelled the rising sensation

of envy she suddenly developed for the lovely and very nice Miss Moore. Rather, she turned her mind to the present problem as she viewed it.

This entire matter would require drastic measures. She would have to consult Hemit, to make certain that his lordship was protected at all times. Perhaps it would help to hire a detective, or maybe one of those fighters she had heard spoken about when gentlemen chatted about the boxing world — which they oddly enough called the Fancy.

Then, she must find someone close to Lord Dancy who had his best interests at heart, someone who would be willing to assist Amelia with her plan. Perhaps Hemit would know just who to ask.

'I say, Amelia, you have the most peculiar expression on your face. I hope you are not hatching another one of your schemes.' Peter again viewed her somewhat askance, and Amelia wondered what he truly expected of her.

'I only wish I could,' she said, smoothing her brow and turning on that polite social smile every girl learned to produce. 'Has Lord Dancy heard anything from his sisters as yet?'

'Said something about his sister Victoria being in the family way and not likely returning to London for some time. Far as I know the others are in the country. Elizabeth is still with her aunt while Julia is yet off painting or something.'

Drat. Then the sisters were not apt to be of any help. Peter had mentioned something about Victoria and Elizabeth assisting with efforts to foil various French attempts at spying in England. Since Amelia was firmly convinced that Lord Dancy also had associations in that direction, she wondered if the villain wasn't someone who had a massive grudge against Geoffrey Dancy.

How she liked his name. She wished it was proper for a young lady to use a gentleman's first name. But it wasn't. Which brought to mind the numerous times that Geoffrey Dancy had used Amelia's first name. So far no one had commented on his slips. While Amelia had said he might use her first name, she had supposed it to be only on that journey to London. She had soon discovered it would not do elsewhere. London was more stuffy about name usage and all that it implied than Macao. Although she was so young at the time she had left there that people had still referred to her as Miss Amelia, and no one appeared to think a thing of it.

What would a drastic measure involve, she

wondered, returning to the problem involving Lord Dancy, while performing yet another country dance. If she were an agent for the government, would she not try to infiltrate his household? Perhaps she could become a maid for a day or two? That would surely be one way to find out the person who best to approach for help.

Chen Mei would offer advice. Goodness knew that she overflowed with that commodity.

The hour was nearing morning when the Blandfords, Mrs Spencer, and Amelia all left Almack's Assembly rooms together. Mr Willis expressed himself most gratified at the pleasure of serving them and complimented the ladies upon the excellent refreshments.

Amelia thought he could take a lesson from them, but then, if his wife poured tea and made the lemonade, perhaps they were merely extremely saving. However it seemed to Amelia they might do better than to serve cakes that had become stale.

★ ★ ★

The next day Chen Mei woke her far earlier than Amelia would have preferred. Rubbing her eyes and yawning hugely, Amelia propped herself up in bed to survey her companion.

'I trust you have a reason for this?'

'You say you velly much want to obtain place in Dancy household. I fix. They need a maid fo day while one is sick. You new maid.'

All thought of lolling about in bed left her. Amelia tossed back the covers, then slid from her bed with great haste. She pulled her nightgown over her head, then impatiently said, 'I imagine you have found some clothes suitable for a maid. I had best hurry.' She scrambled into her underthings and stockings with more haste than care.

'What you going to tell Aunt?'

'I shall tell her . . . ' Amelia gave a vexed sigh, then brightened. 'I shall tell her that I am playing a trick on a friend — to see if she will recognize me. That ought to do it, for you must know that at least half of the *ton* do not pay the least notice of their servants.'

Chen Mei nodded, assisting her charge into a simple challis print dress with a mobcap to cover her lovely blonde curls.

'Is this the sort of thing Lord Dancy's maids wear?' Amelia asked, pivoting about before her cheval glass. 'I vow, the fabric may be a touch scratchy, but it is pretty enough.'

'His lordship likes to see pretty girls, maybe?' Chen Mei stood back to survey her handiwork. 'I think you too pretty. Better turn your back when you see him.'

'Oh, indeed. I intend to do that very thing, you may be sure. I can only hope that he sleeps late, then promptly goes out.' Amelia slipped from her room and down the stairs to the morning room. As expected, her aunt was nowhere to be found so Amelia sat at the desk to write a letter of explanation. It was to be hoped her dear aunt would not think of too many unanswered questions.

Before leaving the house, Amelia entered the breakfast room to enjoy a good meal. Goodness knew whether she would have such at the Dancy household. She suspected that many London homes might request smashing repasts for themselves with little for the help. Although perhaps leftovers might not be that bad, she decided upon reflection. When she considered all the food that was returned to the kitchen after one of the Spencer meals, it might be that the staff ate reasonably well.

How simple it turned out to be to sneak from the Spencer house. With the butler occupied in his morning duties and all the other servants ignoring her, Amelia felt nearly invisible. She knew they were suspicious of Chen Mei, avoiding her whenever possible. When they saw her with Amelia, they assumed the two were off on some errand, and would rather not question it.

Amelia presented herself at the back door

of the Dancy household, hoping no one would have seen her. How she might avoid Evenson, that stately butler, Amelia didn't know, but she would find a way. Perhaps in her new guise he wouldn't recognize her as the same girl who had come here weeks ago with Lord Dancy. She wasn't quite certain if a butler would be one to approach, for all his starch he might prove to be a potential ally. Hemit would know, perhaps.

Using the name of Susan — which happened to be Amelia's middle name — she neared the housekeeper with hesitant steps. From a distance she appeared formidable.

'Mrs Hardesty?' Amelia knew the hierarchy below stairs to be inflexible and hated to expose her unfamiliarity with her position immediately.

'You have come to replace Rose for a time?' Mrs Hardesty replied, less haughty than Amelia expected.

'Yes, ma'am.' Amelia bobbed a curtsy she hope resembled that of the upstairs maid at her aunt's home.

'Hm,' the housekeeper said, glancing away at something before returning her gaze to her. 'Have you served in a gentleman's home before? Or has it been a female establishment?'

'I worked for a lady, if you please, ma'am.'

264

Mrs Hardesty's look sharpened, possibly at Amelia's speech which was hard to disguise. Amelia breathed a sigh of relief when she questioned her no further.

'You will do the dusting on the ground and first floors. Do not go to the second; only the older maid goes there, for that is where Lord Dancy's quarters are located. I was not here when Lord Dancy was in residence in the past. While he has not bothered any of the maids so far, I don't wish to take any chances. You will also polish the brass, open the shutters, clean and blacken the grates. The looking glasses and windows are due for a cleaning. See to them when you finish the other tasks. Mind you, I do not wish his lordship to discover you about when he comes down.'

Paling at the thought of cleaning and blackening the grates, Amelia nodded, then followed the young person summoned along to where the supplies were kept.

'Dusting first,' she told the hall-boy. She had decided that she would put off the matter of the grates as long as she could. When he pointed to the necessary cloths, she carried them along to the first of the rooms she was to clean and busied herself. After opening the shutters, she set about her work.

She took great pleasure in examining all

the beautiful treasures she assumed that Lord Dancy had accumulated during his travels. Either he or someone in his family had loved interesting and splendid things. She particularly admired the sculpture of a pair of twin girls.

'That's Lady Julia's girls,' Evenson offered from the doorway. 'Done by Miss Victoria. Sweet little girls, they are.' He remained to study Amelia as she worked, making her exceedingly nervous.

'I see. It's beautiful.' She didn't know whether to ask Evenson's advice or turn to Hemit. She feared that Hemit might go to Lord Dancy out of loyalty. What she needed to do was to find someone she could trust who would listen to her. So far she had not figured out a way to reach the groom. Not having any reason to be near the mews where Lord Dancy stabled his horses and reluctant to expose herself to possible hazards in that area, she hoped to find him while here. But how?

Evenson watched her as Amelia reverently ran a dust cloth over the sculpture, then went on to the next piece.

'I should like to know what you are about, young miss,' the butler inquired in a conversational manner. 'It's clear to me that you have had no experience as a maid in your

266

life. Suppose you tell me what this is all about?' He actually wore a somewhat inviting expression on his face, a sort of softening.

Since this was precisely what Amelia had hoped would come about, she smiled at the dignified gentleman, who looked as though he had served the Dancy family for a good many years and sighed with relief.

'Is there some room where we might talk without anyone overhearing what is said?' She looked about her warily to see if there was anyone eavesdropping.

Not revealing the least bit of surprise at her question, he gestured to his left, then walked silently with Amelia until they reached a small office of sorts. An etching of four children hung on one wall, and there were surprisingly comfortable chairs for the two of them. He busied himself in a small closet off to one side, then brought Amelia a small glass of sherry.

'Sherry? This time of day?'

'I thought after your exertions this morning, you might be in need of a restoring glass of something. If I request lemonade for a housemaid, there might be a few raised eyebrows. We do not wish that, do we Miss Longworth?'

'Oh, you recognized me.' She took a sip and liked the taste very much. 'Well,' she began. 'It is this way. I met Lord Dancy in Portugal when he saved my life twice. He saved it again when we arrived in Portsmouth, carrying me from the burning inn.'

Evenson nodded slightly, encouraging Amelia to continue.

'So, I am his.' Her simple statement caused the butler to elevate his eyebrows a tiny bit, but otherwise he sat impassively in his oak armchair.

Heartened by this acceptance of her status as Lord Dancy's chattel, she continued to fill Evenson in on all that had occurred to date — from her point of view, naturally.

'I have served the Dancy family ever since I began service as a lad. I would do anything to help them. But I cannot think how to assist you in this.' Evenson pursed his lips while he contemplated the problem at hand. 'His lordship would not take lightly to having someone interfere with his plans. Somehow I misdoubt he will like having someone peering over his shoulder, as it were.'

'Do you think Hemit would go along with our wish to protect Lord Dancy from his enemies? For I know there must be at least two, possibly three of them.'

The butler nodded. 'I daresay he would take on the task with relish. So . . . what do we do?'

If Amelia felt the least bit peculiar sitting with the Dancy butler in his private quarters, detailing her opinions on the gentleman who was even now most likely abovestairs asleep in his bed, she didn't show it.

'Well, I believe we *must* hedge him around with people to protect him at all times. *Never* allow him to go out on his own. Always see to it that he has a friend or two, an extra groom in attendance, and perhaps not drive his curricle about, but take a closed carriage instead.' She gazed at the butler with a hopeful expression. 'It should work.'

Evenson pursed his lips again, then left his chair to cross the room to where a row of bell ropes hung. He tugged at one; they waited until the door opened.

'What's up?' Hemit said in a surprised voice. 'Miss Longworth! You here?' Hemit proved aware that it was not the proper thing for a young woman to enter the house of an unmarried gentleman at any hour of the day. Even a few minutes were enough to compromise her reputation.

'Lord Dancy is quite unaware I am here, Hemit. I tried to think how I might speak with you and Evenson or someone here without Lord Dancy knowing a thing about it. This was the only way I could manage it.'

'She is supposedly taking Rose's place for

the day,' Evenson explained to the groom with a wry twist of his mouth.

'Mrs Hardesty will be in a rare taking if she finds out she's sent a lady to clean the house,' Hemit observed with a look at the prim young woman perched on Evenson's chair.

'That is nothing that can't be remedied. Perhaps we can tell her I did it as a lark, a joke on his lordship or something of that sort,' Amelia offered somewhat hesitantly.

Hemit and Evenson exchanged dubious looks.

'See here,' Amelia said, 'we simply cannot sit about nattering on over this. Any moment now his lordship will come down those stairs and go off into a very dangerous world. You do wish to protect him?'

'Yes, miss,' the men fervently agreed.

'Well then,' Amelia declared with equal zeal, 'let us commence.' She took off her apron, then settled more comfortably on the chair.

The three put their heads together, mapping out a likely guide to Lord Dancy's movements for the day.

Once this was accomplished, Amelia leaned back in her chair, polishing off her sherry. 'There, if I do say so, he ought to be safe for the day.' She saluted the men, then opened the door to peer out into the hallway.

' 'Tis empty,' she whispered. 'How do I get out of here?'

'Leave it to me.' Evenson allowed himself a grin. 'Mrs Hardesty is a bit stuffy. It will come as a surprise to her that the girl she engaged to help has disappeared. Not stolen anything, either. Come, I'll let you out of the front door. No servant would dream of leaving that way, and she'll never see you.'

'Oh, you are an angel, Evenson. I can see why Lord Dancy depends on you so.' She bestowed a flashing smile on the butler, her blue eyes lighting up with her delight.

The dignified man nodded to himself for some unknown reason, then ushered Amelia to the front door, allowing her to slip out to a waiting Chen Mei with not the least sound.

Once at the Spencer household, Amelia found her aunt in the front parlor puzzling over the letter written hours earlier.

'Oh, my love, what a muddle this is. Where have you been? From this letter you left, it sounds remarkably like you have been pretending to be a maid. Surely that cannot be true!'

'Only for a little while,' Amelia admitted with a grin for her dearest aunt. 'I thought I could fool my friend, but my identity was uncovered very soon. And I thought it a very good disguise, too.' At this Amelia twirled about in her mobcap and challis print dress. She bobbed a proper curtsy to her aunt and attempted to appear demure.

'I can see you tried hard enough. I hope that is the reason for your charade. You were in such a bemused state last evening that I had begun to worry about you. You do become involved in the oddest starts, my love. I shouldn't like to think you risked your reputation in some mad scheme to safeguard Lord Dancy.'

'Lord Dancy is somewhat of a trial, Aunt Ermintrude.'

'Is he, now? Fancy that. I daresay you are one of the very few who might venture such an opinion. Most people think he is quite handsome and as a peer, entitled to do anything he pleases.'

'It is easy to convince a wise man, but to reason with a fool is a difficult undertaking,' Amelia quoted from Chen Mei's store of maxims. 'That fool simply refuses to admit he is in danger. Last night I overheard two gentlemen talking — and I do not in the least understand how such dreadful men were allowed to come to our ball. Anyway, they said they intended to shoot Lord Dancy and cursed me for luring him off on that balloon ride that he so unwillingly took. It saved his life,' Amelia concluded virtuously.

'Oh, mercy,' Aunt Ermintrude gasped, fanning herself with Amelia's letter. 'I scarce think Lord Dancy is a fool, my love. He is highly regarded in our circle, you know.'

'Well, I hope that his groom and butler will see to it that he is well-guarded. As devoted to him as they appear to be, he ought to be well-watched.'

Aunt Ermintrude looked as though she would like to inquire just how Amelia knew all this. Apparently she decided it was well not to know, for she rose from her chair and drifted across the parlor to look out of the window.

'Anything interesting?' Amelia asked on her way to her room so she might change.

'Callers. You must hurry to your room and put on that pretty blue muslin with the clusters of forget-me-nots on the bodice and flounce. It becomes you so well.'

'Yes, ma'am. They shan't see my shadow,' she caroled gaily as she dashed from the room and up the stairs.

Behind her, Aunt Ermintrude sighed, looked at the ceiling, and muttered something that sounded like, 'Give me strength, oh Lord.'

★ ★ ★

'Strong coffee. A large pot, I believe,' Lord Dancy ordered in his usual pleasant manner.

He riffled through the early morning mail while he sipped from the steaming cup in his hand.

'Morning, Geoff,' Peter said from the doorway where he paused for a moment as though to gauge his welcome.

'Come in, come in,' Geoffrey muttered none too heartily. 'I trust you slept better than I did. I kept thinking of those two fellows at the ball last night. Wish I'd had a chance to see them for myself. Amelia was less than forthcoming regarding their appearance.'

'True. If a chap is going to be shot, it would be jolly to know what his enemy looks like. Much better chance to beat him to the draw that way.' Peter helped himself to a cup of coffee, grimacing at the bitter taste. He proceeded to add cream and sugar, before pulling out a chair at the table.

'I cannot hide in my room. I refuse to become a recluse merely because of something Amelia overheard — or thinks she overheard.'

'Well, she has been right before. And what about that business of the balloon?'

'Sheer luck.'

'Well, I believe she is telling you precisely what she heard. What's more, I intend to stand guard on you today,' Peter declared with a diffident air.

'I bloody well do not need a nursemaid!' Geoff roared at his good friend.

'Did you wish something, my lord?' Evenson inquired from the doorway in the blandest of manners.

'Tell this buffle-headed fellow that I left short-coats a long time ago. I do not need a guard.' Geoffrey replaced his slice of toast on his plate, looking at it with surprise, wondering how he had come to have it in his hand.

'You can call me a jingle-brained fool if you like, but we had some hair-raising times in Spain and Portugal. If you can tell me that your senses ain't standing on end, I shall drop the matter at once,' Peter said shrewdly. 'I daresay that you will admit that you know you are in danger and in need of your friends right now. Dash it all, Geoff, what are friends for if not to chime in with a helping hand?'

Geoffrey sighed, then nodded. 'Too right, old fellow. I cannot say I like this one bit, however.'

Peter grinned at Evenson as though he sensed an ally. 'I gather you are aware his lordship has been threatened by some nodcock — Frenchie, most likely. Mean to see to it that my friend doesn't come to an untimely end.'

'We are deeply concerned as well, my lord. Hemit and myself, that is. I trust that between Mr Blandford and your groom, you will have staunch accomplices.'

'Hmpf,' Geoffrey replied, waving his hand in dismissal. 'Do you think there is anyone around who doesn't know about this business?'

'I haven't uttered a word, I swear it,' Peter avowed.

'Well, then, since I know that Hemit doesn't come until called, how did my butler become so well-informed about the matter? Pixies?'

Peter frowned, then helped himself to the raspberry jam, which he proceeded to spread on Geoff's toast in generous quantity.

'Wonder how Amelia is this morning,' Peter said after stuffing himself with eggs and a slice of ham plus a third slice of toast.

'You ought to wonder what she will think of next to bedevil me.'

'Now, Geoff, the girl means well. She has your best interest at heart,' Peter argued after downing the last of his doctored coffee.

'I would that she leave me alone. How can I possibly fix an interest with that lovely armful at the opera house with Amelia dropping out of the sky when I least expect her?'

'You know what I think? I think that one day you will miss her.'

'As I miss an aching head. If you have finished demolishing the remainder of my breakfast, I suggest we depart. Tatt's is placing some one hundred carriages on view, with the sale to come up in a few days. I understand a rather fashionable landau owned by a lady is up. Says she only used it a few months. According to the *Post* it's painted patent yellow, lined with light blue cloth trimmed in lace, and has yellow morocco reclining cushions, plated furniture, and patent axle trees no less. I think I just might have a need for such a beauty in the not too distant future.' Geoffrey grinned at his amused friend.

'By all means. I believe Tatt's to be safe enough. It's driving there that might prove hazardous. Listen to reason and do not take the curricle today,' Peter pleaded.

Geoffrey went out his front door, then came to a halt when he viewed his traveling carriage. 'I suspect I wouldn't be allowed if I wanted,' he commented wryly.

13

'Oh, my love,' Aunt Ermintrude sang out in her fluting voice as she drifted into the breakfast room, waving one of her many morning newspapers in the air. 'Napoleon has abdicated! He is banished to the island of Elba. Peace is here at last.'

Chen Mei frowned. She had joined Amelia at breakfast at her insistence so they might better plan the day. It was clear she did not condone so gentle a treatment for the man responsible for thousands of deaths. 'Killing a bad ruler is no murder.'

'Oh, he will be unable to do a thing from Elba, for he will be guarded most efficiently,' Aunt assured them. She looked slightly shocked that Chen Mei would advocate something as strong as murder, even for Napoleon.

The Cantonese woman appeared to think little of that opinion, but she said nothing.

At the end of the table Aunt Ermintrude sank down upon her chair, utterly absorbed in reading the account of all that had occurred and was to take place in the next few days.

'There are to be festivities everywhere,' she read aloud. 'Oh, dancing in the streets ought to be the order of the day with that hateful man out of the way.' She beamed a smile at Amelia, then avidly returned to her newspapers.

'He would be better off dead,' Chen Mei muttered to Amelia. 'A dead man cannot inspire others to rise up so to overthrow.'

'I am not so certain about that, but I suppose you are right,' Amelia murmured back. 'You realize that this will make protecting Lord Dancy enormously difficult. With the press of people everywhere he goes, one slim Frenchman will have no trouble at all in disposing of a hated Englishman.'

'Best lure him away from city,' Chen Mei said practically.

'All of London will be heading toward Paris, or so this says,' Aunt inserted into the softly spoken conversation. 'How I long to see Paris again. Would you not like to travel across the Channel to look the place over, my love?'

'I suppose London will become rather thin of company if that is the case,' Amelia replied, not answering the invitation to travel to Paris. While she might enjoy a view of the French city, she dare not leave Lord Dancy. She very much doubted if he intended to enter the dragon's mouth by making the crossing to a free France. Actually the sparsity of people in London would work to their good, for the parties might not be so crowded. She said as much to Chen Mei, who nodded slowly.

'Good thing.'

'I must go out to purchase some white cockades to do honor to the Bourbons. And I wish to find that scarf I have that has fleurs-de-lys embroidered on it, for I feel sure that will be all the thing. This is enormously exciting. His majesty, Louis XVIII, is to hold a levee. 'Tis said even women will be allowed to attend. What a pity he is such a fat old man,' Aunt concluded with wide-eyed conviction. 'I believe the French deserve someone a little younger and more understanding after the tyrant Napoleon. I wonder if Louis has learned a lesson from the revolution that nearly ruined his country.'

'Indeed, ma'am,' Amelia replied respectfully. She rose in a flurry of blue muslin. 'I shall send a note to Mary Blandford to see if she would care to go for a drive. Perhaps we may see something of the festivities in progress.'

'Invite her brother as well, dear Amelia,' Aunt Ermintrude trilled before returning to the news of the day.

Amelia exchanged a resigned glance with

Chen Mei, then slipped from the room and along the hall. It took but a few minutes to dash off her suggestion, adding her hope that Peter might come along. Perhaps they could make a party of it and invite others as well. Amelia did not wish to encourage her aunt's fond hopes regarding Peter Blandford. He might be heir to the barony, but he did not hold Amelia's interest other than as a friend.

'Dare I invite Lord Dancy?' Amelia wondered aloud to herself. Since Chen Mei had parted ways with her at the bottom of the stairs, there was no one to advise Amelia one way or the other. 'Why not? The worst he can do is say no. I hope Evenson will hide all his other invitations for the day so that he feels compelled to accept this one.'

When the footman returned, he brought a delighted reply of acceptance from Mary; Peter agreed to go with them. Amelia rushed up to her room to dress for the outing.

'Where you go?' Chen Mei inquired as she riffled through the wardrobe of pretty gowns.

'I believe it would be safe enough to visit the British Museum Gardens. It is on the very edge of the city and although usually much sought out, should not be busy today. Any stranger will be noticed immediately. With Hemit and Peter, and my little dagger in addition, Lord Dancy will be as safe as if he were still in bed.'

'Ah,' Chen Mei replied, nodding with satisfaction. She withdrew a gown of peach-bloom sarcenet having three narrow flounces at the hem, followed by a matching pelisse. Once dressed, Amelia set her bonnet in place, admiring the pretty confection lined in peach satin and trimmed with three lovely plumes. She tied the ribands to one side of her chin in a fetching bow. It was a simpler variation of the Oldenburg bonnet made so popular by the Tsar of Russia's sister. Amelia felt quite in style and hoped that his lordship would notice her fetching attire.

She walked slowly down the stairs and was in the act of drawing on her chicken-skin gloves in a delicate peach color when the front door opened.

'Miss Longworth,' Geoffrey said with commendable calm after he passed Grimm, considering that Amelia had cautioned him to present himself or risk death.

'You are wiser than I thought, sir,' she declared as Grimm shut the door behind his lordship, retreating discreetly to the far end of the hall.

Geoffrey advanced on the dainty bit of peach fluff that stood so sweetly at the bottom of the stairs. How could any woman who looked like a piece of candy cause such havoc in his life? He guided Amelia into the front parlor, hoping to keep what he had to say from the ears of the butler.

'We shall endeavor to take very good care of you,' she assured him sunnily. 'I feared that if you went out and about on your own, the wicked Frenchman would be able to shoot you very easily. You must know we could not allow you to place yourself in such danger. So we wish you to be with us. We will protect you.'

Geoffrey stared at the wicked little dagger she pulled from her reticule and restrained a shudder. The richly engraved sheath fell from it easily, exposing a sharply pointed blade.

'Do you always go about with a dagger on you, Amelia?' he asked in a somewhat strangled voice.

'Of course,' came her answer with a straightforward smile directly into his eyes. 'Chen Mei's brother taught me to throw this most accurately at a target. One never knows where danger lurks. I must place your well-being first, you know.'

What was a fellow to do with such honesty and loyalty? Her notion of protection did not quite match his, but how could he scold her — or tell her that she was making him feel stifled? Or how to explain that a chap would rather handle a menace of this sort without an interfering female? Not when the chit gazed at him with such determination out of the most earnest blue eyes he had ever seen. She looked like an angel, but had proved to be a devilishly irritating one.

Geoffrey sighed with defeat. He had not the heart to *again* tell her not to bother him anymore. Or was it that he fancied the girl? No, he assured himself. How could a man be drawn to this aggravating baggage? Not Geoffrey Dancy — never.

Mrs Spencer fluttered into the room, her face wreathed in a smile. 'Is not the news wonderful? That dreadful man is off to Elba, and we may sleep well again. I shall go to purchase our cockades, my love,' she said to Amelia. 'Where do you plan to venture?'

'By all means, tell us what our day shall bring?' Geoffrey inquired with an arched brow that usually intimidated everyone in sight. Not so Amelia. This chit merely giggled and patted him on the arm in a pleasant manner.

Geoffrey gritted his teeth and firmly quelled the desire to shake this young woman until she . . . He put that thought aside as well. Once he had her in his arms he feared he would forget all about chastising her. He had not forgotten that taste of a kiss after his balloon ride.

'I propose that we visit the charming gardens behind the British Museum. We do not need tickets for that, and it is a lovely day.'

Geoffrey gave her a dubious look. But then, with his traveling carriage that Hemit insisted upon driving and the parasols the ladies always carried, they ought to do well enough. If it rained, they could always go over to the Blandford house.

'Would you care for coffee, Lord Dancy?' Mrs Spencer said. 'Cook has baked some rather nice ratafia biscuits.'

'Are we to await the Blandfords here?' he asked of Amelia before assenting to the beverage and biscuits.

'Yes. Mary can be ready in a trice. I fear it is Peter and his cravat that may keep us waiting.'

He conveyed his polite thanks to Mrs Spencer, then watched while Amelia sat down on a backless sofa covered in plum silk. The room had been decorated in a current mode — Greek revival, or whatever it was dubbed. It reminded him of the French Empire style that had raged across that country when Napoleon made it popular. He seated himself rather gingerly in a facing chair, pleased to discover how comfortable it proved.

From this vantage point he had an

excellent view of the young woman who had tumbled into his life and caused no end of mischief. He had to admit that she was the most appealing bit of mischief he'd ever seen . . . or held in his arms. Thoughts of holding her once again began to stir within, and he welcomed the entrance of the butler as a timely restraint.

Grimm brought the tea and coffee with such promptness, Amelia suspected he had anticipated the request. She poured, for Aunt Ermintrude was still absorbed in reading snippets from the columns of her various newspapers to them.

Amelia studied Lord Dancy's face while handing him the cup of coffee, then offering the plate of biscuits. He did not appear to be angry, but she sensed an annoyance in him, one she would do well to lessen.

'I trust you are well-pleased that Napoleon has been banished to Elba, sir. Do you think that will somewhat ease the danger to yourself?' Amelia asked when assured her aunt was not paying the least attention to the conversation.

'It all depends, does it not? If the fellow bears ill will toward me for some reason, Napoleon may not enter into the business in the least.' Lord Dancy demolished several of the biscuits with his coffee, then set the cup down on the table close to Amelia. He appeared not to notice her nervous start when his hand strayed near her knee.

A stir in the front hall indicated that the Blandfords had arrived. When Amelia rose to greet them, she found Lord Dancy right behind her, disquietingly close. He stirred feelings within her that she tried to ignore, for they interfered with her thinking processes. If she didn't quell these odd emotions, she would soon be in a briar patch, for certain.

'Miss Moore,' Amelia said with mixed pleasure, daring a glance at Lord Dancy to see how he reacted to this addition to their group. 'Mr Warwick, what a delight to have you both join us.'

Miss Moore was a vision in mint green muslin with a dark green pelerine. Mary wore a pretty dress of jonquil yellow edged in white lace ruffles. The assessing gaze of each young woman when they encountered Lord Dancy standing close to Amelia made her feel uneasy. How much of her feelings did they guess? She hoped they believed her care for the man was motivated purely by kindness.

Within several minutes they had bid Mrs Spencer farewell, then set off in the Dancy carriage. Fortunately the commodious traveling coach could easily hold them all. Amelia sat by a window where she could peek out at the streets and people as they went.

'I do not see you-know-who,' she murmured to Peter, who sat between her and Miss Moore.

'Wouldn't expect such a thing,' he quietly replied.

Once assured that they appeared to have given the slip to the man who declared he wished to shoot Lord Dancy, Amelia eased back on the seat to enjoy the day. After all, it was reasonable that the man had other things to do besides lurking about in Lord Dancy's shadow.

All declared that the gardens were as charming as promised. The six of them sauntered along the paths, examining the flora as they went. There were a fair number of people about on this day, but not so many they had to worry about a crush. Amelia figured that a man could be easily chased in such an open area, and less apt to strike when he was so vulnerable. Lord Dancy could be better protected as well.

'Oh, how I adore the tulips,' Chloe Moore exclaimed. 'Lord Montague must have been caught up in the tulipmania of some years ago. Look at the vast number that are planted in this garden.'

This phenomenon had to be explained to Amelia, who declared it the silliest thing she had ever heard. 'But since the tulips are so beautiful, I can well understand how a person might become obsessed with them.' She reached over to touch the feathery petal of one striped in red and white.

The garden contained terraces, many carefully tended flower borders, lawns, and gravel walks along which people strolled. The house commanded striking views of the country to the north of London, the fields of Hampstead Heath in particular. A number of trees offered pleasant shade, and Amelia suggested they rest here for a moment.

'What a pity we could not organize a game of cricket. That lawn looks to be perfect for it,' she commented as she surveyed the lush green.

'But ladies do never play at such a game,' Miss Moore reproved ever so gently.

'Truly?' Amelia had played with the neighbor children in Macao. 'What a pity. Perhaps we could play battledore and shuttlecock instead.' Then she straightened as she saw a lone individual not far from where they sat.

'Peter,' she said in a quiet voice, 'does that man appear threatening to you? — the one in the dark green coat with fawn pantaloons and black boots.'

'Sorry. No different from any of the others

that I can see. Are you sure you recognize him?' Peter wrinkled his brow in concentrated examination of the possible villain.

'Amelia sees villains beneath every clump of shrubbery and behind every tree,' Lord Dancy snapped in what Amelia thought a nasty way.

The tranquility of the outing destroyed at this remark, Amelia jumped to her feet and gave him an accusing look. 'We are but trying to protect you, my lord. I am so sorry if you feel it is not worth our while.'

She whirled about, commandeering Mary and Chloe to walk with her. 'Come girls, let us examine those marvelous flowers over there.'

'Fat's in the fire now, Geoff,' Peter said as he watched the ladies march away.

'You must admit this is becoming a bit tedious, always looking for the little man who isn't there. Besides, I worry about Amelia. Do you know that she carries a dagger with her at all times? I don't want her hurt.'

Peter gave Geoffrey a narrow look then turned away to follow the girls.

'What a Cheerful Charlie you are today,' Geoffrey said, strolling along after the group with Denzil Warwick at his side. 'Perhaps it would be best if we left. There are clouds on the horizon.' And that was certainly true in more ways than one.

Amelia scorned Geoffrey's assistance when she went to enter his carriage, preferring Hemit's hand. Geoff noted the glances they exchanged and wondered if everyone he knew was in on this conspiracy to protect him.

The carriage went past the Pulteney Hotel on Piccadilly where throngs of people waited to greet the Grand Duchess Catherine. It had been reported that she had inspected the Whitbread Brewery, which had made the Prince Regent furious. All of the *ton* knew the strong Whig sympathies of Samuel Whitbread, not to mention his extreme opposition to the war with Napoleon. That the Grand Duchess should meet with the Prince Regent's most vocal and radical opponent did not promise well for harmonious relations.

'I wonder what will happen when the Tsar arrives later?' Amelia said to Peter, suspecting Miss Moore would not voice an opinion on anything so ungodly as politics.

'Between the Tsar and King Frederick, not to mention General Blücher and the others, I fear London is in for a spate of parades and festive occasions the likes of which we haven't seen for some time. I wouldn't mind it so much if we could afford them.'

Amelia sobered at this truism, wondering how a country could plunge into such debt while allowing its prince such extravagance.

Miss Moore, then Mr Warwick were deposited at their residences, followed by Peter and Mary Blandford at their house.

Peter exchanged a cautioning look with Amelia when he exited the carriage, but she wasn't sure what it was supposed to mean. She sat in stony silence as long as she could, then turned to face his lordship.

'That was to have been a very pleasant outing for us all,' she said in an accusatory tone.

'You are the one who persists in seeing villains everywhere you look. May I remind you,' Lord Dancy said in a perfectly odious manner, 'that no one else heard that threat against my life.'

'Nevertheless, I did,' she declared with quiet fervency. 'And you shall see for yourself — when you least expect it.' Her look was intended to be censorious, then she recalled her mission. 'Do you go to Lady Titheridge's rout this evening?'

'Since she is my aunt, I had best put in an appearance, I expect. She also happens to be a very dear lady, so I do not mind. I suppose you plan to go?' Lord Dancy gave Amelia a mocking grin, as though he knew full well she would dog his footsteps if possible.

'I do,' she replied sedately, ignoring any

implications she may have merely imagined.

The carriage drew up before the Spencer house and Amelia prepared to get out. She sensed Lord Dancy wished to add something to what he had said, so paused for a moment at the open door, looking down into his handsome face. The most peculiar sensations stirred within her when she stared at him like this. It was as though a flock of demented butterflies had taken residence in her stomach. She didn't much like the feeling, although she confessed — only to herself — that she relished the touch of his hands on her waist when he swung her down from the carriage.

'You will like my aunt, I believe. She is a very independent woman, something like you. One never knows what to expect from her next.'

Amelia caught his glance at her reticule where her little dagger discreetly reposed. She couldn't prevent a small grin escaping. 'I suppose any number of women might surprise you, were you to learn more about their habits.'

'Deliver me from such a fate,' his lordship said with a comical shudder.

'Until later, my lord. And . . . do be careful,' she couldn't resist adding. She noted his grimace and scolded herself all the way into the house.

Up in her room she found the white cockade her aunt had bought her along with a lovely tissue silk scarf embroidered in gold thread with fleurs-de-lys. Chen Mei held up a gown of gold gauze over cream satin for Amelia's approval.

'Day not go well,' Chen Mei concluded when she observed Amelia's preoccupied mood.

'He thinks I am but a fool, imagining the threat against him. He appears to have forgotten that man at Astley's. Or is it that he resents my concern?'

'As it is impossible to please men in all things, our only care should be to satisfy our own consciences,' Chen Mei counseled. It had not been necessary to ask who the 'he' was; there was only one man who obsessed Amelia to the exclusion of most else.

'And that is what I must do. My conscience would never give me peace if something happened to his lordship. I owe him a great deal. I should not have liked to be burned in that horrible fire.' She exchanged a look with her companion that met with a nod of total agreement.

'Missee go to party tonight, see him again. Bad man may try then. You be prepared.'

'I have my dagger. What else could I bring with me? That I could put in my reticule, that is.'

Chen Mei crossed the room to the dressing table to pick up a crystal vial of vinaigrette. She held it up to show Amelia, then removed the stopper. A sniff of the contents brought tears to her eyes, and she hastily replaced the covering.

'This velly strong, throw it at man . . . before you throw dagger.' She dropped the vial into Amelia's golden reticule, then added the dagger along with a comb, a handkerchief, and a few other essentials. 'You find?'

'I shall find it, for it has a peculiar shape to it.' Amelia sank down upon her bed, gazing thoughtfully at her companion. 'Little did I dream when I left Macao that I would be embroiled in an effort to prevent the murder of a man I admire. He must not die, Chen Mei. I do hope he remembers to wear his amulet.'

'You take rest for now, be sharp when you leave for party.'

At dinner her aunt inquired about the outing, expressing dismay to learn that it had ended so badly. 'You may wish to consider forgetting this business about Lord Dancy, my love,' she advised. 'It would seem to me that the gentleman does not appreciate your efforts on his behalf.'

Amelia nodded. 'I cannot please him, I know that. However, I must tend my conscience, dear Aunt. Could I ever forgive myself if something terrible happened to his lordship while I merely stood by and did nothing?'

'I suppose you have the right of it, love.' Aunt Ermintrude gave Amelia a doubtful look.

Amelia suspected that her aunt was not entirely convinced, but changed the topic to the events of the day that had occupied her aunt for hours.

'I must thank you for the pretty cockade, dear Aunt, and this shawl is quite the most splendid I have ever seen.'

'Yes, well,' her aunt said in a pleased fluster. 'I want us to look our best this evening. 'Tis rumored that the Prince Regent will attend.'

Suitably impressed, Amelia thanked her aunt once again for her thoughtfulness, then completed her meal while listening to her aunt's chatter.

The ride to the Titherbridge mansion proved the usual frustrating wait while what seemed like every carriage in London attempted to deposit passengers before the doors.

At last Amelia and Mrs Spencer left their carriage to walk up the red carpet stretched before the Titherbridge front door. A throng of people clustered to either side, admiring or simply staring at the guests while they arrived.

Amelia glanced at them, wondering if the Frenchman hid among them, then entered the house with her aunt hoping to discover Lord Dancy before his enemy did.

Lady Titherbridge had managed to snare Lord Dancy into standing by her side to greet the guests. If London was thin of company, it couldn't be noticed here. Gentlemen clustered about the card room, gossiping, arranging for games of cards, calling for wine, and in general enjoying themselves. A few ladies looked vexed, although a good many of them joined in card games as well.

Amelia greeted Lady Titherbridge with a pleasant smile and a proper curtsy before offering her hand to Lord Dancy.

He totally forgot his manners and used her first name while holding her hand far too long. 'Good evening, Amelia.'

'My lord, how pleasant to see you again,' she replied primly. She glanced about her with concern, hoping no one had overheard his slip.

His aunt appeared to have noticed, but since she said nothing, Amelia could not be certain.

'Geoffrey, why do you not escort Miss

Longworth about. I am sure you could find something of interest to show her.' Her ladyship turned back to Mrs Spencer for a few words before the next arrival came to the top of the stairs.

'You need not show me about, sir,' Amelia protested. 'I well understand how you feel about me.' She gave him a polite look that did not conceal the distress in her eyes.

'You cannot possibly know how I feel about you, Amelia. Even *I* am not certain at times,' he concluded in an undertone that Amelia barely heard.

He placed her hand on his arm, then proceeded to stroll about the handsome rooms, pointing out to her any number of elegant objects collected by his aunt during her travels.

'It is all quite dazzling,' Amelia declared while inspecting a series of tiny animals carved from semiprecious stones. She turned from them to study a tall cabinet. Lord Dancy opened the doors for her.

'See here, different woods are used on each of the drawers.' He gestured to several rare woods.

'Most remarkable,' she replied, trying not to notice his warm clasp on her arm when they resumed their walk.

'So here you are,' Peter said in an amused

tone when he joined them. 'Doing the pretty, Geoff? Evening, Amelia. Geoff, your aunt has more clutter in her rooms than even Prinny manages. Wherever does she find them all.'

'She collects them on her travels, Peter. How she gets them all back in one piece mystifies me.'

Amelia listened to the details of his aunt's fascinating life when she suddenly observed a man acting rather oddly. Instead of simply walking straight up to where they stood, he sidled and edged, quite as though he hoped to move close to them undetected. He might have succeeded but for his dress, which was so boringly dull that he stood out like a weed in the midst of a bed of petunias.

Not bothering to disturb Lord Dancy, Amelia slipped one hand into her reticule, closing her fingers about her vinaigrette. With stealth, she removed the crystal vial, took off the stopper, then waited.

The flash of metal proved what she waited for. Before the Frenchman — for that was who she firmly believed the man to be — could cock his gun and take aim, she tossed the contents of her vial in the villain's face. He sputtered, cried out in distress, and waved his gun about in the air.

'Amelia!' Lord Dancy exclaimed, then immediately understanding what was afoot, dove at the villain, knocking him to the floor.

Peter quickly dropped to the fellow's side, pinning his arm while removing the pistol from his hand. The flow of French was such Amelia was glad she was not accomplished in the language.

'Someone fetch a man from Bow Street,' Geoffrey demanded. 'I'll tie this chap up in the meantime.'

In the distance music could be heard, with an unusual hush from the guests.

'His Royal Highness the Prince Regent has arrived.'

'It wanted only that,' Geoffrey moaned as he turned his gaze to where Amelia stood prudently returning her empty vial to her reticule.

14

Everyone froze, Geoffrey tightly holding the Frenchman with both hands. In the next room the murmurs of the pleased guests could be heard as the Prince made his way through the throng of people.

Peter darted a look at Geoffrey, then said, 'I'll go. They most likely won't believe a servant. Who would, with a wild tale like this?' He strode from the room, escaping before the Prince came along the hall that led to the card room.

Amelia took a step in the same direction, thinking to fend off His Royal Highness. Surely there should be someone to warn who could prevent the Regent from straying into this room.

There wasn't time. Before she could accomplish her intent, the Prince had paused in the double doorway, staring in perplexity at the peculiar scene before him. Amelia sank into a curtsy worthy of a royal presence. Then she backed toward the wall, hoping to go unremarked.

'I say, dashed odd behavior, Dancy. What's going on here? We should like an explanation.' The portly first gentleman of England advanced a few steps into the room, one of the lovely cedar-paneled anterooms in Lady Titherbridge's London home.

Geoffrey straightened, attempting to keep a firm hold on his prisoner and yet give due respect to his prince. 'Please stop where you are, Your Royal Highness. This man just attempted to shoot me. I believe he is a French spy.'

The Prince halted in his steps, unsure whether Lord Dancy was being amusing or meant what he said.

A gentleman at the Prince's side murmured something in the royal ear, and the Prince nodded. 'Bow Street on its way, I trust?' His Royal Highness inquired as he turned to quit the room.

'May it please Your Royal Highness, I should like to tie this fellow up before they arrive. He's an elusive one.' Geoffrey looked about as though in search of a sturdy cord or something else that would serve the purpose.

The Prince merely waved his hand as a signal of sorts that he fully concurred, then left the room, murmuring words to the effect that Lady Titherbridge had invited rather uncommon guests this evening. Not one of the men remained behind to help Lord Dancy, all assuming that he had things well under control and needed no assistance. The wretched man wouldn't ask for help, either. Yet Amelia well recalled how the Frenchman had slipped just like an eel from Chen Mei's grasp when at Astley's.

Amelia waited until the Prince and his party ambled along the hall to the card room, then dashed over to snatch a length of drapery cord from next to the window. 'Here, this ought to suffice.' She watched from a prudent distance as Geoffrey tried to wrap the cord around the fellow. It was an awkward business at best.

'Maybe I could tie the knot while you hold him still?' Amelia inquired at last.

'No,' Geoffrey snapped. 'Keep your distance.'

Amelia took an alarmed step backward as the Frenchman suddenly wrenched himself from Geoffrey's hold, then lunged for the gun that Peter had placed on a nearby table.

Geoffrey dove after him, but was too late to prevent what followed. The Frenchman grabbed the gun, then aimed it at Geoffrey. In slightly imperfect English he said, 'I should shoot you now and be done with it.'

Crouching warily, Geoffrey slowly straightened to his full six feet in height. When the other man held a gun, height mattered not in the least. 'What do you wait for?'

Amelia desperately looked to the hallway.

There had been only the three of them in here and Peter had gone. Now there appeared nothing she might do to save the man to whom she owed her life. It seemed that people either hovered about the Prince Regent or clustered about in the main salons. Not a soul ventured along this particular hall.

'Please . . . do not shoot him. What has he done to you that he ought to die by your hand?' she pleaded.

'He was a spy. Had he not been in Spain, in Portugal, in France, many lives would not have been lost,' the man snapped back at her.

'He was so important, then?' Amelia said trying to stall for time, although she had no idea what she might accomplish.

'He drew maps, talked to the people. He is a devil, for he knew when our generals planned to strike next.'

'I do not see why you must shoot him for that,' Amelia said in a reasonable voice. 'You would have done the same thing. In war all is fair, I have heard tell. Put down your gun, and the charge will be less,' she coaxed. 'I feel certain that plotting against a peer of the realm is not as great a crime as actually killing one.'

Geoffrey took a step closer to the man.

'Do you not have a family in France? Someone who will miss you, worry when you do not return?' Amelia pressed. 'For you must see that you will die. In England you simply cannot kill a man and then walk off as though nothing has happened. Why do you not hand me the gun?' She spoke in a soft, almost mesmerizing voice.

'Silence!' the Frenchman shouted. 'You, woman. Come closer.'

With a glance at Geoffrey, Amelia took several hesitant steps toward the madman. At least, he seemed utterly demented.

Suddenly his arm snaked out to clasp her to his side. He sneered at Geoffrey. 'I take your lady with me. She will guarantee my freedom. You,' he said to Amelia, 'you have spoiled all my plans. I will take you along, then maybe I will shoot you when I am done with you.'

His little chuckle chilled Amelia right down her spine all the way to her toes. It occurred to her that this lunatic might actually shoot her, and she trembled. What else he might do to her did not cross her mind as yet.

Somehow — and Amelia never understood quite how — the Frenchman — with his gun close to her ribs managed to whisk their way along the hall to the rear of the house where he propelled Amelia down the stairs ahead of him. '*Rapide*,' he kept murmuring in their mad scramble.

Once they had gained the narrow street that ran by Lady Titherbridge's home, he forced Amelia into a small carriage that waited for him. A spate of French to his small, wiry companion followed, and then the carriage tore out along the street at such a rate that Amelia figured that no one could possibly have followed them.

Huddled against the shabby squabs of the musty carriage, Amelia listened to the two men discuss what they ought to do with her. It seemed that her interference could cost her life this time.

The carriage turned a corner, and Amelia's heart sank. With so few lights any possible pursuer would have had a difficult time to follow them. Now they had altered their direction, there was no way she could be trailed.

★　★　★

Geoffrey paused at the side gate at his aunt's home, then ran to her stables. He ignored the carriages, for there was no time to harness one. Instead he grabbed the reins of a horse that apparently had been out not too long ago and had not yet returned to his stall.

'Lord Dancy,' the coachman cried in some alarm.

'In a hurry, Soames. Explain later.' With that terse remark, Geoffrey and his mount dashed from the stable. He urged the horse along the same street that Amelia had been taken not long before, turning where he thought he had seen them turn.

There was but a small sliver of a moon, not enough for much help, but the lights here and there offered a little benefit. Geoffrey persisted. It was unthinkable to just do nothing when Amelia had saved his hide so many times. First there was Clarissa and her scheme, then came the danger at Astley's, followed by the damage to the curricle. That was not enough, but she had goaded him into the balloon ride that had most likely prevented his being shot. Taunton and his card cheating had been exposed, thanks to her, and now this evening. He would be safer if she disappeared, he suspected. She seemed to attract danger.

She also attracted him, but that was all it could be — attraction. Good grief, fancy being married to a woman like Amelia! It was enough to make a strong man turn pale!

The street before him was empty. Not a carriage to be seen, not even a person moving about, much less a Charlie he might ask. Quite obviously they had turned once again, the darkness covering their direction.

Geoffrey kept going, pausing at each street intersection and alley to stare into the night, searching, hoping to see a clue.

Nothing.

At last he turned his horse toward his aunt's house. If only he'd had something better than a slippery drapery cord to use; the fellow had slithered out of that like melted butter. If only the Prince hadn't arrived at that precise moment, Peter would have been able to help. If only Amelia had not been present, or at least not so close. He suspected that once again she had saved his life at risk of her own. If only he had been able to save her from being dragged along with that lunatic Frenchman.

The thought of just what that man might do to Amelia before shooting her spurred him to action. He tore along the streets back to his aunt's, then up the back stairs, hunting for Peter or a man from Bow Street.

Back in the anteroom he found them both looking puzzled, with the Robin Redbreast sounding annoyed, saying something about a wild-goose chase. Geoffrey plunged into the room, coming to an abrupt halt beside Peter.

'He managed to escape, taking Amelia with him.'

Peter cursed the man in several languages. While none of them was known to the runner from Bow Street, he could guess at the meaning with no effort. He hastily identified himself to Geoffrey as Ben Tobin. 'Do you have any idea at all where they might be, milord?' the runner asked.

'Geoffrey,' his aunt said upon charging into the room, 'I just heard the most astounding thing from the Prince. He said something about a spy being held in here by you, of all people. Poor man. He must have been imagining things.' She stopped, glancing from Geoffrey to Peter to the stranger in the red vest.

Geoffrey shook his head, giving his aunt a grim look. 'Fear not. Chap has been giving me a spot of trouble. Now he has bolted, taking Amelia with him.'

'Dear me,' Lady Titherbridge replied. 'And I had thought India to be a dangerous place. What will you do now?' she demanded. Having traveled about the world much of her adult life, few things daunted her. She was accustomed to taking charge of events that crossed her path and looked to be fully prepared to do the same here.

Geoffrey began to pace back and forth as an aid to thinking. He rubbed his chin absently while his mind frantically searched for a clue he might have missed.

'Nothing. I cannot think of a blessed thing

he said that might give an inkling as to where they intend to go. He said he will shoot her once he has finished with her,' he baldly declared in spite of his aunt's presence.

'Good grief,' the lady said in a fading voice, for she well understood the implications and the effect on a gently reared girl.

'You may as well know,' Geoffrey said in an aside to Peter, 'that she saved my life yet again. Stepped forward to argue with the chap, just as though he didn't have a gun, or wasn't a raving lunatic. Talked him out of shooting me and ended up being taken hostage. He wants a free passage from England with no promise that he will give up Amelia — unharmed or otherwise.'

Lady Titherbridge murmured her excuses, for she had a houseful of guests and the royal prince to entertain. She promised to inform Amelia's aunt in such a manner that the dear lady would not have an attack of the vapors.

Geoffrey realized that he had totally forgotten Mrs Spencer. He thanked his aunt, then returned to the serious problem at hand. He, Peter, and soft-spoken Ben Tobin put their heads together to formulate some sort of plan.

In short order Geoffrey led the two men along the route the abductor's carriage had gone. They peered into shadows, rode along for a way down each street, but it was hopeless. Amelia and the Frenchman had vanished.

★ ★ ★

To the north of London Amelia warily made her way along the steep stairs to what appeared to be a loft above some shop or warehouse, propelled by the Frenchman. His name appeared to be Claude from what she could make of the conversation between the madman and his helper.

'Take care,' she said in English, not wanting him to know she could understand his French, or Portuguese, for that matter, although neither of the men attempted it now.

Inside the door at the top of the stairs she discovered a rather stark room with three wooden chairs, one cot, and a small wooden table that looked to have legs of varying lengths. The Frenchman thrust her onto one of the chairs, after which he tied her in place using stout rope that Geoffrey could have used to advantage.

Amelia pressed her reticule to her lap, finding a small comfort in the knowledge that her little dagger reposed within.

Across the room the two men argued about

311

what to do with her.

'I am tired,' Amelia said at long last, wishing she'd had the foresight to have eaten something before being carried away. 'Permit me to sleep.' She glanced longingly at the cot without a thought to what might evolve.

The men laughed and made crude remarks that prompted Amelia to wish she had kept her mouth shut. So, she didn't pursue the matter of sleep. Eventually she nodded from sheer exhaustion, but it was a fitful drifting in and out.

She woke to find one of the men had disappeared, and the Frenchman sat in another chair contemplating Amelia with a look she preferred to ignore. Dismissing it from her mind was better than dwelling upon possibilities.

When morning arrived, it brought her one roll and a cup of bitter coffee, brought up by the accomplice. Apparently they had decided to keep her alive for the moment. Perhaps, she thought with rising hope, they intended to use her as a means of exiting the country. Then she recalled that Claude had also announced he would shoot her regardless. It did not look to be a good day. She wondered where Geoffrey Dancy was, and thanked the heavens he, at least, was safe.

The day seemed interminable. She had

begged twice to use a necessary, and had been shown to a closet with a chamber pot within and precious little privacy.

It seemed that Claude and his accomplice — named Henri, Amelia deduced from their conversation — could not agree on the next step in their escape. Nor could they agree on whether they ought to go to France and hope to fade into oblivion, or possibly to assist Napoleon to flee Elba, or if perhaps they ought to find some ship sailing to America. Henri had heard that New Orleans offered possibilities for the French.

But all that day they ignored Amelia. She grew hungry, and she was more tired from the strain than she had ever been in her life. But as long as they left her alone, she would not complain. She listened and watched and remained silent.

When darkness fell Henri grudgingly brought Amelia a cup of bitter coffee and another roll, allowing her the freedom to eat by releasing her hands. Apparently they felt that merely tying her to the chair was sufficient to keep her quiet — that and keeping a perpetual watch on her movements. Where could she go in this neighborhood and be safe? For Amelia suspected she was far from Mayfair.

★　★　★

313

'I do not see how you allowed that man to simply disappear with my niece, Lord Dancy,' Mrs Spencer declared. 'I am glad I have discouraged her interest in you. I doubt you would make a fit husband. No doubt you would lose your wife before you left the church!' She shredded a cambric handkerchief as she perched tensely upon her sofa. Her worried gaze sought that of Amelia's devoted companion.

Chen Mei sat upon her ottoman, her almond-shaped eyes staring at Geoffrey with such dislike that he felt chilled. 'I not there when she need me,' the Cantonese woman stated in a bleak voice.

'Believe me, I would rather he had shot me than taken Amelia, Mrs Spencer. With his temper, he might have proved to have terrible aim, and we would both have been spared.' His attempt at a bit of levity fell flat.

'But that poor girl,' Mrs Spencer continued as though Lord Dancy had not spoken. 'She must be utterly terrified.'

Geoffrey recalled the words spoken by the Frenchman and shuddered. 'Terrified' would scarcely cover Amelia's reaction if those men lived up to their threat.

'The wise place virtue in thought,' Chen Mei offered, then proceeded to follow her own maxim.

Ben Tobin was ushered into the Spencer salon by Grimm. The Bow Street runner appeared to have had a good night's sleep, for he looked fresh and ready to do battle. Neatly attired, his red vest spruce and brushed, he greeted Mrs Spencer with the kindest of smiles.

Geoffrey wondered how the man could have slept when Amelia was in the hands of that lunatic. Then he realized this was merely a job for the man. Amelia didn't have reality for him other than a name. Geoffrey had fared badly during the night, finally falling into an exhausted slumber, only to have a nightmare about Amelia. She had screamed as those two men reached for her, and Geoffrey had awakened with a heart full of despair. In a city the size of London what chance did they have of finding one girl cleverly hidden away?

'We have been combing the area where the French émigrés tend to congregate,' Mr Tobin informed them all. 'There are several men who meet your description, but only two of them are recent arrivals to the area. One has lived there for some years. Nevertheless we shall investigate all three.'

'I will go with you,' Geoffrey declared. He hated the inactivity and feeling of helplessness.

Ben Tobin eyed Geoffrey, then nodded. 'You may as well. At least I'll have you under my feet instead of going off on your own.'

Mrs Spencer rose from the sofa, offering her hand to Lord Dancy in farewell. 'I trust you to bring my girl back to me, my lord. I depend on you.'

Rising from her ottoman Chen Mei tottered to the door, declaring as she went, 'I go, too. Tian Li may have need of me.'

Both men gave quick shakes of their heads and began to deny her.

Mrs Spencer put a hand on Lord Dancy's arm. 'Please allow her to go along. She is extremely clever and seems to have an uncanny sense about some things. She may be of help to you. Besides, she will drive me to distraction here with her habits, the least of which are her wails that frighten the maids.'

Geoffrey turned his gaze to the runner. 'Mr Tobin?'

'You never know,' replied the soft-spoken man. 'Let her come.'

So when the search continued, it was with the addition of a Chinese lady dressed in her usual outlandish garb.

But two days passed, with the trio growing more and more frustrated when the leads proved futile. Finally they had one hope remaining. A man who delivered coal

316

reported some French chaps had let the loft above a hat manufactory in Marylebone.

Upon that clue the three based their expectations. Chen Mei withdrew the dagger from her sleeve. Ben Tobin glanced at it, shared a look with Geoffrey, then made his way quietly up the steps, one at a time. At last they all reached the top.

'Allow me,' Geoffrey said grimly. He reached out a hand to push open the door.

Chen Mei shoved him aside and darted into the room, dagger at the ready and aimed for the man she hated, Claude. In moments it was all over. Chen Mei cut the ropes to free her Tian Li.

It took a few moments for Amelia to regain feeling in her limbs. She bent over to rub her ankles, then rose from the chair. She rushed into Geoffrey's arms, taking refuge there, seeming to relish the feel of his body as he wrapped his arms about her in a crushing embrace.

'Are you all right?' were his first words after he searched her face, as though there might be some indication of the ordeal she had endured written there.

'I am now,' she whispered, her throat sounding tight.

Across the room, Ben Tobin efficiently tied up the accomplice while Chen Mei held her dagger to the throat of the Frenchman. She looked determined that he wouldn't be allowed to slip away from her again. Geoffrey wagered that the fellow would have a scar — for as long as he lived — from the pressure of that little dagger.

A second runner joined them and took over the guard on the Frenchman.

'His name is Claude, and he intended to take me with him to Dover. I was to be his insurance.' Amelia turned away from the sight and sound of the Frenchman being led from the loft. He raved and ranted against the English, Dancy, and Amelia in particular.

'Your aunt is anxious to have you home.'

'It has been days, but it seems like years.'

'For all of us. Poor Chen Mei nearly drove Tobin mad with her demands. She will undoubtedly not allow you out of her sight for some time to come.'

'And you?' the whispery voice said hesitantly.

'Not now, Amelia. We shall discuss all else later when you have had a decent sleep and food in whatever order you please.'

Chen Mei had followed the men down the steep stairs to make certain the chap didn't get free again. Geoffrey and Amelia were now alone in the loft.

'I knew that you would save me. You always

have,' Amelia said in a tremulous voice.

Geoffrey felt her melt against him and a rush of tenderness overwhelmed him when her slim arms encircled him. Poor Amelia, now safe and in his arms. When she lifted her face to give him a tentative smile, he did what any gentleman of sensibility would have done. He kissed her gently, then more fiercely as he remembered what he had gone through to find her, how worried he'd been, wondering, hoping she would somehow survive untouched and unscathed.

She leaned her head against his chest, then said in a very contented-sounding way, 'You may take me home now.'

Rather than permit her to attempt the stairs in her weakened condition, Geoffrey scooped her into his arms and carefully carried her to the ground level and out to where the carriage awaited them.

Tobin gave a salute and said something about seeing him later. Geoffrey merely nodded. He had to tend to Amelia.

She nestled in his lap all the way to the Spencer house. Chen Mei kept an eagle eye on the pair across from where she perched. Her eyes missed nothing, not even the rosy glow on cheeks that ought to have been ashen.

Grimm opened the door and gasped, for

once definitely shaken. One of the maids sniffed into her apron, then disappeared from view.

Mrs Spencer hurried from the salon where she had spent most of the days Amelia had been gone, dabbing her handkerchief at her eyes even as she barked out orders to one and all.

Geoffrey carried Amelia up the stairs to her room. Chen Mei had darted past him and now had the bed covers drawn back and awaiting her charge.

'I shall see you when you are fully recovered. I fancy you need sleep as much as I do,' he joked.

Amelia studied him, then turned her head away. 'As you please, sir. And,' she added as Geoffrey turned to leave the bedroom, 'Thank you for saving my life . . . again.'

He paused at the door, meeting her gaze. 'That makes us even, I believe . . . again.'

★ ★ ★

It took two days for Amelia to feel more the thing. She ate a breakfast of tea, toast, and marmalade, then slept around the clock.

On the third day she knew she could not postpone what had to be any longer, and she sent for Lord Dancy.

'My lord,' she said when the polite amenities had been observed. 'I believe you wished to speak with me.' Her heart was so full of hope. Her love for this man had sustained her all through the incredible hours of her capture. But now, looking at that handsome face of his, so closed, so shuttered, she began to fear the worst.

'Dash it all, Amelia, this is exceedingly difficult for me.' He rose and began to pace the floor, looking everywhere but at Amelia. Her heart sank even further.

'Do go on,' she replied evenly, giving no hint of her emotions.

'When I saved you from danger while in Portugal, I was performing a rescue of sorts, and while I did save your life in Portsmouth, it was nothing that any gentleman would not have done given the same circumstances. Since then,' he plunged on after a moment's reflection, 'you have pulled my chestnuts from any number of fires.'

Amelia frowned, unsure of what he meant by this expression.

'You have extricated me from several awkward and dangerous situations,' he explained when he observed her confusion. 'That business with Clarissa was admittedly difficult. The curricle race — now that I might have managed on my own, you know.

As to Astley's, the chap ran away and later missed me at the balloon ascension thanks to your coercing me into taking that sail. Not that I didn't enjoy it once I recovered from the height,' he admitted. 'The affair with Taunton and the cheating, now, well, I might have been able to expose him myself, had you not been so precipitate. But this latest, when you were placed in such terrible danger — Amelia, this must cease.'

'I suspected you would say as much, my lord,' Amelia replied formally.

'Then you agree? We are settled once and for all. You will no longer dog my footsteps and make my life a terror for fear that some disaster will befall me, and you as well?' He paused, staring down at her from his green eyes with such anticipation that Amelia felt her heart grow cold.

'Is that how you view it? I cause apprehension when you see me?' Amelia repressed a sigh, knowing it might well lead to the tears that were rapidly gathering. She did not want his final sight of her to be one of a watering pot.

'I propose that henceforth we shall be as polite strangers,' he suggested in a coaxing voice that nearly finished breaking Amelia's shattered heart.

'By all means, sir.' She rose from the sofa,

praying that her trembling knees would not betray her. Extending her hand in a graceful gesture, she concluded, 'I trust you will excuse me, I am still a trifle tired. Perhaps some country air will improve my spirits. Goodbye, Lord Dancy,' Amelia said, firmly controlling those still-threatening tears. 'And do take care,' she could not resist adding for one last time.

Amelia swept from the room, chin high, legs steady. She marched to the bottom of the stairs that led to the second floor and paused to see him slowly make his way down to the entrance hall and out the front door.

He was gone from her life, forever. He wouldn't change his mind. She had driven him to distraction.

Tearing up the stairs and around the corner, she burst into her room to throw herself on her bed. A good bout of weeping would heal the wounds, Chen Mei had said when Amelia had hurt herself as a child. Amelia felt as though no amount of tears could heal this wound to her heart.

15

'You were quite right, Chen Mei. The man is a fool. He does not wish my help, even though I love him dearly and want only the best for him.' Amelia leaned against the headboard, scrunching pillows behind her so she might be more comfortable. Her bout of weeping had been brief. Indignation had taken its place.

'Remember,' her companion said, 'it is the beautiful bird that gets caged.'

'You mean there are compensations. Perhaps. Although I fail to see what the compensations might be in this case. You think that I might find someone better?' Amelia considered that idea for several moments, and finally nodded. Her innate honesty compelled her to agree. 'I imagine there is a man who might suit me more admirably.' Her tone implied that it would be next to impossible.

'The man who fail to appreciate your devotion is not worthy of you,' Chen Mei declared with narrowed eyes.

Amelia caught sight of her companion fingering her dagger and hastily said, 'You will not do anything foolish, Chen Mei. I have no wish to learn that Lord Dancy has expired of a dagger wound. Besides, I have decided you are correct, and I shall turn my attention elsewhere.'

'Good.' The Cantonese woman gave a decisive nod, tucking the dagger back up inside her sleeve.

'Remember I have served his lordship as was proper, yet it did not nurture his regard. It is for the best that I forget him. I shall agree that I owe him nothing more.'

A soft scraping on the door was followed by Aunt Ermintrude peeking around the corner. 'My dear little love, what has been going on here? You look very much as though you have indulged in a bout of tears.' She stood near the door, gazing at Amelia with some caution.

'Never fear, I shan't turn into a watering pot.'

'Good. I wish you to join me in a theater expedition this evening. There will be any number of important people there, and the program is touted as being exceptionally brilliant.' She approached the bed with a hesitant smile, as though uncertain what reaction Amelia might have to her suggestion.

'Aunt . . . ' Amelia protested, not feeling much like going out where she could possibly see Lord Dancy. Even if she intended to turn her interest elsewhere, she needed a bit of time first.

'No silliness,' her aunt scolded, wagging a finger at Amelia. 'I suspect that you have decided that you and Lord Dancy are not destined to make a pair. In that event you ought to be casting about to see upon whom you will decide. For you must, you know.' Her aunt plumped herself on the edge of the bed, taking one of Amelia's slim hands in her own soft, pudgy one. 'Your papa wishes you to marry well, and to please both of you it is necessary to find a man who has both a proper background and will cherish you, for I know that is what you wish.'

'True. I have been rather obsessed by Lord Dancy, have I not? Although not as fatally as Lady Caroline Lamb with Byron, I should hope.' Amelia grimaced at the very idea.

'Gracious, no. Now, I suggest we make an expedition to the milliner's shop. Buying a lovely new bonnet is just the thing to cheer a girl.'

Determined not to fall prey to the green melancholy, Amelia slid from her bed and permitted Chen Mei to help her dress for the outing. Before leaving her room, Amelia paused to issue a caution. 'I shall be fine, and there will be no thought of retribution against

Lord Dancy. Is that clear?'

Chen Mei agreed, although most reluctantly.

Joining her aunt in the carriage, Amelia considered the devotion of her companion and hoped that she obeyed Amelia. While angry and hurt, Amelia still cared too much for the dratted man to permit him to be injured or worse.

Later, after a successful trip to the milliner's, Amelia beamed a smile at her aunt and confessed, 'You were right. I am tremendously cheered.' And, she added to herself, she had not observed Lord Dancy out and about, although the Spencer carriage hadn't gone anywhere near Bond Street or St. James's, where the clubs were located.

It was with a lighter heart that Amelia dressed for the theater that evening. She wore a pretty gown of celestial blue satin that had an overdress of silvery spider gauze. In her blonde curls Chen Mei wove an arrangement of silver leaves and blue silk flowers. While drawing on her long gloves, Amelia glanced at the looking glass, well pleased with what she saw reflected.

The streets around the Drury Lane Theater were clogged with elegant carriages and people pressing to enter the premises. When at last she and her aunt were able to go inside, she found the noise considerable.

Amelia searched the lobby for a familiar face and was relieved when she saw Peter and Mary Blandford with Chloe Moore and Denzil Warwick. She suspected that Peter revealed more than a passing interest in Miss Moore, and if so, fine. Amelia liked Peter. But that was all. Mary appeared attracted to the somewhat stuffy Mr Warwick, but then, Mary was a trifle on the reserved side herself.

Of Lord Dancy there was no sign. Following a few moments to say hello, the parties went their separate ways. Their boxes were not close, and Amelia did not expect to see them during the intervals. Besides, Mary looked so uncomfortable, as though she wondered about Lord Dancy and feared to inquire.

During the first act of the tragedy Amelia took the chance to study the audience. She had not wished to when they first came in, for if Lord Dancy was there, she was not certain she wanted to know about it. Now she did.

It was as though her eyes were drawn only to him, for she discovered where he sat on the far side of the theater almost immediately. He looked well, she noted with relief. Then she observed that a woman shared the box with him when he leaned over to whisper something into her ear.

Even from this distance she appeared beautiful. Not in the sprig of youth, nevertheless she glowed with a radiance that a woman has when showered with the attentions of a handsome gentleman. Diamonds glittered about her throat above the black gown that dipped low over an ample bosom. She appeared an expert at flirtation, using her fan with skill.

Stupid man, Amelia said to herself. Resolution firmed within her heart. Henceforth he would cease to exist. Amelia would search elsewhere — far away elsewhere.

Calm in her determination, Amelia faced the stage where the drama unfolded. She paid little attention to the acting or anything else for that matter. Plans were formulated in her mind only to be discarded immediately. At last, about the time of the final curtain and just before the farce, she decided.

'I should like to travel in England, dear Aunt,' Amelia announced after comments on the drama had trailed off and there was relative silence in the box.

'I suppose you saw Dancy and his lady friend over there and now wish to do something foolish,' Aunt Ermintrude said in dismay.

'Not really,' Amelia replied judiciously. 'But what about my uncle? Could I not visit him? To tell you the truth I have not been that drawn to any of the young beaus I have met in London. Perhaps I might find a country gentleman more to my liking? I think the prospect of a husband who might gamble away my fortune rather distressing. And most all the London bucks gamble.'

'On curricle races and cricket matches and the like,' her aunt said with a nod. 'I daresay what you point out has merit. Not that country gentlemen do not indulge in gaming. Horse racing and other temptations exist there, too, you understand. I fear I shall miss you dreadfully when you depart. You truly feel that you must?'

Ignoring the hopeful look on her dearest aunt's face, it took but a glance in the direction of Lord Dancy's box to firm Amelia's resolve.

'I shall leave once you write my uncle to inform him I should like to make an acquaintanceship.'

'Your mama's brother is the Viscount Quainton. Lord Quainton is somewhat of a recluse, preferring plants to people.'

'Intelligent man,' Amelia said with a final glance at Lord Dancy. 'You *will* write to him?'

Her distress obvious, Aunt Ermintrude nodded most reluctantly. 'If I must. He took in those servants, most likely he will take you in as well.'

During the week it took for an express to reach her uncle and his answer to reach Mrs Spencer, Amelia packed her belongings, shopped for a very few things, and endured a call to Mary and Peter Blandford.

When Peter left the room to fetch his map of the countryside so Amelia might have a better notion as to where her uncle resided, Mary moved closer to her guest.

'Amelia, you are not leaving because of that dreadful woman Lord Dancy was with at the theater, are you?' Mary reached out a comforting hand to pat Amelia's arm. 'Perhaps it is for the best, for I suspect he did not appreciate your concern for him.'

'Chen Mei said the same thing. No, I merely long to see a bit of the countryside and visit my uncle. However, you must promise me that you will not reveal my whereabouts to anyone, particularly Lord Dancy.'

'What's this?' Peter asked as he returned. 'Dancy giving you a spot of trouble?'

'No more than usual. I want you both to promise me that you will not tell anyone where I go,' Amelia repeated for Peter's benefit.

'She means Lord Dancy in particular,' Mary added.

Both promised to do as Amelia requested, although Peter did not look happy about it.

'Dash it all, Amelia, you and Dancy go well together. He didn't mean anything serious by attending the theater with Mrs Hawtaine.'

Amelia bestowed a level look on her friend. With a half smile she said, 'It matters not in the least. I decided I would look elsewhere for a husband. Since Lord Dancy has freed me of the obligation I owed to him, I may search the country.'

She studied the map Peter remembered to offer her. The estate was located in Wiltshire. 'It is not far from Salisbury, so I shall have delightful shopping and who knows what else? Although I suppose the assembly rooms are not open in the summer.' She parted from her friends a bit teary-eyed, but resolved.

★ ★ ★

When the viscount's reply arrived that he would accept a visit from his niece, Amelia packed the last of her belongings, prepared to set out at once.

'For,' she explained, 'I wish to travel in comfort and it will take days to get there in safety.'

In total agreement, Aunt Ermintrude gave a final dinner party for her dear girl, including not only Peter and Mary Blandford, Chloe Moore and Denzil Warwick, but a number of other interesting people Amelia had met while in London. Lord Dancy was not present.

The trip was most pleasant, although the dust from the roads was dreadful.

When they arrived at the front gates to her uncle's home, Amelia was impressed. The iron gates swung open and her post chaise brought her to the front door of the house. A man she presumed to be the butler hurried across the terrace and down the steps to open the door and escort her into the house. Behind her Chen Mei gave orders as to the disposal of Amelia's belongings.

In the long central hall Amelia was turned over to a housekeeper who took her up to a lovely bedroom decorated in shades of lavender. Once alone, Amelia hurried to the window to see that she overlooked a wandering stream where three swans leisurely paddled along.

'Oh,' she exclaimed to Chen Mei when her companion tottered into the room, carrying a collection of parcels, 'this is a splendid house and has a marvelous view. How odd that my uncle did not come to greet me. Perhaps I had best search him out.'

With her companion's blessing, Amelia set off to find her elusive relative.

The butler directed her to the gardens off

to the west of the house. 'His lordship is overseeing the trimming of the topiary, miss. You can't miss him.'

Intrigued by the idea of a topiary garden, Amelia wrapped her shawl about her, then left the house in search of the special garden.

It didn't take long to discover that the entire grounds were planted with magnificent specimens of various shrubs that lent themselves especially to topiary. She encountered a hornbeam hedge with rectangular holes cut at intervals to form an arcade of green. Yet trees clipped in amazing shapes were everywhere she looked. Topiary garden? Why, the entire estate was a topiary garden. How was she to locate her uncle?

The swans, followed by an assortment of ducks, gracefully paddled up to greet her near the edge of the stream. The grass had been trimmed right up to the water's edge for a neatly elegant walk.

Amelia marveled at the exquisite topiary animals that loomed before her as she rounded the corner of the hornbeam hedge.

'Here now, this is to be a giraffe, not a tree,' scolded a deep bass voice.

Peering around a pyramid, Amelia encountered a tall gentleman with a mop of unruly white hair. He wore a shaggy corduroy frock coat that certainly had seen its best days long ago. But there was an air about him that led her to suspect that he was indeed her uncle. When he turned, she found celestial blue eyes trained on her with disconcerting directness.

'Uncle!' Amelia cried with pleasure. He was much as she remembered her mother — the blue eyes and the sameness of expression. She stepped forward to offer her hand.

'Ah, you are like your mother. Welcome,' he said. He shook her hand with an absent-minded bow of sorts, then returned to scolding his gardener.

Taken aback at his abruptness, Amelia decided to study what she could see of this part of the garden. To her left grew a magnificent peacock, or what ultimately would be a peacock, for the tail had not quite reached its ultimate length. There was a frame over which it was to spread.

What appeared to be an extremely fat pig marched with a dog of noble proportions. Some distance away she observed a series of boxwood cones and pyramids and cubes in the more basic shapes seen in a topiary garden. She gave the plant on which her uncle and the gardener worked a critical inspection. A giraffe — yes, she could see the potential, but it had some ways to grow first.

Turning around she found a chair formed

of greenery, with a fountain and a sundial not far away. 'Oh my,' she declared with amusement.

'You like my garden?' her uncle inquired.

'Indeed,' Amelia replied, a little stunned with the magnitude of the place.

'Come along and tell me why you decided to visit in the country when London society is at the peak of its glory. Some man, I'll be bound.' He motioned her in the direction of a pretty little summer house built to look like a tiny cottage ornée with a thatched roof and elaborate decoration.

'Not in the least,' she declared stoutly and too quickly, confirming his views, she feared.

A footman materialized with a large tray holding tea, sandwiches, pastries, and bowls of fresh berries with a pitcher of thick cream. Amelia realized with a start that she was utterly starved.

'Gardening is hungry work, I find. But it keeps a man fit. How's your Aunt Spencer? Haven't seen her in an age. And your father, child? How did you leave him?'

'Aunt Spencer is fine. When I last saw him, my father looked tired, but he has been doing quite well, I believe. There is some problem with the opium trade he fears will lead to serious trouble.'

'And so he sends you to England to find a

suitable husband. Quite right, too.' Lord Quainton stared at her a moment from beneath his white beetle-brows, then smiled.

For a time they both concentrated on the exquisite repast, Amelia appreciating the scents and sights when she raised her eyes from her plate to look out from the little cottage.

'Your trip to England . . . uneventful?' he inquired when he had reached his bowl of berries.

'Not in the least,' Amelia replied with animation. She proceeded to tell him the tale of landing in Portugal, then the fire in Portsmouth.

'Speak Portuguese, I suppose, after living in Macao all this time. French?'

'And Cantonese a little as well,' she added with a nod.

'Your aunt said you had a Chinese woman with you. A companion?'

Amelia agreed, then explained how she had been raised by Chen Mei following her mother's untimely demise.

'Well,' he said as he concluded his small meal, 'I must return to my giraffe. Heaven knows what that villain of a gardener will make of it if I am gone too long. Make yourself comfortable. I trust you are here for the peace and quiet, for there won't be any parties or balls or the like. I live simply. I like it that way.'

He bowed, then strode off in the direction of the topiary giraffe in the making, bellowing for his hapless gardener whose name it seemed was Puddy. Her uncle's tailless coat flapped in the breeze, and his hair looked even wilder after he had run his fingers through it another time.

Amused, Amelia returned her teacup to the saucer, then leaned back on her chair. She had done it. Knowing how she might feel compelled to interfere in Lord Dancy's life, she had made the necessary break, left London, and now had to work out a future of sorts in the depths of Wiltshire.

Leaving the pleasant shade of the little summer house, she ambled in the direction of the stream. Here she reclined against a stately elm to watch the ducks and swans feast on whatever it was they ate.

After the hustle and excitement of London, could she cope with the dullness of a country life? Of course, she declared firmly. None of these die-away airs for her. She would explore the gardens, make the most of seeing what she could of the surrounding countryside, and enjoy herself.

When she reported to Chen Mei, it was with a cheerful visage and good account of her moderately eccentric uncle.

'One generation plants trees, another sits in their shade,' Chen Mei said in Cantonese in an effort to find a maxim to fit the situation.

'Well, I scarce believe one sits in the shade of that giraffe, but it is charming nonetheless.' Amelia submitted to having her gown changed for dinner and wondered all the while what her erstwhile lord was doing in London.

★ ★ ★

Geoffrey stared out of the window of his home at nothing in particular. He was free. He had not seen Amelia Longworth since that evening in the theater when he had attended with the elegant Mrs Hawtaine.

'Chattel, indeed,' he muttered.

'You wished for something, milord?' Evenson inquired from the doorway. 'Something to eat, perhaps?'

'I am expecting Mr Blandford. Show him up directly when he comes.' Evenson had been nattering after Geoff to eat for days, but nothing had appealed in the least.

'Of course, milord.' The butler left the room on silent feet, allowing Geoffrey to return to his musings at the window. At last he spoke aloud.

'She's an elegant armful, but I'll wager she's dashed expensive,' he said to a passing chaffinch.

'Who is? The Hawtaine?' Peter entered the room, crossed to stand by Geoffrey, and looked out at the scene below. 'Something in particular you wanted, or was it merely my company you seek?' he said when he'd decided that there was nothing of interest to view.

'Spot on,' Geoffrey replied, shaking himself from his lethargy. He ought to be celebrating, and by Jove that was what he'd do. 'Have dinner with me at White's. A bit of cards and then the opera?'

'Well, I am to take Chloe and her mother to the theater this evening. Tell you what, make it tomorrow. I'd like to go out to Lord's and watch that game. I have placed a few bets on it.'

'Just the thing,' Geoffrey replied. He settled his friend in a chair, joining him in a glass of canary while they chatted about casual concerns.

It seemed to Geoffrey that Peter was seeing more than a little of Chloe Moore. She was a pretty girl, but her eyes lacked a certain defiant sparkle, and she seemed far too docile for Geoff's tastes.

'You knew Amelia had gone,' Peter inserted into the conversation. 'She is visiting a

340

relative in the country.'

'I hadn't seen her for a time and wondered if she had returned to Macao or whatever.'

'And you have Mrs Hawtaine,' Peter observed.

'You don't have to make her sound as though she were a serious disease,' Geoffrey objected. Lila Hawtaine might appear a trifle haughty with her superior attitude, but underneath Geoffrey suspected she was warm and inviting. Certainly her eyes met his with a clear invitation in them. He had not decided whether to accept that invitation as yet.

The men set a time to meet on the morrow, then Peter strolled off to prepare for the evening while Geoffrey decided he would attend that rout for which he'd received an invitation. He'd accepted, then later repented. Now, he would go after all.

He knew it was a mistake the moment he crossed into the drawing room of the Haversly household. The rout was less well attended than in the past, no doubt because of the exodus to Paris. The young women who remained fluttered lashes until Geoffrey wondered that the candles stayed lit. They giggled and flirted, behaving in general precisely like what they were — husband-seeking girls. *Insipid, the lot of them*.

He'd have none of it. At least Amelia

hadn't indicated she had wanted to marry him. All she had ever said was that it was her duty to care for him. There was a difference, was there not? He rather thought so.

He left early, drove to White's where he gambled until far too late, but winning an enormous sum.

'Lucky in cards, unlucky in love, old boy,' said one of the men, thinking himself a great wit.

For some reason the remark hit Geoffrey as unpleasant, and he abruptly bid the gentlemen good night, hoping he'd feel more the thing tomorrow. He left the room, recalling the night that Amelia and Chen Mei had dared to enter the club. She had been helping him, exposing that cheat Taunton. But what a chance she'd taken. None of those simpering misses he had met at the rout this evening would dare such action, not even to help the man they loved.

Loved? Where had that word come from? Amelia didn't love him, although she should, given the number of times she had rescued him from one thing or another. Perhaps that was why she left? She became tired of rescuing him. Her face had turned pale when he suggested they become as strangers. Had he really meant it? He supposed he had at the time.

The next day he met Peter and they drove to Lord's cricket ground. They left the carriage beside one of the buildings in the care of Hemit, then sauntered over to join several acquaintances. The betting was heavy on the team Peter favored. Geoffrey had great hopes for his team, the underdog.

The day was hot, ideal for the batsmen. The wicket looked to have a bit of the devil in it, and the bowling was outstanding. It was the second day of this game; the innings had been running around 200 runs each with the teams very close in their scores. Luncheon was served at two, and they dawdled afterward, chatting and walking about to confer on one thing or another. The play resumed shortly after that and continued until the stumps were drawn at six-thirty with his team declared the winner.

Geoffrey found himself the recipient of a sizable amount of cash. His team had won. Amelia had not appeared to spirit him away from the grounds, nor had Chen Mei turned up with her dagger to ensure that his bowlers did well.

Peter clapped Geoff on the back, then good-naturedly walked with him to the carriage. They drove home in good spirits, but Geoffrey found himself wishing he could see Amelia's face when he told her the sum he'd won without her interference.

They drew up before Blandford's house. Before Peter left the curricle, Geoffrey said as casually as he might, 'You told me that Amelia has gone to visit her cousin, I believe. When is she due back?'

'I don't recall saying it was her cousin, old man. And I have no idea when or even if she will return to London. She said something about finding a good husband in the country.' Peter grinned, then walked smartly up to his door.

'Oh,' Geoffrey said, reflecting that his good friend was less than forthcoming with any information.

Two days later Geoffrey engaged with another friend to do a curricle race from London to Brighton. The hour arrived and the race began with no celestial blue-eyed blonde to prevent it, nor a check for hugger-mugger of any sort.

He won the race. He tooled around Brighton acknowledging the acclaim of friends for the brilliant bit of driving. All the while he drove he found himself searching for that unlikely pair of women, the dainty blonde with her outlandish Chinese companion. They were not to be seen.

He endured a round of parties, more simpering misses — Lord, would they ever cease that drooping eyelash trick to display demure demeanor? — and at last decided he had best return to London. Brighton might be gay to some; to him it appeared sadly wanting.

It proved to be no better in Town. Dinner seemed uninteresting; he had no appetite at all. Without Amelia around to liven up his life, it scarcely seemed worthwhile to get out of bed. Life had become as dull as a dead dog.

But . . . what could he do about it?

16

'What do you mean, you will not tell me where she is?' Geoffrey demanded of his good friend Blandford.

'Well,' Peter said, shifting uneasily in his chair. 'Dashed if I can think of why she insisted we keep mum about where she went, but she did.' He looked across the morning room at White's as though wishing he were somewhere else — anywhere.

'You mean she really did not wish me to know where she went?' Geoffrey was stunned. He had young women flirting with him wherever he went, billet-doux by the score landing in his pile of mail. Never had he been told a woman not only did not care to see him, but refused to let him know where she had gone. And this wasn't any woman — it was Amelia!

'But she is mine, and you bloody well know it!' he raged at his friend.

Peter merely shrugged, concealing a smile beneath a hastily raised hand. 'You should have told her that.' He thought a moment, then added, 'No need to ask Mary, because she ain't going to tell you either.'

Geoffrey's mouth firmed, and he rose from the comfort of his leather armchair to pace back and forth across the fortunately empty room.

'I take it you went to see her aunt?' Peter studied a pattern in the rug with great intensity, looking quite as though he was trying not to laugh.

'She gave me some cock-and-bull story about Amelia wishing to visit a few of her relatives. Mrs Spencer claimed she could not remember which one Amelia went to see first. A likely story!' Geoffrey kicked at a chair that happened to be in his path. He shoved his hands into his pockets, contemplating the view beyond the bow window with unseeing eyes.

'Guess you had better forget the girl. She always caused you a devilish amount of trouble anyway. Can't imagine why you wish to find her,' Peter said with a perfectly straight face.

'Because . . . ' And here Geoffrey paused in his striding about the room to stare at Peter for several moments. 'Because life without her is deadly dull. Can't think why, but I miss her infernal interference in my life. And she did save my hide a few times, you know,' Geoff reminded his friend.

'That she did, at risk to her own, I might

add. Lord, do you remember her scheme to unmask Clarissa Filbert? Never laughed so hard in my life as when we saw their faces. Well and truly flummoxed. And I thought that Sands would have compromised Amelia. However, that companion of hers had him to rights quick enough with her little dagger. And then there was the matter of your curricle. Have to admit she sensed trouble there.'

'Yes,' Geoffrey said, 'I'll allow as how she does seem to have a premonition of trouble. Perhaps it's because she brings it on?' He grimaced at the memory of the damage to his curricle and how he might have been seriously injured but for Amelia and her blessed interference.

'Well, she sensed it sure enough at Astley's. You'd have been put to bed with a shovel long ago had she not interfered then. And that balloon ride sure enough saved your hide.' Peter steepled his fingers beneath his chin while he contemplated his friend.

'What about Taunton? He was no threat to my life.' Geoffrey plopped down on a chair facing Peter to challenge him.

'Aye, but what if you had issued a challenge to the man without knowing for certain those cards were marked? They were devilishly hard to spot. Taunton is known to be a deadly shot. And that Frenchman, well, you proved about even there, rescuing her from that room up in Marylebone,' Peter concluded.

'When I think of the disgrace she could have brought on us all if she had been recognized at White's, I have a case of the shudders.'

'So I repeat, why bother to find her?' Peter rose from his chair and sauntered to the door. 'It appears you are foxed at any rate, for no one will tell you a thing.'

Once alone in the room, Geoffrey sank into deep thought. Peter was right. For some peculiar reason no one thought he had a right to find Amelia. Why, he'd need a sleuth-dog to locate her at this rate.

At which thought he sat up straight. His mind working at a feverish pace, he charged from his chair, dashed past the startled porter and out of the door to hail a hackney.

'Bow Street,' he snapped to the driver before they set off.

At the famous Bow Street office Geoffrey encountered Nathaniel Conaut, who proved sympathetic but scarcely as helpful as Geoffrey might have wished.

'Sorry, old chap. Ben Tobin is on a case at the moment. Missing heiress. Family thinks she has eloped with a ne'er-do-well half-pay officer. Younger son of a baronet. Without prospects, but handsome as the devil. Has a way with the ladies. Also has a record of eloping, then being paid off to forget the entire thing. Family wants him bought off and shipped out of the country.'

'How soon will Tobin be available? He has some knowledge that ought to prove helpful in my search for this missing person.'

'An heiress? There seems to be a rash of them at the moment.' Sir Nathaniel squinted in speculation, listening politely to the man opposite him.

'I suppose she's an heiress. Never gave it much thought. I need her for other reasons,' Geoffrey admitted.

Sir Nathaniel nodded, rubbing his chin while he contemplated this problem. 'Well, best wait. I will send Tobin over to see you when he returns.'

Geoffrey left the Bow Street office feeling frustrated. To one side sat Covent Garden Theater, looking odd in the harsh light of day when he was accustomed to seeing it at night. Around the corner stood the Drury Lane Theater, resplendent in its rebuilt glory following the fire that had destroyed it a few years back.

All Geoffrey could think about was Amelia, and that he couldn't find her. Only when the realization that he was in an unsavory part of town hit him after he was jostled by a rough-looking fellow, did Geoffrey come to his senses and hail a hackney.

'I've been a fool,' he admitted to the interior of the hackney. 'But I shall find her. I believe I love that interfering minx.' With that momentous admission he sat back, somewhat dazed, to contemplate life with Amelia.

★ ★ ★

Ben Tobin did not present himself at Geoffrey's door until another week and a half had passed — a frustrating time during which Geoff tried every means he could think of to uncover Amelia's whereabouts. Nothing he could dream up sufficed to convince Mary or Peter to part with what they knew. He quickly gave up on the vague Mrs Spencer. She would merely smile and wave her hand in the air as though to swat him away.

Baffled, confounded, perplexed, Geoffrey was prepared to do violence when Ben Tobin entered the library at Dancy House.

'Tobin! The very man I wish to see.' Geoffrey suspected he pumped the man's hand a bit too enthusiastically, but dash it all, he was a sight for sore eyes.

It didn't take long to explain what was needed. Ben Tobin sat on the chair facing

Geoffrey, his face a mask, his eyes alive with curiosity. For a Runner, he was a strange one, his soft-spoken and polite manner at odds with what Geoff knew about the force of detectives.

'Well, I am more at home tracking down a wanted criminal or a runaway, sir,' he said when the assignment had been outlined. 'I confess I don't mind a change, however. Since I've met the young lady, I'll need but a few particulars before I begin pursuit.'

He proceeded to ask a great number of questions, causing Geoff to believe Tobin was far too conservative in his use of the word 'few.' Geoffrey handed him a small leather pouch containing a sum of money to aid in loosening the tongues of reluctant witnesses. He'd found that in most cases money proved helpful — except for people like Mary and Peter who were above such things.

Once the Runner left the house, Geoff felt at loose ends. He had run into so many stone walls in his hunt it was a relief to turn over the search to another. Yet he felt lost — useless.

He stood staring at the empty hearth while recalling the conclusion of that infamous balloon ride. She had been so sweet in his arms, and her lips had responded so deliciously to his touch. Why had he let her go . . . only to tell her that if she did something like that again, he would beat her? Guaranteed to charm the lady for sure, he berated himself. He vowed to make it up to her . . . his Celestial Delight.

Someday he would take her on a balloon trip. She had wanted so badly to go up in one that fateful day. And she had tears of worry in her lovely blue eyes when she faced him in the middle of that field.

Oh, he had been the veriest clunch, a dolt not to see where his heart was leading him. And he had the stupidity to tell her he believed they ought to be as strangers! Small wonder she had issued orders to one and all to keep her direction a secret.

The following days were the most difficult Geoffrey had ever endured. Even the forays into enemy territory to gather information for Wellington had been a snap compared to this. He contemplated the scar on his leg, relieved it had healed so well, yet knowing that if he didn't succeed in his search for Amelia, there would be a scar on his heart that would never heal. He fingered the precious silver amulet that always hung about his neck, wishing he could speak to the one who had given it to him.

When Ben Tobin again presented himself at Dancy House, Geoffrey was more than glad to see him. Friends had complained to Geoff that he had become a sorry fellow, downright blue-deviled. Most likely they were being generous in their remarks.

'So, what did you find,' Geoffrey demanded before the Runner could even be seated.

'She is out in Wiltshire not too far from Salisbury. I found out her direction from the post boy who went with her on the first stage of the trip. After that it was relatively simple to go from stage to stage. The post boys were willing to talk for a sum.'

'Clever. I ought to have considered that. She did not travel in her aunt's carriage, nor did her uncle send one for her?' His frown might have daunted a lesser man. The Runner ignored it, well accustomed to reactions from worried family.

'As you say, milord,' Tobin replied. 'His lordship has a right fancy place, although he's a bit of a recluse. Don't entertain none. Don't go about in local society, either.'

'His lordship?' Geoff had latched onto one word that struck him as interesting.

'Viscount Quainton be his title. One of the Kenyon family, I gather.'

'You say he is a recluse? Is he mad?' Alarm for Amelia's safety in the house of a demented man clutched his heart.

'Not unless you think making all sorts of

topiary figures mad. Place is a forest of crazy shapes. Animals, birds, cones, you name it. I could see some of it from the gates, the rest I learned from a Quainton groom while at the Star and Garter down the road a piece. Seems Quainton is a nice enough chap if you ignore his mania for trimming hedges and clipping trees.'

'And Amelia is there. Tell you what, I suspect you had best come with me when I travel to Salisbury. I have a hunch you may come in as very useful.'

A gleam lit Geoffrey's eyes that promised a prime bit of mischief, to Tobin's way of thinking. Having a liking for the young gentleman, he nodded his agreement, then found himself faced with a determined man.

'We shall eat first, then take off. You can leave immediately?'

Accustomed to hasty trips, the Runner agreed. Since Geoffrey had been packed for days, it needed but to inform his coachman to have the traveling coach made ready and notify Hemit they must depart.

Within an hour the men were on the road out of London. They left by way of the Bath Road, then at Marlborough turned to head southwest toward Salisbury. The closer they came to his objective, the more anxious and nervous Geoffrey became.

To Tobin the man looked nothing so much like a bridegroom waiting to say his vows and as nervous as a cat too close to a rocking chair.

Once they achieved Salisbury, Geoffrey selected a neat inn on New Canal off Catherine Street in the heart of town. Across from the Market Square, he figured that he might even spot Amelia strolling along the street. He had not failed to note the presence of a circulating library close by on Catherine Street. Amelia liked to read.

The following day, having had no sight of Amelia, Geoffrey decided he would travel out to see Lord Quainton. Tobin would go with him, in hopes the sleuth could pick up some useful information while Geoffrey went inside. That is, if the man would see him, and Geoff had doubts on that score from what Tobin had said.

After a pause before the impressive iron gates to give his identity and desire to see his lordship, Geoffrey was allowed to enter.

'I see what you mean about the topiary — looks like some sort of green menagerie,' Geoff commented as they passed a boxwood turtle.

At the front door Geoffrey found himself escorted inside with a pleasant greeting, then down a long hall that resembled something one might see in a cloister, with elegant windows along one side. Statuary, treasures, and paintings were placed along the other wall and between windows. Definitely a man with taste and the means to indulge it.

'His lordship will be with you shortly. Since it looks to rain, he elected to work at his records this afternoon,' the butler said by way of explanation. Given what Tobin had said about the viscount, it seemed a day indoors was rare enough to cause comment.

Geoffrey chose to stand by the window rather than sit. He stared out at the lovely scythed lawns and the various fantastic shapes in view. A gentle stream flowed past with a few swans and a great number of ducks paddling about. Did Amelia stroll along that grassy bank to watch their antics? Was she even now a floor away from him in her room? He drew an impatient breath, turning when the door opened.

The man who entered didn't surprise Geoffrey very much, given the background from Tobin. White hair in wild disorder and a corduroy frock coat with bulging pockets fit the image Tobin had given Geoffrey. A no-nonsense country man of the soil, hardly the notion of a viscount that most people possessed.

'Sir' — Geoffrey plunged immediately to

his concern without the finesse he'd have used on a mission — 'I have come about Amelia Longworth.'

'Fancied you'd show up sooner or later from what she's said. Sit down, my boy. What may I do for you?'

'I would like to see Amelia, if I may,' Geoffrey said politely, calming down now that he was so close to his objective.

'Indeed? Pity, that, for she'll not see you.' Lord Quainton massaged his jaw while studying Geoffrey as though to assess the effect of his words.

'What?' Geoffrey exclaimed, nearly starting from his chair. To be so close and denied a chance to redeem himself was more than he could tolerate. 'But she must see me! I mean, I refuse to accept that. I believe the young lady cares for me, sir. And I care for her as well,' Geoffrey said, deciding he might as well lay his cards on the table.

'Oh, I have no doubt as to the truth of that. You have the same lovesick look that she wears when she thinks I'm not watching her. But she is a determined young woman, and I respect her wishes. She said she will not see you if you come to the house. Mind you, if you were to casually bump into her when she goes into Salisbury tomorrow to exchange her books at Fellow's Circulating Library, it would be different, don't y'know.'

Hope rose within Geoffrey at the encouraging words from Lord Quainton. It seemed the elderly lord had sized up Geoffrey and not found him wanting, and for that Geoff could only be grateful.

'She goes into town every Tuesday to shop and exchange her books. Good gel, likes my topiary and the swans. They even seem to like her, and they are rude birds as a rule.'

'I am most grateful for the information, sir. Now if I can just persuade Amelia to listen to me, my battle may be won.'

'She'll have that Chinese dragon with her,' his lordship warned. 'Don't envy you taking her on. I vow she has a maxim for every occasion. Some of them are downright uncomfortable.' He gave Geoffrey a companionable smile.

'Ah, yes. The indomitable Chen Mei. She's rather handy in a fight. Her ability with that dagger she carries up her sleeve is quite amazing.'

'Indeed? I hadn't known about the dagger. I see I shall have to use care not to offend her.' The beetle brows drew together in an amused frown. 'I gather you have had occasion to observe its employment?'

'She uses it to defend and protect Amelia.' Then, beguiled by a new listener who appeared sympathetic to his cause, Geoffrey told Lord Quainton the entire tale, how he had met and dealt with the determined and loyal Miss Longworth.

'Chattel, did you say? Good grief,' his lordship muttered at the conclusion of the story. The telling had involved some time and several glasses of excellent port.

'She is as honest and direct as a May day is long. Inventive and protective, too,' Geoffrey reflected.

'I suggest you slip out of here before she sees you. Don't want to warn her in advance, y'know. As I said, she's a good gel and deserves a good husband.'

'I am pleased you allow me the chance to present my case to her.'

'The least I can do for you, my boy.' The viscount rose and offered his hand.

Geoffrey, who had been the head of his house and not called 'my boy' for many years repressed a grin at this. He welcomed the chance to shake hands, then said, 'Thanks to you again. Wish me luck on the morrow.'

'No doubt you'll need more than luck. Better devise something that will further the match.' He walked with Geoffrey to the door, clapped him on the back, then watched as Geoff strode along the hall to the front door like a man with a mission.

Oh, to be young and in love again, thought the viscount as he gently shut the door, walking to the window to stare out at the stream. A misty rain fell, but his thoughts were with a certain lady, now long gone, who had denied him many years ago. This young fellow deserved a chance, one that Quainton had not been given.

In the carriage, Geoffrey consulted with Tobin, sharing with him the viscount's advice.

'Sounds as though his lordship knows what he's about. But, what to do?'

The two men discussed the matter all the way back to the inn. At the Rose and Crown, Geoffrey and Tobin settled in a private parlor with a bottle of the best port.

'What will be the best approach?' Geoffrey muttered, staring out at the falling rain through the mullioned window.

'You say she comes to your rescue?' Tobin said, savoring the excellent wine the likes of which he rarely got to taste.

'True.' Geoffrey pivoted about, frowning while he considered something at length. Then he grinned and eagerly crossed to seat himself at the table where Tobin watched him with a speculative gleam in his eyes.

'This is what we shall do, my good friend.'

* * *

'What a blessing the rain has ceased,' Amelia said to Chen Mei while she gazed out of the window with satisfaction. 'I have looked forward to our weekly trip to Salisbury too much to be put off by it, but it does make it a deal pleasanter to have sunshine.'

'Do not anxiously hope for what is not yet come; do not vainly regret what is already past,' the companion quoted in her usual Cantonese from her reservoir of sayings.

'Who says that I am regretting what is past?' Amelia cried, whipping about to challenge Chen Mei. She wished to deny what was all too obvious to her, that she did regret turning her back on Lord Dancy. For one who was always truthful, it was rather difficult to pretend otherwise.

'Long face tell all,' Chen Mei smugly replied.

'Well, I shall have to take care that I smile when I go to town.' Amelia slipped on her peach pelisse, trimmed down the front with dainty bows of a deeper shade of peach. Her plumed bonnet was the latest thing, and when she peeked in the looking glass on the stair landing, Amelia felt pleased with her appearance. Not that she would see anyone she knew in town. Because of her uncle's uninterest in company, no one had come to call these many weeks, nor had she met any one who appealed to her.

It wasn't like London, she admitted. There, Mary and Peter and Chloe had filled her spare hours with laughter and fun. And Lord Dancy had . . . Amelia resolutely rejected the very mental image of the man, an image that had haunted her dreams every night, lurked in her mind in the day. It had become so trying that she sometimes imagined she saw him while in town. A gentleman dressed to the nines with a jaunty walk would catch her eye, then disappoint when it turned out to be someone else.

The ride to town was as uneventful as always. She thought back to the dashing times she had known in London when Lord Dancy had needed her protection and care. Oh, she missed that, she conceded. But that man . . . to tell her they would be best to be as strangers after all they had shared.

The coachman left Amelia and Chen Mei off at the corner of Catherine Street. On such a lovely day Amelia wished to saunter along to admire the objects for sale in the shop windows.

She was astounded when a gentleman spoke to her while she studied the contents of a millinery shop window. It sounded so much like the voice she had heard in her dreams that she was afraid to face him, preferring the shadowed reflection seen in the window. How much this man looked like Geoffrey. Then he spoke again.

'Amelia, I know you are upset with me, and rightly so. Will you not give me a chance to redeem myself?' he pleaded.

This time his voice seemed too real to ignore. Hoping she was not being foolish, Amelia decided to hazard facing him.

'Geoffrey!' She met that familiar green gaze with a fluttery heart. Her hand went to calm the beat within while her eyes searched the figure before her. He appeared well, although he seemed to have lost a bit of weight.

'I finally found you. And I do not intend to let you go,' he declared in a low voice that thrilled her. Only Amelia had dreamed this too often. This was not a dream, but reality. In real life Geoffrey had scorned her and her love, even though she had never told him that she loved him.

'My uncle might not agree with you,' she answered, feeling quite perverse now that she was close to Geoffrey again.

'Perhaps not. But I am not so bad a fellow as you may think. I own a rather nice place north of London I long to show you. And my family is acceptable. I've told you all about them. If I hadn't become so involved with a certain Miss Longworth, I'd have been to see them before this.'

'Had I a family, I would wish to see them after being gone so long,' Amelia couldn't resist chiding. She had no intention of allowing him to talk her around to his point of view. But she wouldn't be rude to the man, for he had obviously come some distance to see her.

'I have had a great deal on my mind, as you may know. How could I go haring after them when I needed to find you!' He glanced about with a hint of desperation, quite as though he looked for someone.

'What is it?' Amelia asked at once, her protective tendencies where he was concerned springing to life.

'Do you see a chap behind me? Wears a dun-colored coat, dark hat tipped over his eyes. Not very tall, sort of inconspicuous, you might say.' He lowered his voice to a conspiratorial whisper.

Amelia grew alarmed, for the very person he mentioned lurked near a tree across the street. He looked decidedly suspicious.

'I do see him. What a frightful-looking man. Are you in trouble again?' she demanded, subtly positioning herself so she stood between the two. One never knew when a gun might be drawn from concealment

— or a knife, for that matter.

'The thing of it is, I don't know. The chap looks to be a Bow Street Runner. Do you suppose that Taunton's been found dead and I am blamed?'

With a gasp Amelia placed her hand on Geoffrey's arm, leading him along with her toward the circulating library. 'I thought that dreadful man had fled the country.'

'But we don't know that for certain.'

'Come with me. There is a back way out of the library that we may use. From there I shall take you to my uncle's home where you will be safe from harm.'

Chen Mei tagged along behind, darting looks at the Runner, then at his lordship. No smile crossed her lips, but her eyes appeared to dance with amusement had Amelia chanced to look at her.

'Here.' Amelia thrust Geoffrey ahead of her into the circulating library, peering around the door to assure herself that the man still lurked in the shadows across the street. 'You stay here, Chen Mei. If he dares to come inside, use your dagger. Lord Dancy and I shall escape out of the back door.' She tugged his sleeve, then drew him along with her past the rows of books until they reached a hall. From here she marched along to the door.

A clerk bowed respectfully to the young

woman known to be the niece of Lord Quainton. Even though a recluse, he still garnered deference. He held the door open for the pair, watching as they hurried down the alleyway.

'Now, you ought to be safe. Where do you stay? Is Hemit with you? Will you be able to come to my uncle's with me and not cause comment where you now stay?' She led him along the alley until they reached Brown Street. Swiftly drawing him along with her, it was but moments and they were at the side of Lord Quainton's crested carriage.

'Hurry. Who knows when that dreadful man may decide to explore a bit.'

Once inside the carriage, they set off toward the west and Lord Quainton's estate.

Geoffrey turned to study the determined little face at his side. 'You do care for me. I am certain of it.'

'Well, and I would not wish anything to happen to you, sir,' she primly replied, folding her hands neatly in her lap.

All of a sudden Amelia found herself picked up and deposited on his lap. His arms wrapped around her in a most beguiling manner, and before she could protest — although she actually had no desire to do so — she was most thoroughly kissed.

She melted at the onslaught. It was beyond

her to fend off the kiss when she had ached for this very thing for so long. Her arms crept up to cling to those broad shoulders, and she returned his kiss with all her being.

At last, content for the moment, she was permitted to lean against his chest. She sighed with delight.

'We are going to be married. I'll not take no as an answer, my little love,' he stated firmly, holding her tightly against him as though he feared to lose her. 'Once married, I hope you will agree to some time at my country home, for things there have been sadly neglected while I chased after you.'

She made no answer, for indeed it was quite beyond her at the moment.

'What? No contrary reply? No words of denial?'

'Think twice, say nothing,' Amelia said.

'She comes along, too,' Geoffrey murmured as he gathered Amelia even closer and proceeded to convince her that he never again intended to be parted from his Celestial Delight — even if she led him into one escapade after another. With Amelia life would never be dull again.